THE BROKEN
SHORE

THE BROKEN SHORE

BY
ARMAND LANOUX

TRANSLATED FROM THE FRENCH BY
ALAN DAVENTRY

E. P. DUTTON & CO., INC.
New York   1965

Je ne savais pas qu'une guerre
n'a jamais de fin pour ceux
qui se sont battues.

Malaparte

To Katia Tolstoy

To the Canadians who sleep beneath the
maple leaf in the cemetery at Bény-sur-Mer,
to their comrades in the war for
liberty, to their enemies who died loyally
for an evil cause.

'YESTERDAY AT le Havre, at a little past ten o'clock in the foyer of the offices of the newspaper *Paris-Normandy,* which had been elegantly but discreetly decorated for the occasion, the directors of the paper were hosts to a hundred and twenty-one French Canadian visitors, from Quebec and Montreal.

'Under the auspices of the Canada-Normandy Association, our guests who had come ashore an hour earlier from the liner *Samuel Champlain,* had come to visit the Normandy of their ancestors and in particular to make contact with the descendants of the families which carry their own names. So it is that there are twenty-four called Leclerc, a wonderful family name found very widely in our region, on the list of this unusual tour. One interesting detail is that among the staff of *Paris-Normandy* who attended the fraternal ceremony there are three Leclercs: our sporting editor, the ex-soccer international, Maurice Leclerc; a foreman from the paper's printing house, Antonin Leclerc; and Mlle Etiennette Leclerc, one of the oldest of the employees.

'Councillor Daniel Durand, deputy mayor of le Havre gave a moving speech in which which he extolled the Franco-Canadian friendship forged in those battles for liberty to which the great military cemeteries bear witness, such as the one at Bény-sur-Mer.

'After toasts all round in wine—and cider—the French Canadians left for Caen by road. They will visit in particular the Permanent Exhibition of the Disembarkation at Arromanches and the remains of the Mulberry harbour.

' "*Bon voyage,* dear cousins from Quebec," Monsieur Durand said when closing his speech. "And may the fraternal amity of the Leclercs endure forever across the waves of the Atlantic." Among those present were . . .'

At Verville, a fishing port situated between Courseulles and Bernières, in the *rue du Soleil Levant,* the elder Arnaud, red in a check shirt which was even redder, pushed aside the paper which carried the date: 27 May 1960. Then with studied truculence, he said:

'What the hell does it matter if they're called Leclerc, Smith or Muller? Not at all, eh, Bébé? That's the truth, to be sure.'

The girl whom the landlord had addressed in such a familiar fashion was a slender young woman, with a catlike face. Only her eyes were made up, in the manner of ballerinas. She gave the appearance of a blonde Nefertiti. She was much too elegant for this rural bistro, which proclaimed itself with a sign which imagination had furnished for the name *Père Magloire.* But she did not seem to care. She was looking a long way away, far beyond the counter, beyond the glaring shirt of the *patron,* beyond the tree-lined terrace towards the sea. A thin young man in blue jeans, his back towards her, was shaking a pin table ornamented with swimsuited pinups.

'Leclerc's a nice name, when you think about it,' she said, dreamily.

Part One : The Roses of Arromanches

CHAPTER I

HIS NECK, shoulders and torso made up a single forbidding mass; and Abel felt the others pushing up against him. There was a smell of sour apples. The sharp pleasing sense of joy which had buoyed him up at Port Winston an hour ago had now gone. Abel recognised the warning signs; his heart beat against his ribs. No, he shouldn't have come into this damned hole! He wanted to swallow but his throat was much too dry. He stifled a sobbing cough. He was thankful that Valerie was not there to witness his discomfort. She had stayed at the hotel. Thank God for that! Valerie was really beginning to get on his nerves, with her fine manners, her regal deportment—and her 'Hero's Grave'!

This last phrase struggled from him like a huge bird caught in an electric grid. A sequence of warning bells rang right up to the farthest frontiers. General Intelligence was alerted, for no signal could get by them.

At his back a nervous laugh broke out into a low feminine voice:

'Ferdinand! Ferdinand! What do you think, I've forgotten to get the hens in.'

In front of them there was nothing, nothing but a vague milky rectangle. The attendant came back and spoke in a fine deep voice:

'Push up closer, lady! That's right, that'll give the men a treat. I've got to shut the door because I must have complete darkness.'

And all at once it became appalling. In the pitch darkness harsh cries arose. There was a creaking sound, like iron gates at the end of a graveyard, moans from the chained slaves under the whips of a crew of convicts. The horror came into focus: it was nothing but the seagulls.

The seagulls were calling in their immemorial manner, the white gulls of death who watch over the dunes. He saw them now as he had done long ago, on that indistinct line at the very frontier of life where the waves die, in the disputed territory between the last of the seaweed and the first of the thistles, the inaccessible Promised Land of dry sand.

Abel shook himself. The mechanical deception became obvious. This was nothing more than an inferior recording of sea birds, such as he would never want to use in his own broadcasts.

'The Artauds' cook is going to have a fine old time,' said the woman.

Her companion whispered a few words in her ear and they stifled a laugh. A cough sounded, then a child's cry. A feeble light filtered through, suggesting an immense yellowish expanse. At the same time the spectators grew wildly in stature, becoming giants before this sandy mound which gleamed in an eastern light. Abel recognised it, like the gulls. This was the dirty violet light which, for him, would always be mixed up with daybreak.

A big voice, a station announcer's voice, barked out:

'We are in the night of the 5th June, 1944. The Normans, who never despaired, are now sleeping. They are sleeping in their farms behind closed shutters, while in the gun emplacements of the Atlantic wall, with their noses pressed against the barrels of their guns, the soldiers of Hitler . . .'

Meanwhile, the sunlight rose steadily in the sky, etching out every little variation of the soil. It was like seeing the windows of the shops in Quebec in the days when Abel used to stand amazed before them as he came from the banks of the Chaudière with Mamie Jolicoeur, Abel's eyes would open wide; he was the poor boy who knew that Santa Claus was not able to give good French Canadian children everything they wanted.

The windswept dawn shone wanly on the cubes of the villages and the isolated farms, on the ribbons of road, the carpets of woodland and the pools of the fenland. *Total surprise . . . The preparation for the most enormous invasion ever known to military history . . .* Two villages were illumined, bearing odd names which Abel recognised although he had forgotten them long since: Ouistreham and Troarn. Searchlight beams crossed one another and the parachutes of the pathfinders came down between the two extremities of the fan-shaped region of death from Ouistreham to Troarn. The child who had been whimpering was pushed against Abel's leg. There was now enough light for Abel to pick out the kid's blonde hair, cut very short, to perceive the curve of the cheek and the thumb in the mouth. Abel ruffled the cropped hair. Aircraft throbbed. The German siren sounded. Everything within him, in spite of him, was once again at war.

The dawn lightened into mauve. The day broke. A gangling dark-haired man, six foot four at least—and that's taller than me—was telling his beads. It was the butcher from the *rue St Vallier,* murmuring his prayers. A spume of

13

foam stopped his mouth. He spat it out and finished his prayers in a frenzied torrent of curses! I laughed frantically! I was nineteen and I'd only made love to one girl at the side of the St Lawrence; and she wouldn't let me take her virginity! I was going to die without knowing love, for Jennifer had refused me! I'd have got away with it, if it hadn't been for Jacques. I'd pushed her at him, pushed that Southampton barmaid into the arms of Jacques! Jennifer, Jennifer! All pink and white, lively smile, blonde curls—and lips which smelt of toothpaste!

Lieutenant Petitjean, who was yelling through a megaphone, chased my girl away.

It was H-Hour. H. H is for hatchet, to chop off your head. The hatchet of my Uncle Jolicoeur, Dad's brother, who had gone through the 1914 war without a scratch and was very proud of the fact. He used to snap his finger and thumb and say: 'Not even that much!' And then he goes and gets himself crushed by a tree, near the *Baie des Ha! Ha!* in Saguenay in 1950. Shakespeare is right, as always. Clowning and putrefaction, that's what life is made of.

The sullen day got going and the Norman countryside opened up its jaw on the West, from the mouth of the Seine to the Cotentin. Soon, the men, sickened by the stink of fuel oil and by the pitching of the barges in a filthy cross-swell, tumbled down into the water or clung to the nets, amid the thunder of naval armament. A trumpet was sounding crazily in the beaten-up old barge; and the hungry gulls were circling above the boats, the crows of the sea. 'They're waiting for feeding time,' Simeon blurted out, with a disgusting laugh from his toothless mouth.

'The most enormous invasion the world had ever known was about to break on the Normandy coast. No one will be able to forget those dramatic hours. The destiny of a civilisation was being played out on five beaches, shortly to be trans-

14

formed into artificial ports. The Canadian troops unleashed the first assault . . .'

The vast machine of war pulled on chains, hauled on winches, drove out trucks, The tanks came out from the depths of the past. During bombardments, I wanted to get up and go. But I couldn't. Because of the shell-bursts, naturally; but also because of the M.P.s. And then what sort of spectacle should I have made? I used to get sick of it. You listened. You counted. It was crazy. But just try and reason with a coward like that! As for the bombing raids, I got to know them later: the multi-coloured flak bursting like rockets, the insignificant puffs of the explosions, the orange shafts of tracer ammunition, and the fighter planes in dog-fights overhead, flashing like fish. A real Brock's benefit! But fear, plain dirty funk, withering funk—as Jacques said —that we kept for the tanks. What was it, the Normans say? 'If you want to be happy, live between Caen and Bayeux.' We used to laugh about that between Bayeux and Caen. But no one laughed about the tanks. Even ours. Anything, anything was better than getting flattened by those huge ponderous moles—you never knew where they were going to aim. And neither did they. And then they'd go and leave you to it. All of them, even ours . . .

The bunker, which had been blasted by shell fire a few moments earlier, was pissing out a blackish liquid. Suddenly a man came out. He was holding something. We didn't have time to see what. Our lads bawled out. There was a luminous jet. Liquid fire from the flame-thrower enveloped the German. He was carrying a piece of white cloth. Too late! He ran. The jet of flame followed him like a spotlight following a comic across a music-hall stage, then let him go after a dozen or so yards, directing itself back at the silent bunker. The man ran directly across the line of the Canadians who did not even think of firing. His legs spun about, his arms flailed. Fire, like the flame from a punch-bowl, was rising up from this man who ran, ran, ran, kept on running, stumbled, ran, grew smaller, ran twenty five, thirty yards, and ran again, and went out of shape, broke up, disintegrated, sizzled and at last collapsed, surmounted by a sickening yellow glow. Abel dug furiously with his nails. When he got control of himself again, he spat out sand from his mouth. Where the German had fallen, there was only a burning bush. The little tank had disappeared. And the bunker started firing again! By his side, and on all fours, Jacques was shaking convulsively, like a cat who had just swallowed a bone.

The distorted sound of the diorama brought back the terrifying memory of the lines of tanks. Shermans, Panzers, Tigers, Churchills; then there was the crazy tanks, the 'funnies': tank-trucks, caterpillar trucks, Bren carriers, Buffaloes, self-propelled guns, jeeps, Dodges and hideous bulldozers which drove interminably over pebbles, beaches, woods and roads, smashing down trees and houses. The infantrymen crept along, their mouths soundlessly, uncontrollably open. And the machines, stinking of burnt oil, left behind them flattened-out bodies, with heads an inch thick and a foot and a half wide, with helmets looking like orchids made from metal.

Abel had completely lost the thread of the story when the voice recalled the storm of 19 June. That was true, there was a storm. It uprooted the corn with its blasts while they were slogging towards Caen. It had even messed up the two Mulberries. But Abel didn't give a damn about the Mulberries. The war, for him, had been narrowed down to a little willow forest which some swine of SS troops were holding, knocking out everyone who budged with rockets, mortars, heavy machine-guns and their eighty-eights. Seen from his point of view the storm had been something of a blessing. '*The*

16

treacherous sea had become Hitler's ally!' Get away! That's a lot of hooey!

The sun went down, drawing its fantastic cavalry into the stables of the night. The bellying clouds of the storm were travelling off towards the continent which they, too, were besieging. Abel, in an orchard, gathering apricots. He chucked one up to Jacques. Jacques spat it out. It's true, I forgot about the storm. My crazy memory just stores this fact and rejects that one at random. But I've just seen Jacques again, Jacques, with his clear countenance, freckles, high cheekbones, baby smile, even his dimples and his blue eyes. 'They're not ripe,' he said. About the apricots. That was all. But he smiled at me. He understood. He liked me. He forgave me. Deepening his dimples and crinkling his eyes, he had returned for an instant from the other place, to smile at me—sixteen years later.

'The Seventh and the Eighth Canadian Brigades finally took Caen.' The tape recording was coming to an end. You could guess as much from the increasing theatricality of the diction. The huge luminous V-shape lay upon the molehill of sand which, for some minutes, had contained the summary of an important part of the history of the world.

'The way to Paris was now open. It was Victory. But at what a price! The heroes' names are forever written in our hearts as they are written forever in the pages of history.' The names of heroes are written down. My God they are! Written on their graves. That is, when they could be found! But Abel fought back the emotion aroused by those three words: 'In our hearts.' Words!—Words! Words! Clowning and putrefaction!

'Come to this museum and the great cemeteries with reverence. They will bring home to you the price of liberty.' The door opened. The keeper with the white hair had an amiable smile on his well-shaven face as he said:

'This way out, ladies and gentlemen.'

'Hallo,' said the little boy, 'In the dark I didn't recognize you.'

The little boy made a pleasant picture, with his freckled skin, his tousled hair, his fine little unangelic urchin's head, his sky-blue eyes, which looked straight into those of the grown-up, a nose which wrinkled over difficult words and a tooth missing in front.

'Hallo, Olivier.'

'I wanted some soldiers with parachutes, but mama doesn't want me to have any soldiers, she says she's seen enough of them.'

A tall elderly lady, dressed in black, with her hair gathered in coils, called him.

'Olivier! Don't worry the gentleman.'

In spite of her severe voice, the old lady had rosy cheeks like a wrinkled apple. It was thoughtful of her to have baptised the boy Olivier.

The clear light of every day was bathing the Mulberry which stretched from Asnelles to The Chaos. The colours, dove-grey with stripes of white grease-paint, dissolved into shimmering reflections. Away to the horizon it stretched, like shot-silk, on which the shrouds of giants seemed to float, the velvet traces of the seaweed.

A young woman was looking at Abel with an open smile and a laugh in her eyes. She had got to know well that expression which they all got inside, this appearance of sleep-walking. And here was another of them.

The visitors, for a moment stunned to silence, spoke to each other. Country people, townsmen, Whitsun tourists who were just taking advantage of the opportunity. It could equally well have been a museum of head-dresses or of butterflies. A large forbidding fellow came across the room, a tall man with a very long body, sharply creased trousers

18

and ridiculous little legs. Obviously a G.I.; and he dragged round behind him a red-faced girl, in a dress of apple green.

Abel was looking at a model of a service woman. Severe in her uniform of navy blue, not a strand out of place, she presented a picture of war which was antiseptic and domestic. The title said: Women's Royal Naval Service. The war, his war, had been a bit short of the female corps. The big American looked for the model's behind under her skirt, made a grimace and aroused a horrified shock from the scandalised company. Then he went away, laughing his head off, but not before he had given Abel a wink. He had recognised, God knows how, another being who would understand English.

'Hi, fella! The fun of it!'

The female naval auxiliary smiled her eternal smile.

The majority of the photographs which were displayed outside the Gates of War portrayed as their subjects the moments immediately after the landing. Helmeted, with cigarettes in their lips, the well-ordered Rangers went down a gangway from a landing craft into very calm water. Suddenly, Abel stood stockstill. Amongst all these pictures, one image shrieked out. The enlargement was technically poor, but it breathed such a spirit of life that it might have been a newsreel. The title said: 'Gold Beach, 6 June. In the background the troops are lying down to shelter from the German fire which is enfilading the beach.'

In the foreground, on the left, a man was going forward, bent down under his equipment, his helmet sliding forward, his camouflage net loaded with a motley collection of objects, his knapsack like a camel's hump. The base of the picture cut off the face at the chin (but, since it had been taken from above, you could see the man's back). He had a long nose. Bulging eyes. A twisted mouth. At the side, in profile, an N.C.O. was shouting. He had his haversack in front. You could see he was shouting because of the way his mouth curved inwards. A man followed him, another broken-down furniture remover. Still farther behind were three men in a group. The man on the left had a red cross on his arm and was holding a Bren gun; no doubt the weapon of the fellow in the middle who was dragging a leg and turning an anguished face to the camera, a face not much bigger than a postage stamp, but on which could be read the whole suffering of humanity. After this group, and behind them, the column made a sharp bend as the men avoided the water. The infantry, standing up, on their knees, lying down, sitting, leaning one upon the other, became more and more numerous, and harassed. They made an unhappy procession which stretched right to the edge of the picture, where you could see a pale white star on a truck. The column broke up once again then turned left, making a Z. The men were now microscopic, bent down under the enfilading fire mentioned in the caption, like misshapen mice, some standing on their hind legs, others partly immersed. Finally, in the space between the huge helmet in the foreground and the procession of figures at the rear, a soldier was falling, his hand open before him like a flower. The carbine with the short bayonet had just left his hand and the weapon hung in mid-air. The man and the gun were going to plunge into the still water in which the scene was reflected. But the moment went by and the man had not fallen. He stayed in the air, together with the carbine. As long as this strange picture lasted, so long would the soldier be falling, immobile, in an eternal stillness which was more terrible even than death itself because when death has passed, forgetfulness begins.

That was when Abel heard the music. And he was hearing it in reality. The music existed in this present world on Monday, 6 June, 1960 at Arromanches. It came out of the loudspeakers arranged around the square. The record, put on by

20

chance by the technician who was looking after the sound for the show, was not altogether appropriate. However, the Canadian had never again been able to hear the *Ritual Fire Dance* without associating it with his war.

I've done my fighting on the beaches, in the ripe corn and in the orchards and I whistled, hummed and tapped my foot to the *Ritual Fire Dance.* As though the apple trees could bring forth olives! There it was, though! A sombre figure beat the earth with his heel, turning up a doleful face to the sky, and then bending it down to the ground. That was the war dance. War swerved to left and to right and came back, right along the twisted column in the picture. The dead returned on this, their day, and they danced.

Dragging his apple-green popsy behind him, the G.I. with the tiny little feet reappeared, an involuntary tight-rope walker, shouting, guffawing, giving voice to a revolt which could find expression in no other way; and then departed.

What were they selling in this hall, in this lost past? Memory? Hope? A good conscience? Or merely the joy of not being dead?

At the entrance stood the cheerful guide, who oddly resembled Maurice Chevalier, with gleaming complexion under a blue cap which he often removed, with smooth cheeks and white hair.

'This way, ladies and gentlemen,' he said. 'The tour is continuing. It was at Quebec in 1943 that the landing was decided upon. It took place on the sixth of June, 1944 and that is just sixteen years ago today. It's fortunate that it succeeded, otherwise we none of us would be here now.'

He laughed, glad to be there.

'You can still see a few *caissons* of the port across these bays. That was the Mulberry which was laid down and finished by the eighteenth of June. In just twelve days!'

The young woman was still looking at Abel. She judged

21

him to be a big man, well above the five foot six which, in France, is the average size of men of good height. Yet he did not seem to be slim. Stocky, rather, and barrel-chested. His shoulders rose up almost without interruption of line to the top of his head. It was an animal shape which gave a dangerous attractiveness to his whole personality. A superb beast! She made a slight movement and the Canadian turned towards her. But he did not see her. He was like the Hercules by Bourdelle, but without the curly hair. In fact, this Hercules had no hair at all! He had a squarish forehead, well drawn but rather wide, and his baldness laid bare a round shining head, with a prominent nose, a tight mouth and brutal chin. Bourdelle's? Certainly. Or more likely something from primitive sculpture, such as the granite heads from Saïs.

She gave a start. An unpleasant voice murmured in her ear:

'One can lose the weed from the fountain and still keep it round the tap, eh Bébé?'

The young woman's face, until that moment very gentle, became hard.

Abel went up the steps. He saw before him a pitifully thin torso above the delightful curve of a backside which moved beneath a light cotton print on which were illustrations of yachts. The legs were covered by seamless stockings, the insteps were arching, balancing on stiletto heels. He reawakened to the existence of the world outside.

A ragged military band sounded forth. Churchill's round face, with the cigar in the mouth, took over the screen. In this commemorative film, Arromanches appeared just as it had remained in the Canadian's memory, much more authentic than this smart resort was today. Arromanches in 1944 had been like an ass's jawbone washed white by the rains. But already history had carried them away, victory had snatched them up, the sappers had rolled out a road through the

22

flooded land. *'Attention! Alert! Alert! The engineers' road in the floods. Alert, danger, danger! A pint of gas is worth a pint of blood.'* Once again, the Central Intelligence made its warning too late. The squat colossus on his armchair gave out a muted groan. Jacques. Jacques, my old Jacques . . .

A clammy hand rested on his hand, shook it lightly, and as it withdrew, caressed him with fingertips. It was nothing, nothing more than a feeble hand resting on the strong hand of the man, but the life of Abel Leclerc had just revealed the fissure which it had hidden for sixteen years. His life was falling apart, like those Norman houses which held up until after the bombardment and then suddenly caved in before the breath of a comforting breeze from the sea.

From a life-size picture, General Patton stared at Abel Leclerc. The general just wasn't happy! Old Blood and Guts! Four stars on the collar and, on the helmet, one on top and three below. An etched-out face. Wrinkled eyes. *A pint of gas is worth a pint of blood!* From the other side of the Gates of War, General Patton considered Leclerc with the icy scorn of the brass-hat for the poor soldier.

'What's that?' asked Abel, as he turned round.

In a friendly voice, the elderly guide said, 'I was only saying that if you want to sit through a second time, it won't cost you anything.'

Abel saw, without seeing, the face before him, even redder now under the blue cap and the white hair, with a paternal smile. He shook his head, uncertain. Entering through the walls, the floors into the belly, the inhuman, incessant sound-track started up again, accompanied by the antediluvian cries of the seagulls: *We are in the night of the 5th June, 1944. The Normans who never despaired, are sleeping . . .'*

Abel passed his hand over his brow and then dropped his two hundred pounds into a chair. Bending over, he found breathing difficult and put his hand to his heart. He tore open

23

his shirt, uncovering a hairy chest and breathed deeply. Then, after some time, amidst the hubbub of curiosity, he lifted up his face and his strong Herculean head reappeared as though corroded by a long time under the sea, while his sight, unsteady and wandering, was seeking out the surroundings and the actors of a vanished world.

The young woman in the marine print leaned her swelling breast on him. That was better. Things were coming back. Now he saw the lovely anxious face of this young woman directly from the front. In profile she had a perfect cameo beauty; but full face, there was a little irregularity which made it less than perfect, but much more alive.

The disappointed visitors were hesitating to depart, hoping for more.

'You're not American?' asked the young woman.

'Canadian.'

She pursed her unpainted lips, impudent but innocent.

'And I'm Norman. Going to be all right?'

He stood up, leaning heavily on the back of the chair. He was a lot taller than she.

'You're a big fellow! Good. Well, I'm off. You need some air. Come around to Verville. That's where the oysters are. I'm often there myself. Good luck, Canada.'

She was delicate, matching the preconception he had formed of France.

He went to the door. He stopped for a moment on the threshold, refreshed by the sea wind which smelled healthily of seaweed. Then he was lost in the crowd.

Behind the Gates of War, the old guide shook his head.

'Every year they come back,' he said to the younger guide. 'Sometimes, they stay for hours . . .'

'Don't you tell them to go? If it's time to close, you won't see me worrying myself.'

'You'd have told that lad to get out?'

'Well, perhaps not. He was built like an ox.'

The elderly man's fine voice spoke softly.

24

'Especially in winter. Sometimes they give the impression of not being here. And if you look, you'll understand them. But that comes from the effect that's produced when there's a wind and the dummies sway about.'

He coughed. He had lost his well-set-up air.

'Another batch,' he said. 'Well, it's the last.'

He hesitated. The young man seemed so lacking in comprehension. However, he went on in a low voice:

'For my brother-in-law it was Dixmude. Dixmude. Every year for forty years and more . . .'

Then, more quietly still he said with a shamed tone:

'For me it's Verdun. Verdun. The Old Man. Pétain. That's right, the Marshal. The trenches and the bayonets. Le Mort-Homme?'

On the old man's face, which until now had been so jovial, the young man saw the same icy shadow pass which a few minutes earlier had masked the Canadian's. He did not understand because he was thirty. The whole thing bored him. He was a nut, this old man, him and his Marshal. It was a good job, being a guide. It wasn't tiring. You could take it or leave it; but the annoying thing in these museums of the Landings or the War or Victory was the old soldiers. Obviously, they'd had enough! But all the same! He'd better do the decent thing and go and do the last batch himself. He slipped off, resigned, towards his group of tourists.

The upset dummies in the boxes remained alone, with the old guide just as still, his stare fixed before him, like the slaves at the doors of the Pharaoh's palace.

BENEATH THE ENORMOUS and poorly conceived statue of Notre Dame du Débarquement, in the Place de la Libération, you might have thought an agricultural show was going on, with this assembly of Sunday-best clothes. But it also had the air of a fourteenth-of-July procession and of a fairground, on account of the already numerous bathers, the Parisians who, for the next three months, would peaceably take over these beaches. In the freshness of the early June Sunday, the crowd had put on a festive spirit. It was dotted with the *coquelicots* of the choirboys who were jostling the old leather-skinned men, stuffed into their clothes, the young lads-of-the-town and the old soldiers, moustachioed like ancient Gauls (And God knows if they'd done any fighting since the days of Vercingetorix). The crowd was happy yet subdued, brought together by a memorial ceremony in which was mingled, unconsciously, the pagan summer festival. And so Abel loved it as he had loved, at home, the gatherings of St. Jean. If it had not been for the vernacular, he would have been able to take them for his neighbours along the banks of the St. Lawrence or the Chaudière. It was not an immense expanse of water which separated Arromanches from Quebec, but a vast amount of time.

With its turret open, a tank was attacking the coast, amid the stink of hot oil. Two girls in light green beach suits went past him, laughing aloud, greeted encouragingly by the lads.

At each higher step the sea came more into view while the village retreated. The machine took its last turning before its final resting place in a position dominating the Permanent Exhibition of the Landings, at the level of the roof of a turreted and quite out-of-time château of 1880 vintage. The wind from the open sea stirred the harvest wildly and whipped the flags which the bearers were pressing into their bellies. At the back, climbing as best they could, came the lame, the sick, the injured, the silver-haired warriors crammed into their mufti, with flowers in their buttonholes, two hundred grizzled veterans.

'General Rouvillois,' whispered one man to his girlfriend who was pale with boredom. 'One of Leclerc's companions. And there the general's son, beside him. He's got thin.'

It was becoming hard to go forward. The crowd got stuck. One lady, as wide as she was tall, with hips like a mare, got in the Canadian's way. A little girl, with a doll-like prettiness and eyes the colour of periwinkle, was leaning on the mother's arm. With her other arm the mother was trying to grab an urchin of about four years of age, a tough little animal. The *Marseillaise* burst out in a riot of false notes. The little fellow stopped and clumsily made the sign of the cross. He had sensed that he should do something and he behaved as he did in church. The dust placed on his cheek a peach-like bloom.

In the front of the rigid ranks of serving soldiers, with their helmets on their eyebrows and their chinstraps on the points of their chins, the heroes had drawn themselves up. These heads, now being sawn off by starched collars, those deeply etched mouths were relics of the Druids, the Franks, the Vikings and the companions of Merovius! For the official photographs the municipal council made a horseshoe around the mayor, the general, the young Leclerc and a personage completely dressed in leaves. The only gay note was struck by three local girls in Norman head-dresses, looking pretty but hot under their heavy woollen bodices, striped skirts and *fichus* like table lace. This was the Dame of Calvados and her two maids of honour. They seemed disinterested and would have preferred to be at the dance. A bugle call sounded out. A bright yellow trawler at sea beat out the rhythm in common time, heavily accented. The shadow of a cloud slid over the bare heads.

The drums beat sonorously, an imperious citation to the dead.

Towards Asnelles, Graye-sur-Mer, Verville, Courseulles and St Aubin, bells were sounding the carillion. In each of these rejoicing towns there just had to be a *Place du 6 Juin,* an *Avenue de la Libération* or a *Boulevard Eisenhower*! And, especially, a parade! At the town halls, the cemeteries, the churches, the municipal parks and the monuments to the dead. The trumpets tore the air. The crowd began to cough, to laugh and chatter.

Abel went up to the caterpillar vehicles, the tanks and the gun decorated with the white star. He read the name on the tank. He was certainly out of luck. 'That reminds me of a Sherman I used to love,' he scoffed, with a taste of bitterness in his mouth. But he took the blow full in his chest and he went along the shore. The flood of people which was starting to pour out towards the village was attracted by the thoughts of apéritifs, oysters, brown bread, salted butter, underdone roasts, Muscadet, creamy Camembert, and the pleasant Marie Harel and the ceremonial wine. Abel grumbled: 'Hell! Hell! Hell' half sincere, half self-mocking at his position as a stranger, at his Canadian accent. Hell! On the side of the tank, he read the name *Vimy.* At Vimy, more than forty years before, another Leclerc had taken a bullet right through his chest and he had spent fifteen years in dying, in 1931 when his son Abel was only six.

Coming down the steep slope, the standard bearers rolled up their flags and the gilded lances of their staves menaced the passers-by. At the top, the official party had placed two wreathes of red roses on the old heap of camouflaged iron. The tank alone had started to rust.

*　　　*　　　*

At the other end of the *Place de la Libération* was the Hotel de l'Escale. There is always an *escale,* a port of call, somewhere, and it's always a bistro. The press of drinkers went there for the sacred ritual of the *apéritif,* a libation to the gods of the good things of life. Beyond, a long concrete passage opened, skirting the shore, level with the oyster-coloured sea, far off, washed over the scanty black remains of the half submerged Mulberry 2.

Abel dropped into a chair, sighing with relief. He no longer felt the malaise which had overcome him in front of the Gates of War. The waitress came at once, a willowy brunette with a long nose and small sparkling eyes which could not have made uglier her heavily ringed eyelids, her drooping bosom and her large hips which supported the white apron, still in its folds of the morning.

'I'm done for, Yvette has done me down. She's pretended that she can talk American and she's gone off with one of them; there's a delegation of them. You want a "perroquet"?'

It was convenient, this complicity over the *'perroquets'*.

'I certainly do. Has the, er, the young lady come down yet?'

The hesitation was unavoidable. How was he otherwise to speak of Valerie?

'Oh, she's been gone at least an hour.'

'Simone! Simone!' Someone shouted from the hall.

Simone put her hands on her hips.

'Coming! Those lads there are worse than the Yanks. Film people!'

Abel glanced over at the shouting men. You might have thought it was a western saloon in the good old days.

'They've hired the *Marie-de-Mai,* a sardine boat which is just about falling apart. For three weeks' hire, they're paying enough to buy the boat. All right, all right! I'm coming!'

She was rough in her work but she'd be gentle enough at play, this Simone.

'Have a drink with me, Simone,' he said.

'I've still a lot of work to do.'

One of the bright lads from the film crew, which had grown impatient, now appeared in the door. He was wearing a pull-over, green squares on a ground of Chinese red which was enough to put one's teeth on edge.

'Come on, beautiful,' he said. 'We've got quite a thirst, you know. Give us the whole bottle of whisky, honey.'

The affectation of virility in his boisterous mode of address was completely destroyed by a high-pitched lisping voice. His legs had come up in goose-pimples from the sharpness of the air.

Simone went to the bar, laughing a little, her apron flying behind her. A new shadow passed across the town, brought by a cloud in the shape of a four-masted barque, as white as Simone's fresh apron. Simone! In Quebec Abel's girl was called Simone. She was a saleswoman in a supermarket. She washed her teeth with a vitaminised mint and whatever she ate came out of a cellophane pack. Since the boat had arrived at le Havre, he'd completely forgotten about her!

The other Simone came back, very brisk, carrying two *perroquets* of a cloudy green in the glasses. Suddenly the child Olivier appeared, kicking something with his right foot, his left foot in the air. Then, plunging down like the goal keeper in ice-hockey, he gathered from under the table all the tops which were used to cap the bottles of soda, beer or Coca-cola.

'Move your leg and shift your feet.'

The missing middle tooth made him lisp no more notice-ably than the waxen-legged film man. Within a few seconds, Olivier had gathered up a dozen bottle tops. Then his grand-mother arrived, quite out of breath.

'So this is where you are, you scamp! He'll be the death of me! Now just throw away those dirty things!'

Already Olivier had taken himself off with his loot.

The sky had become blue once more. Towards Caen, the barque had changed shape into an heraldic boar, rampant on its hind feet. Abel lifted his glass. Shaking her hair, frizzy from its rural perm, Simone shook off her tiredness.

'If madame or her mother sees me, they'll tell me off good and proper. They're ruining the hotel and they don't know anything about business. Well, it's all because of the war damage.'

'War damage?'

'Of course! The original owners died when the dump fell down and their heirs took over when there wasn't any more risk!'

On the first day Simone had said to him, 'Would you like a *perroquet*?' She had to explain to the Canadian this mixture of *pastis* and *sirop de menthe*. The *perroquet* was a real discovery. Before the liquid filled his mouth with the elaborate flavours of the south of this France which resembled the faded checker pattern red of a tiled Norman kitchen, it gave out its strong aromas. He drank, closed his eyes. His throat felt at the same time the coolness of the herbs and the warmth of the alcohol, a subtle taste of the *anis* and the chill scent of the *menthe*.

'Inevitably, everything round here was destroyed. You got "war damage" to reconstruct with. The sharp ones bought up property for a song when no one else had any confidence in the market. And they set themselves up in houses four times as big as the ones that had been demolished! They really "put it over", I tell you, and not only once!'

She emptied her glass.

'To "put it over", amongst these business men, that's a question of doubling your capital.'

'Putting it over a girl is a different matter, eh?'

'Oh, monsieur Abel, what would your . . . your young lady say?'

He was enjoying himself. He played like an actor who was aware of the effect he made.

'Simone, she would say: "Abel, when are you going to give up this habit of drinking with everyone you meet?" So, then, if I understand it rightly, the war has done some good?'

'For certain people. Now, there was a chemist at St. Fé . . .'

'Abel?' It was a melodious but imperative voice which called. 'I wonder when . . .'

'. . . when I will give up the habit of drinking with everyone I meet. Hallo, Valerie!'

Valerie must have been a sight for sore eyes around the campus when she was at the university. There was no make-up on her pale fair face. Her cheekbones were prominent, her features regular and severe, her ears were small and around them she swept her long hair, drawn back into a well-ordered chignon. She was dressed in a grey tailor-made, very well fitted, but in that impersonal cut which typifies the uniforms of air hostesses in all the airlines of the world.

Abel drained the last drops. He stifled a desire to laugh in deference to this chilly young woman. The Valkyrie in horn-rimmed spectacles crossed her ankles. Ostentatiously, he shook his empty glass with a movement inspired by the ship-wrecked mariners of the Medusa's raft.

'That's the third, I suppose?' she said.

He made the Churchillian gesture of victory.

'Two. And I haven't even drunk the second one. I'm ordering it now. Look here, Valerie, it's the sixth of June and that demands a drink! Don't you realize they're going to drink like fishes, our worthy liberated Normans? It's the famous Norman thirst!'

'You must be a true Norman, yourself. A true Leclerc! Have you found any Leclercs here?'

'In front of the tank. A general's son.'

Simone came back.

'Simone, another *perroquet*. Fruit juice for mademoiselle. Pineapple or grapefruit or tomato or apricot. Or carrot. Or beetroot. Or turnip. Or cucumber. Or even potato. Well, any-way, see what you can get.

Since Valerie's arrival, he had taken on a new personality.

32

His voice had become fine, strong, the accent lightly stressed but from time to time made heavy. His syntax did not differ from French French, but his intonation rang differently, singingly, noticeable in the slight displacement of the major stresses and the accentuation of the vowels. It was the famous 'Normandy-Picardy' accent. It was a voice which gave a suggestion of haymaking and of the cowshed but which also suggested, to the continental ear, the stage yokel.

Valerie made up her mind to smile. When she smiled, spring came to warm the cold lands of the North.

'Abel, Abel, Abel, you are a badly brought up child, a two hundred pound child.'

'Two hundred and two! What's new in church?'

'There's nothing new in church, of course. Only a lot of people. I did not know that the French were such Christian people. I did not want to look at your museum. I went for a walk along the cliff. And that gave me a good idea. It's full of inscriptions. Shall we go there before lunch, do you think?'

Valerie's wishes were orders to be carried out at once. They got up. She was tall, but beside her, the man's strength returned to him, the strength of a lumberjack. He held out his glass in the direction of the bay, then drained it off at a gulp and held it upside down with a theatrical gesture.

The sun went behind a cloud. The wide beach, now splashed with foam became dark.

This promenade also carried the obsessive name: *Quai du Général Leclerc.*

'This isn't a family, Abel, it's an ant-hill! Jacques also had a Leclerc in his family, his lumberjack cousin'!

She pronounced 'Jacques' in the Canadian fashion, accentuating a long 'a'.

The wounds on the houses became more frequent; walls pock-marked by bursts of machine gun fire, scars of a pinky red, villas reduced to rotting stumps, encircled by fences overcome with nettles. Absorbed by the game, Abel was looking for evidence of the past, among the nameplates of the lawyers and the 'For Sale' notices which carried the slogan 'Complete With War Damage' in the gaping excavations and in the rusting barbed wire.

'Recognise anything?'

'Heavens, no.'

She was pursing her lips with the expression he knew so well. Everything about Abel got on the young woman's nerves, even to his manner of walking with his head lowered. 'Anyone would think you were going to beat someone up!' Today, however, he had replied: 'It's all too obvious. It's because I have beaten someone up that I walk like this.' Since then, she had recovered herself by diverting the conversation to other topics, chiefly to the old Dunhill with the chewed stem whose gurgling noises indicated a blockage; then the *perroquet,* followed by his curses, his resounding laughs and all those masculine habits which seemed to her to be just so many sacrilegious assaults on her world. But something else was worrying Abel, more worrying than the temper of Valerie Chandoisel, bachelor-girl, who was imbued with a triple sense of superiority, as an intellectual, as a teacher and as a free woman from the American continent. *He could recognize nothing.* General Intelligence, so eager to communicate disagreeable portents and tiresome news, was obstinately silent. The past war was uncovering itself and what had seemed so easy in Quebec, when they were chatting about their trip, on the Dufferin Terrace, now appeared to be of an insurmountable complexity.

'By the way, Abel, you've asked me to tell you how I got to know Jacques.'

Abel had just read a road sign: 'Tracy-sur-Mer.' This Tracy-sur-Mer no longer meant anything to him.

'It's a veritable novel. Or a lament, rather, a complaint . . .'

He made an effort to come to terms with her. The story nevertheless interested him but she was at one remove from

34

the lost soldier, a soldier as lost as he had been once before on this same green and shining land.

'Génevieve de Brabant, the Complaint of Génevieve de Brabant. That's your second name, isn't it? Génevieve? I see you transformed into a doe.'

'I'm not a doe. Men adore doe-like creatures, don't they?'

'Some little thing's upsetting you, Valerie. Your liver, perhaps?'

'Since I've been in France, I can no longer breathe fully.'

'You're missing your maple syrup, perhaps.'

'I don't like this country.'

The seagulls flew screaming above them. This was interesting, this reaction from the tough woman.

'Is it Normandy, or . . .'

He hesitated. The word appeared to him to be too big.

'. . . or France that you don't like?'

She stopped, turning her back on an expansively vulgar house, corseted with bulging balconies, painted in an acid lemon yellow. Some happy children chased after a dog who was barking furiously.

'I love the France of books and painters and the radio and the lecturers. But I don't like the France which I've seen for the past week, this little France of the little pot-bellied customs men in their absurd uniforms, with its little fields, its little roads, its little cars, its drunks, its dirty songs and the shameless women who hang about the streets. Do you know, Abel, at Rouen, one of them actually said that I could get off with her. Me! Me! *Me!*'

For Valerie, in her precisely tailored suit, with her military walk, her breasts in harness, to be accosted by a happy little homosexual tart, that was really something!

'For a student of sexology, this is a wonderful country in which to experiment, Valerie. I sometimes wonder if you have the *true* scientific spirit!

'Clown! No, I don't like the France of the cafés, this

35

France which smells of fried onions, this France of servant girls who'll go to bed as soon as look at you.'

He ignored the transparent allusion.

'All the same, there must be some characteristics in common between these two Frances?'

'I feel ill at ease on this continent.'

'Why?'

She knew, but she hesitated to speak.

'The men. It's the way they look at you.'

'Of course, Canadians never look at women. They don't even wolf-whistle when they see something that appeals to them . . . especially from behind!'

'Men are the same everywhere. But here, they've got . . . well, how shall I express it? . . . they've got a definite certainty of their own superiority.'

'Well, well!'

He dropped a statement flatly:

'Acteon complex.'

Valerie pricked up her ears. Was this a complex unknown to her?

They were on a new narrow cement road, as new as the handrail, as new as the house which carried an absurd name invented by some self-satisfied wit: The Five Ascetics. As new as Arromanches. And a small clubfooted man was coming towards them. This dwarf, in a white cap and a reefer jacket with gilt buttons, matched in height the four ponies which followed him and on which were riding four grave children.

'It's a good day, for lovers.'

Valerie reddened and was quick to return to the subject of this known complex.

'Acteon? That rash fellow who was changed into a stag because he saw Diana . . .?'

'In her skin.'

'Oh, your French origins are never far away.'

'And I'm glad about it, you may be sure, Valerie.' Now

listen to me. Acteon has the luck to surprise Diana and her maidens while bathing. He gets quite an eyeful. Put yourself in his place! But he forgot the great military principle: see without being seen. And he is seen! So, then, Diana is enraged and changes him into a stag. Now, truth demands that this is underlined: A bit of Acteon had already been animalised by the charming spectacle . . . the doubly charming spectacle which was given by Diana and her companions and he . . .'

'Abel!'

'So, then, you understand? At one stroke, Acteon became a stag completely. You follow me? But the stupid dogs threw themselves on him and devoured him.'

'That's fine then. Where can I find your complex in all this?'

'My complex is in Diana, Valerie. Diana acted in anger. She wishes to punish impertinence. To punish this audacious man. She succeeded in bestialising him. But, oddly enough, she did not want to get him eaten up. Her unconscious—hum!—made use of the situation. You follow me? Diana had not foreseen the conditioned reflex of the dogs. It's fortunate that I've arrived. No one so far has understood anything about this edifying story!'

What had she in mind when she came to France with this tub-thumper? She could have come in a hundred other ways. For example, the Children of Mary were just finishing at this moment a mass visit which did not omit a single Gothic cathedral; not Rouen, nor Amiens, not Chartres nor Paris. Yes, she had to admit that that wouldn't have been too amusing. She needed Abel. It was humiliating. But he was necessary. For the moment, she just had to go along with it. When she was finished, she would change him into a stag and whistle for her dogs.

CHAPTER III

There was a stencilled notice which read:

> Maintenance Commander—Offices
> 6 N 1900

The English sector! Then where was the Canadian sector? He deciphered the signature of a certain Porter, some regimental numbers, a few unit names under a blue cross. He certainly was in English territory. He went back to Valerie. This didn't add up at all!

'Well, what about this love story?' he said, hiding his preoccupation.

'It was a real novel, Abel. Our families were the Lafleurs and the Chandoisels. You could find Lafleurs and Chandoisels everywhere. But the two families hadn't been able to get on together, not for a long time.'

She became expansive amongst these memories which were lightly gilded with a sentimental patina. At last she was living.

'In my family, they used to say: "as crooked as a Lafleur." I was a student. He was employed in a British bank. For, as much as they hated each other, the Lafleurs and the Chandoisels had one thing in common. They had to go out and earn their living at an early age.'

'Naturally, I don't know how our ancestors set about things when they founded the city, but they have certainly made some pretty poor investments since.'

She did not smile. What he had said was of no importance. All that counted for her was her unfinished film, her lost romance.

'I met Jacques in a private school where I was an assistant in French. We'd got on well together before we got to know each other's names. When we did learn them it was too late. In 1830, the Lafleurs had thrown in their sympathies with the revolutionaries. And it hadn't been forgiven in seven generations! They lived near the *Voûtes Jean Talon.* We used to stroll interminably in the little streets which line the hillside, under the arches. You know the *rue Sous-le-Cap,* Abel? We went along it a hundred times! We played like kids, we behaved like tourists, we might have just come from the end of the world and seen that street for the first time! We savoured the *rue Sous-le-Cap* as one might sample the flavour of life itself.'

Abel had a soft spot for the *rue Sous-le-Cap,* with its ramparts and its docks bristling with cranes, its painted façades and its obese walls, its terraces and the walkways in wood or iron which span the street. The dogs, the overhanging houses —just like Rouen—its loud-voiced population and the washing hanging from window to window. In one respect it was a street which was a bit like her:

'Half in the air, half on the ground! In one of those corners where they sell antique junk to American tourists, on one of the first days of 1943, Jacques kissed me. My feet were frozen. I went home with a cold and told myself that it was a fine thing to have met the man of my life.'

'Without your glasses,' he said, gently teasing, 'one might almost find something human in your expression.'

'That is the impertinence of France speaking—your accomplice, Abel! In Quebec, I'd never have told you that. Oh don't deny it, you and France are as thick as thieves.'

The promenade narrowed into a *cale,* a slipway about twenty feet wide and perhaps thirty feet deep, just a termination of a road which ran at right-angles to the sea, a refuge accessible at high tide. The water was slapping sharply on the stones, sending up spray. The blue plaque carried the words:

Commune de Tracy-sur-Mer
Cale du Général Eisenhower

They leaned against the parapet, buffeted by the wind.

'When we found out who we were, this stupid hatred between our families was excitement to us, Romeo and Juliet for ever! There wasn't a single one of my friends who could boast of having a lover hated by her family. So I put religion aside. They were Reds, the Lafleurs. I spurned Canada. I said I was stifling there. But the proprieties weighed heavily.'

He did all he could to stop himself from laughing. Valerie as the enemy of cant! That was just too rich!

'We thought we were avant-garde. He admired Picasso. And he had a communist friend! Is it true that one Frenchman in five is a communist, Abel?'

'At least, one in five votes communist.'

'How extraordinary! Anyway, we believed ourselves to be emancipated. A free union, that was to be the solution to the hatred between our families. Oh, we talked about it. But—but, we never did anything about it.'

Amongst some other remarks about Jacques—Jacques—which came to him in scraps and through these confidences, Abel imagined with tenderness the lovers of Quebec, timid, passionate and virtuous, who talked about sex and revolution with the persistent application of good students of the catechism.

'Jacques was always talking of you, Valerie. May I be frank? I may? Well, he was not always discreet . . . he told me that you and he . . . Well, it wasn't always platonic, was it?'

She sat down on the parapet, took off her glasses, so that her eyes seemed naked, younger and less severe. But she breathed on the lenses, wiped them meticulously, put them on again and said:

'Basically, I was deceived by papa. He allowed himself to be governed by my mother. Papa always said: "When we are in agreement, Louise does what I want. When we differ, I do what she wants. We're very happy." In general, a young woman seeks in a young man a reflection of the father she adores and respects. With Jacques, I was looking for a father who was more . . . more manly!'

Jacques, Jacques . . . Exactly. She was full of her Jacques.

'One Sunday night I found myself alone with Jacques, without very much more to learn!'

In Arromanches, overwhelmed by the statue of Notre Dame, the coaches were gathering together their gangs of passengers with long blasts of the horn.

'It was the desire to anger papa, because he was over-submissive to my mother, that threw us into each other's arms.'

'Yet afterwards you desired him?'

She jumped down on to the tarmac, now put out of countenance.

The walk came to an end in front of a worm-eaten staircase. There was the beginnings of a path which lost itself a hundred or so feet away in the sand. The cliffs plunged down vertically on to the heaps of huge rocks. They were at the world's end, at the Chaos. And the topographical conclusion was inescapable. *This was not where they landed.*

General Intelligence was still silent. However, something was stirring. It was the impulse that moves wild horses and sends them galloping off, the impulse that alerts every animal and is reawakened in a few wartime days in the city-dweller. Abel was sensing with his whole body, as he did at the time when his skin depended on the speed of his reflexes. Then there had been tracks, menaces, dangers; and he sensed them with his shoulders, with the back of his neck, with his spine.

He had senses everywhere. Eyes in his back. Awakened by the infantry battles, in spite of his sixteen years of city living in between, all sorts of hereditary influences still haunted him: Vikings landing on the Norman beaches, then leaving again for England, soldiers of the Hundred Years War, mercenaries, conquerors of Canada, warrior monks, pioneers fighting against the Indians, the forest, the snow, the bears, the English, then at war again against the Boches in 1917 and against Hitler's fanatics. His hunter's senses, awakened in 1944 in Normandy, although without object in peacetime, had not left him. How many times had he tossed a grenade at hazard, only to find a target? 'At hazard.' Uncle Jolicoeur, as he sat under that odd picture of a big angry peasant woman who was going about her business with a sword in her hand and who was called Marguerite in the family. Uncle Jolicoeur used to say that when the Indians lost something, instead of looking for it by reasoning and by methodically scouring the countryside, they sat down, concentrated together, head on the knees, knees in their arms. Then they would get up abruptly and go straight to the lost object. It sometimes worked. There remained in Abel, to a greater degree than among the majority of the 'civilised', a primitive man, revealed by the war, whose sixth sense, an awareness of natural things, was highly developed. Now, since his arrival in France, this sixth sense had been silent.

'Goddam!'
'Abel!'
'I'm sorry, Valerie. But I am completely lost.'

He turned to orientate himself. The sea was certainly to the North, the Cotentin to the West and the mouth of the Seine to the East. So? Well, this was now becoming mad. He returned to the quay, shook his shoes and cussed the sand, then went right up to the first street sign. Still Tracy-sur-Mer. It was only the general who had changed. Montgomery. That was one who lost out a lot. They'd had him as C-in-C before Caen-Caumont when they'd been held up by the SS of the Hitler Youth Division. Monty! That madman who used to make them do P.T. every morning at six, in the open air, and who gave an example himself, dressed in those madly chaste shorts which only the English know how to design! Monty! The man who had never smoked, who had never had a tart, who had never been tight . . . Quietly, he whistled the Davy Crockett tune.

So they had given him a quay! At Tracy-sur-Mer. But there had never been a Tracy in the Canadian sector. Now let's see, Tracy was on the flank. On the right. No doubt about it. The state of the tide helped him. He remembered it better when the sea was up. Yes, Tracy had been on the right, on the right of their sector. Now, Tracy, on the Michelin map, was clearly on the *left*!

'Perhaps it was even farther right,' said Valerie without moving.

'Farther right? What nonsense!'

She stood up, took the map, spread it out in spite of the wind, put it on the ground and fixed it down with stones. She pointed out Arromanches; then, quite clearly on the left of Arromanches, were Tracy-sur-Mer and, on the right, Courseulles, Verville, and Bernières, St Aubin and Ouistreham. By the *right,* she was thinking of the East and on the left, the West.

'But of course you're right, Valerie! I was looking to the right and all the time it's on the left. Towards the mouth of the Orne, towards le Havre . . .'

And still she did not understand!

'But, Abel! These places are on the right. You're looking at the map upside down.'

The explanation burst on him. Valerie had come from the interior of the land. She was looking at Normandy as the French see it, like travellers, like children with the North absurdly 'up there', Tracy 'on the left' of Arromanches and

Asnelles 'on the right'. But they, the attackers, had come from the Ocean.

They saw Normandy in reverse. That very morning, even, in the diorama, he had seen the countryside from the sea in the conditions of the invasion. This was how his war happened, landing from the North, facing south, with the menace from the Cotentin on his right hand with the Rangers getting beaten to hell, the Normandy coast in front of them, extending to the south, flat and treacherous; and, afar, on the left, the invaders' left, the Orne, the Seine, the Pays de Caux, Belgium. The reflexes had been dinned into him in England, just outside Southampton, in front of the sand models, the mock-ups, the aerial pictures and in all those exercises which preceded D-Day.

A gust of wind carried off the map and he ran after the large piece of whipping paper.

'Jacques and I,' she went on.

She had just taken up again the interrupted story which was eating away her life.

'It's coming back to me, you've disturbed me. I wouldn't have you think . . .'

The story of Valerie and Jacques no longer interested him. He showed his wit:

'. . . that you were living in sin?'

'Twice,' she replied, ignoring the irony. 'Twice only. The second time was in the country, in the autumn of 1943 when the apples were ripening. Near the *Ange Gardien* . . . Jacques told me that he'd joined up. Anyhow, Abel, Jacques loved me.'

Abel knew many things about Jacques which she did not, but how could he be sure of them, tie them together, confront them, elucidate them? How could he talk of them, even if he were sure?

'Jacques loved only you.'

44

'Then why did he leave for the war? I gave myself to him because he was going away. Because he was leaving.'

Making love to Valerie must have been really gay, what with her sense of sin, her contrition and her remorse! She had no doubt been beautiful then, for she was still very lovely, but for Jacques it must have been like going to bed with the North Pole!

The seagulls were gliding, the distant bells rang out their peals; and the quays stretched forth empty, geometrical, abstract under the fierce sun. Suddenly, it had got very warm.

It was very warm in the narrow streets, with a thick heat which the breezes from the St Lawrence did not succeed in sweeping away. When he went on leave, Abel had been so happy to be alive that he left as late as possible the interview with Jacques's fiancée. Every evening he swore he'd go the next day. The next day passed, and now there was Valerie before him, young, tall, serious, intimidating.

Dressed in a black suit, she was giving a French lesson to three boys. She had known for some months. She had had a personal letter from Colonel Mathieu; but the Angel Azrael had assumed for Valerie the figure of this big hockey player, dressed in khaki, awkwardly twisting his stiffly pressed beret in his fingers. She sent her three pupils out to play. A wasp hung about, attracted by the smell of ripe fruit.

She had sat down. The wasp was not going to leave although the window was open. In the street, the kids were playing about, overjoyed at the unforeseen break. There was an expression almost of anger on her perfect face.

Abel put Jacques's brief case between a French grammar and a dictionary. She took it. Her fingers were trembling. She did not open it and dropped it into a drawer.

He did not recall how he had gone out, but he remembered clearly, in retrospect, the air in the street which he had breathed with relief. That day he had kept two pictures of Jacques, his share in their friendship. The first showed him in mufti in front of the Maison de Montcalm with its barred

45

windows and its roof of a piercing blue. He had walked there carelessly, blooming with the joy of living. He had no doubts. The other picture showed Valerie and Jacques, no doubt at the *Ange Gardien*. This was probably the day of the 'second time.' Already she was wearing her hair in chignon. Jacques was displaying that fuzziness of feature, that imprecision, that indefinable but definite sign whose warning character did not become apparent, until it was too late; and then you could read it into the photographs of those who died young with a violent death.

A radio sounded out with trumpets and drums, and the husky voice of a woman:

> Ce n'était qu'un simple soldat
> Sans nom, sans papiers, sans mystère . . .

They came back by way of the *Câle Général Eisenhower*. Some wit had christened an old tub *La Riflette*. An old warrior, no doubt, like all those who felt obliged to talk loudly at this time, at all the counters of all the bistros. Some of the boats carried feminine names. *Suzanne* or *Marie-Louise*. Ah, *Evangéline*. A Catholic land! In a shaded corner, there was a big boat, freshly painted in white and lilac, smelling of linseed oil, standing on stays. Its name became legible as they got nearer:

LIBERTE

'There's a rope to make this Liberty secure,' he said in a surly voice.

He had never had these reflections when he was nineteen, when he was in this country with Jacques. This, then, was all that life had brought him in sixteen years: bitterness!

There was one last boat, high and dry at the top of the slipway laden with blood coloured nets. It was called:

We Three

They stopped. Above their heads, the seagulls shrieked. There was an interminable pause before Valerie spoke again.

'Are you superstitious, Abel?'

'Of course.'

'I'm not. But I think that we all live in the middle of signs which we do not know how to read. We are lazy in our heads . . .'

They looked at the boat with the red nets. *We Three.* He went aside as though he was going to get trapped by these nets.

'You think with your head, Valerie. I think with this.'

And he beat his chest with his two fists, breathing in at the same time so that it made a hollow boom. He was doing the 'gorilla' act.

'I've always thought that you were some kind of animal,' she said thoughtfully.

Three jersey-clad fishermen set about launching *Evangéline*. One of them released the blocks. The three pulled together with a grinding of pulleys and Abel went to help them. Then Abel and Valerie set off again for Arromanches. In the tobacconist there was one local man with fair hair and red complexion, who was sniffing at a green apple and shaking his head earnestly, in front of a jovial patronne with apple-cheeks, apple-breasts and fists like apples on her broad hips. As they went out Abel laughed. She asked him why. Quite unabashed he said: 'These Norman women have such big backsides.' Not another word was uttered between them before they got to the Escale!

But a hundred yards from the hotel, in front of an abandoned house, he gathered up some roses, once-cultivated roses which returned to the wild state. They were little climbing roses, pink, fleshy, gay with prickly leaves and stalks, the roses of Arromanches.

CHAPTER IV

ABEL AND VALERIE had hired a little drive-yourself car. It was a lively little toy which bravely attacked the steep path which led to the Vimy tank and passed beneath the huge statue of the Virgin, looking as though it were carved in lard, then between the pines and the acacias. Valerie, wilful and abrupt, was giving the engine hell without being aware of doing so. She was self absorbed. In one field, a band of crows was exchanging untranslateable insults with a group of gulls. Through St Côme, then Asnelles with its low spreading buildings, blooming with hydrangeas around its church spire. They stretched in a line between the backdrop of green fields and the dunes. The blue of the sky and the pink of the road wove themselves into a gentle pastoral against which the cows stood out as though made of cardboard, small ones, big ones, some with huge horns, of every shade of white and red, fawn, chocolate and tobacco. Normandy possesses an eclectic cow.

Valerie braked violently. A cart, drawn by a donkey, had come suddenly out of a side road. The car slipped into a skid. Valerie controlled it by accelerating and went off.

'No doubt you noticed that the donkey was complete,' said Abel.

She did not understand him.

'I mean that this is a fine donkey, a true donkey, a complete donkey. There isn't an ass in the Acteon complex,' he went on, with his eyes crinkled teasingly. 'But there is one in Shakespeare. "Clowning and putrefaction." Do you remember? The queen of faery, Titania, falls in love with

48

Bottom when he is transformed into an ass. Ass, stag, bull . . . You ought to study these variations on one zoological theme.'

The young woman's hands went back slowly onto the steering wheel and she sat up straight with her lips tightly closed.

'Titania and Bottom, that's very important, Valerie! By the way, don't you think it absurd that the French never translate the name "Bottom", in their adaptation of the *Dream*? "Bottom" has a very definite meaning for the English public! Titania is in love with Bottom. The French never understand. But if you were to say: "Titania's in love with my arse," they'd understand all right. Free translation, of course.'

He stopped and then said, sweetly:

'You don't seem to want to talk?'

After Ver, the Pearl Coast stretched before them, punctuated by the remnants of the pontoons which drew in dots the shape of the ghosts of the Mulberry. Near Graye, there was a shed which spewed out a number of highly coloured wooden horses, an immobile cavalry of childhood.

'Valerie,' he said in a changed voice, 'we must stop here.'

The sea was again only a hundred yards away. They got out and walked. In front of them the dark wet sand lay in contrast with the whiteness of the foam. He looked hard. The wind was whipping a wild, cropped vegetation, of thorns, broom and of sea pinks. He breathed down deep into his lungs the strong scent of the seaweed. He hesitated for a long time, floating on the high tide. Then he stood up, his mind sadly made up. He returned to the car. She came after him. He began to drive off without a word, skidded in the sand, got out, put newspaper under the spinning wheel. Slowly, almost regretfully, he crossed the bridge over Rives, which comes just outside Verville-sur-Mer, and stopped the car in front of the new Casino, not far from a Calvary.

'Didn't you make any notes?' she asked.

He returned to her a fishlike expression.

'I did keep a war diary. It was very short. *"Journal of Abel Leclerc. Enrolled . . . Arrived in England . . ."* I don't remember the dates. That's the end of Abel's Journal.'

Workmen, indifferent to the Landings, dressed in brilliant yellow oilskins with high boots—the sanitary squad. They set to work in the tanks where a notice said:

JAOUEN'S OYSTER BEDS
Oysters Bred
Sightseeing Tours
THE OYSTER
Pearl of Health

Nets lay about the catwalks, close to a beached boat. On the other side of the channel was a grey hulk on which one could still read:

T.173   U.S. ARMY

Three girls passed, arm in arm, in blue jeans, with long greasy hair dangling round their shoulders.

Abel went to and fro, striding over the damp rubbery mounds. He climbed up again on to the sea wall and sniffed the wind. At the top of the channel a blockhouse commanded the beach in enfilade. The bathing cabins bore old fashioned names: *Heloïse, Amanda* or *Léopolda*. However, he felt the crisp dry wood with his hand and found it a friendly touch. He stopped, took off his shoes, and rolled up his trouser legs. The blue shells of the broken mussels, the cockles buried in the sand, the dead crabs—that's just how it was. There were ten yards of dry sand in front of them, at high tide. And they were in country of wet sand, engulfed, near to the moving frontier of the primeval weed, seaweed as old as time. He came and went, from the dry beach to the wet sand, where old women in dusty black were talking loudly without looking at the sea. A chubbily prosperous woman was dipping bread in her coffee and giggling like a small girl being

50

tickled. He sat down in front of a mummy-like old man. Valerie installed herself near him, arranging herself as all women do at the seaside, drawing her calves up to her thighs, knees held together with her intertwined fingers.

'Have you found what you're looking for?' she ventured. He chose his words.

'No. No. Valerie. Not at all. I used to tell myself that a place where your very life was once in danger . . . that you would never forget. Valerie, when we disembarked on these nightmarish beaches, we were all certain we'd be killed . . .'

A mist came into his eyes, disturbing, a sign of doubt, of weakness and disquiet in this amiable colossus.

'I'm sorry, Valerie. I'm . . . I'm talking nonsense. I said "we". I believe I am speaking for him.'

What an intelligent man, for all his brutishness! For this was the quality in him of which she was becoming more and more conscious. She had to keep from herself the idea that Jacques was concealed in Abel in some way, that he was the means by which Jacques would be able to return.

'These nightmarish beaches . . .' The chubby young woman was trying to give the eye to a solitary white-haired man, in white shirt and grey flannels. Two young girls were roasting themselves. Children were making sandpies.

He pulled some skin off his lips. Now, he would have to explain himself and that annoyed him.

'We went forward yard by yard, with our bellies in the water. Crawling on our bellies! And as the tide rose, the water came with us.'

'Jacques as well?'

Drily he replied:

'Jacques like the rest of us.'

Then with a great tiredness:

'You must try to understand me, Valerie.'

'For three days now,' she said, 'you've taken me through a lot of villages. And everywhere you've said: "No, it's not there".'

51

'We were part of a detached commando. Most of them now are dead. I tried to get in touch with the rest, five years ago. Only one answered. He could remember nothing.'

'You didn't even find out the name of the village?'

'It was a name that ended in "ville", that's all. In Quebec I've always been able to keep every detail of the countryside in my head. So I thought I would be able to locate myself again here. By instinct. You know, by smell. What nonsense that was! There's only one thing that agrees: this flat beach, with its seaweed, its sandfleas, its gulls and the tide. But that goes on for dozens of miles.'

'But the place where Jacques was killed is inland, isn't it?'

'Yes. The other side of Caen. It was a place which ended in "ville", as I've said. And there are hundreds of them. Normandy consists entirely of Leclercs and towns whose names end in "ville".'

Abel shut his eyes. If only he could be somewhere else! Anywhere else! It was like the day of the wasps. He felt as if he were the victim of a practical joke. He was unaware that thousands of men had experienced the same sinister game of blind-man's-buff, like their fathers after Verdun, Dixmude, la Fè-Champenoise, les Eparges or Vimy; like their grandfathers and their grandfathers before them right back to Thermopylae; had experienced the same impossibility of making memory agree with the world which continues and which can go to blazes! On one hand, memory hardens its images against oblivion. The world itself, throws healing tissue over the scars of the trenches, regroups the cemeteries, divides up, buys and sells the damages of war! Life casts away its dead on the desert islands of time and sails along before the wind.

His deeply lined brow became smooth under the effort of his sombre reflections.

'A name which ends in "ville". A very pointed steeple. I

had a shock at Asnelles. The one there was the very brother of my steeple. Mine was in two sections, one square, at a wider angle so that it could serve as a plinth, and the other section had eight sides at an acute angle. The roof of the church, out of which the steeple rose was brown. The roof of the steeple was blue. I expect the growth of the parish had compelled the priest to enlarge his buildings several times, because three annexes were added under roofs with an increasingly shallow pitch. As for these roofs . . . They were like this. You see? The pitch of the steeple itself was almost vertical. A needle. Then, it was broken halfway down into an angle of 45 degrees. Like that. Then there was the tiling and, in four successive steps, the church merged gently with its churchyard.'

She was amazed by the obsessional, grief-laden quality of this vision, almost lightheaded in its precision.

Unaware of her, he made a drawing in the sand with the tip of his finger.

'The church is very old. Its successive grafts had made a living thing of it, as I knew it, which is still waiting for me somewhere, with its cemetery, its porches, its sacristy and its lantern window like evidence of an intelligent life which looks out like an eye.'

He sighed deeply, his forehead damp.

'And then?'

Valerie did not move. Her mouth was dry from the excitement aroused by his description.

'And then?'

'And the graveyard. In the graveyard the tombs were higgledy-piggledy. There was a broken down wall, a little bridge and, right beside it, the meadow. Cows were bellowing because they'd not been milked. Their udders were swollen yellow. It's heartrending, a cow which bellows. The meadow was full of orange coloured blossom, wild marigolds, probably.'

'Did you stay long?'

'I don't know. Twenty minutes? An hour? Oh, not more than an hour. Quite near us we could also see hedges and very old apple trees. The apples were green. An acid green. The village was like an island, you know. Not a big place. A few cottages, low and long with sloping walls to catch the sun. The lantern and the steeple. For this place made a frame round its red, brown and blue church, which stood out against the mackerel sky. Now understand that we were not in the village. It was some four hundred yards from us. More or less. But for us, it was the end of the world.'

'Jâques?'

'Jacques was dead.'

Yes, today was becoming as ghastly as the day of the wasps. For the same reason. It was his fault, after all. He had settled nothing on the day of the wasps. So the abcess formed once more. But he had not been more than twenty, that day of the wasps. And what does one know of death at twenty, even when one has escaped it?

He began again, as though talking in his sleep.

'Four hundred yards from the village. Jacques saw that village. He saw it but he never went into it, never. The apple trees were being strangled by ivy. As for me, I had just been thinking: "I'd like to be an apple tree." But they were cut to ribbons, those trees. And . . .'

'And? . . .'

She tried to lead on his narration much as one prompts the semi-conscious.

'There was water everywhere, right out of sight. It was water which hardly made a reflection, it was so filthy.'

'That's a very precise recollection. Especially the church. Very precise, indeed.'

'What?'

He raised his head.

Valerie paused for a moment.

'Is that where his grave is?'

He sprang back. It had been hell! He'd just described

54

hell! Not the village, not at all. That on the contrary, seemed to them to be a haven, where they'd find a drink, cider, bacon and eggs, camembert, warmth, life. But hell was this swamp between them and the village, this putrid bog made by the Germans' flooding, the reflection of the steeple in the grey water, and the crows which the motors did not succeed in frightening away. He had just looked again at hell and this little fool talked about a grave. Why not a monument?

Where on earth was this stinking road? Like the artificial ports, vanished. Swallowed up in the grasses, because it wasn't an honest road! It was a wartime road in the land of France, an imported road, an engineers' road thrown across the mud, with appallingly bad foundations, a one-way track to supply those who were up ahead. That was hell and ever since they'd started to look for villages 'with names ending in "ville",' they'd found nothing but small towns bathed in a golden glow of peace!

'We first went to Drainville,' she said, sensing his opposition to her. 'I made a note.'

She noted, did she? Ah, if only he had made a note! But he'd behaved like one of Uncle Jolicoeur's Indians. He need not surround himself with advice. He need not reason it out. He would go straight to Drainville! But instinct had betrayed him. What would they have done in this instance, those Indians? They would have abandoned the track. They were not logicians. If they didn't find what they had lost, it would be because it did not interest their gods. But the Indians didn't have a squaw with them to call the tune.

He sat up again and faced her.

'No. It's no good, Valerie. No good at all! You're putting the cart before the horse. First of all, I must locate myself. By starting at the exact spot of the landing. That's not going to be easy.'

'But it's here, isn't it?'

Well, no, that cannot be quite definite. He saw in the young woman's eyes the desire to beat him.

'I could do with a stiff Calvados,' he said.

A cold glance from Valerie told him her opinion, that this was not so urgent.

He took his pipe out of his pocket, the old Dunhill, and caressed the knotty briar, once so black and now scorched by long use; and, with a familiar gesture, he rubbed it on the bridge of his nose to bring a shine up on the bowl. Clogged up, the bastard!

Valerie was getting fidgety.

'So?'

'So? Ah, yes. Well, then, by starting again at the beginning, that's to say from that charming little beach. I shall end up, perhaps by making my drunken memories agree with a location . . . a completely sober location.'

He had an attack of hiccups. He held it back. He was trying to escape from the persistence of his companion by taking refuge in parody, in self-derision.

'Is there anyone on this earth, Abel, someone who has been a friend of Jacques and who does not drink so much calvados?'

'No one. Not even one who does drink too much calva. Or even whisky. Out of a dozen in the commando, Valerie, only five of us knew Jacques well. Lieutenant Petitjean, Tit-Rouge, Siméon, Vadboncoeur and myself. I was the last left with Petitjean. All the others are dead, Valerie. Valerie, listen to this. It's instructive. Tit-Rouge was murdered by the SS. He was taken prisoner and then shot.'

'Oh!'

'When we saw it, we did not take a single prisoner that day. Do you still understand? Siméon. Siméon was a little swine. But this poor little swine died in the Ardennes. A wound eighteen inches long. You could see his ribs and his guts inside. The lungs! Red and going in and out . . . like a pump.

Vadboncoeur was the last. In Germany, on his birthday. A rocket. The rocket was fired by a kid. Hitlerjugend. Nothing remained of either of them. Except for Petitjean, they are all as dead as a doornail, all of them.'

He hammered out:

'Valerie, I'm going to do everything I can to find Jacques' remains, once again. But for God's sake give me a little peace! Go and eat shrimps. Have a swim. Read Freud and let me work out the direction of this trip, if it has one. With or without calvados.'

She bit her lip. Sitting down, leaning on hands which were buried in the sand, with her head back, she followed a white bird with her eyes. She had taken the wrong direction. She was the one who had been outmanoeuvred. She had fallen into the trap. No, it wasn't going to be easy, with this intelligent brute!

First, the port of Courseulles, the twin port of Verville, only larger, did not teach them anything. Then Bernières rose up in its setting of greenery. A memorial stone stopped them, facing the land, like the prow of a ship which has run aground.

Here, on 6th June 1944
the Heroism of the Allied Forces
liberated Europe.

On 6th June 1944, at seven in the morning, the Allied armies including the Canadian Régiment de la Chaudière, commanded by Colonel Paul Mathieu, landed on the beach at Bernières-sur-Mer, so creating the first bridgehead for Victory.

'They know about these things,' he said between his teeth. But this tough cynical fellow could not stop the tears streaming down his face. The tears trickled down his primitive, Herculean, hunter's face. He could do nothing to stop it, stupefied at this turning on of the taps. Valerie turned away her head and wondered why she felt ashamed.

Abel wiped his eyes several times, in vain; but an ancient dignity transfigured him. Only then did he notice a detail which he never afterwards forgot. Leaning against the monument to the Allies, sixteen years later, precisely, was a half-moon shaped shrimp net about to plough through the shallow waters. Beside it, washing his car with a bucket, was a stoutish little man with bare feet, his trousers rolled to the knee, whistling under his breath. Now and again he cast a glance at the sea. He was waiting for the tide to go out . . .

'My God,' said Rifleman Leclerc, 'there's a shrimp net leaning against the Monument to the Dead!'

CHAPTER V

WITH SUNKEN EYES War was lying in wait for them from a stoutly built cube of a house, with a roof of broken tiles, which displayed its timbers like bones. A fisherman was sitting on the quay playing a harmonica listening to himself, as only mouth organ players can do. This fellow watched them coming from the corner of his eye.

'Did the Canadians land here?' asked Abel, sitting down beside him.

The old man shook the spit out of his instrument.

'The Canadians? Good gracious, yes. They come by here like a drill squad. They were all smashed up.'

He pointed to the big broken villa and took up his harmonica again. The tune he played was a gay one, an old music hall song, and the mouth organ music had overtones of the bagpipes.

'Was it tough?' asked Abel.

'Tough? It was good and tough. But after a couple of hours, about ten o'clock, the lady in the château poured them out some cider. They were really hot, poor sods. They went off into the village.'

He lisped his 'r's, because of the gaps in his teeth.

In spite of the anniversary of the Liberation, black-dressed women were throwing seaweed into antique carts which, nevertheless, had pneumatic tyres.

'Tight at ten! So the old lady of the château said to me: "Sabastian, I suppose you'd like some cider too, you rogue".'

Sebastian grumbled a few unintelligible statements and then there was nothing left within him but the fire of an old man's spite to warm his weariness in the sun. Ah, yes, lady, he'd seen the Canadians! The ones who didn't speak French. And them, well, you didn't take any notice of them. Almost as though they spoke English! And the others, those who spoke French. Bernières had been liberated by the ones who spoke French:

'You could understand everything they said, these Chauds! That's what we called 'em here, the Chauds. There were Chauds here, Chauds there . . . Look, they didn't talk quite like us round here. More like the people inland.'

He shook his head.

'Wasn't very nice to see. There was all them poor devils in khaki all bleeding so much it took a doctor to put 'em back again. I used to do the garden of Doctor Horovitz. And he never stopped. No more did the Boche doctor. Big skinny wolf of a man. Grey all over. Grey eyebrows which came down to here. And he cut and trimmed and sewed 'em up. These Canadians, they told the Boche quack: "You've done enough. Take a rest." He said: *"Ja, Ja."* He showed them 'em his silver teeth and just went on.'

Sebastian moved his legs, one at a time. One could almost

perceive a very old little naughty boy hidden inside the old man's skin.

He thought.

'I was wrong to call him a Boche. He was a German; a good man. There were a few. A good man. He didn't spend any more time with the men in grey than the ones in khaki. He was a man, I could have kissed him.

'The wounded came in here from all over. They could get them back on the boats one by one. Specially they came from Bény-sur-Mer. Round here, it's sometimes called Bény-on-Mud. You see, there's no sea near it.'

He laughed for a long time with his eyes closed. This witticism doubled him up.

'Well, Doctor Horovitz had a red apron on, like a butcher. A real butcher, you'd have said. And the German didn't sleep for forty-eight hours. And me . . . I was washing, all the time, how I washed, just how I washed! I saw more blood in two days than during the whole of the war of '14!'

He spat between his legs.

'There's a cemetery full of them, at Bény, the Canucks.'

Abel offered him a cigarette. The old man turned the packet over in his wrinkled hands, laughed at the gilded camel and said, with respect:

'It's not the same picture, but it's the same smell.'

He lit one of them with a lighter of German tinder which stank in spite of the open air. He drew on the cigarette, astonished by the taste. After a minute, he put it out, carefully, tore off the paper, heaped up the tobacco into his hand, rolled it up, stamped it together and popped it into his mouth.

Abel went off, with a friendly wave. Sebastian waved back, champing away with his molars.

'You were wrong to be impatient, Valerie. It's over two miles of this coast that the Régiment de la Chaudiére attacked. The Chauds! Do you understand? My regiment. The Chauds. Now it's very simple. Jacques and I were put ashore a bit farther to the right.'

He burst out laughing. He was relieved.

'That's my own right. Oh, these conditioned reflexes. They really made us into good robots for this to persist for sixteen years. Fine! Valerie, all we have to do now is to go over this coast with a fine toothcomb, on the right from here. That's to say, the left on the map. Understand?

Clouds, like shoals of fish, assaulted the sun and set a rapid succession of light and shade running. At the empty base of the dune, he took his suede jacket off, like battle-dress. He whistled the tune which Sebastian had put into his head. A cracked bunker was half extracted from the sand, like a rotten tooth. A little farther, on top of an intact blockhouse, grass was growing, destroyed here and there by cinders, the traces of picnic fires. A manhole opened up on top. Abel let himself down through it. He lit his flashlight, and went into the shelter. A strong smell of ammonia attacked his nose. The passage opened out into a larger room, higher, lighted by the observation hole for a machine gun so that it could sweep the beach in a scything action. The walls were studded with swastikas. Soldiers' names, dates, Friedrich, Hofer, Horst . . . Someone had painted the words Lili Marlene in tar in gothic characters. There were some words in an unknown alphabet, Greek or Russian. Then, at one side: *Claudie et André P.L.V.* So André had made love to Claudie on this sand, suffused with blood, in spite of the defecations of the living and the memory of the dead. The earth was strewn with bones of an oblong shape. It took him several moments before he could identify them. They were fish shells brought in by storm tides.

It was a personnel shelter, armed with heavy machine guns, perhaps the very ones which had pinned them down for so long. He went to the firing slit. From there, the 'charming little beach' stretched out, studded with living dots which were bathers, women sitting in deckchairs, children running

61

and jumping . . . Sixteen years earlier at the same hour! What must it have been like then, with the stench of burnt cordite! Once more he saw the barrage balloons and the dives of the escorting aircraft. He smelt in his nostrils, the rotten-egg smell of the explosions, while the flame-thrower tanks and the crocodiles began to disembark their iron and fire. He saw the Chleus, as the French called them, burned by machine guns which fired by themselves as the barrels became red-hot. The blackened faces, the streaked eyes and the faded blue eyes. The blue eyes of men who had come from the East and from the land, who were machine-gunning other men with blue eyes who had come from the West and from the sea . . .

A harsh voice shouted at his back:
'*Wer da?*'
Abel turned round, leaning forward. In the opening which gave on to the neighbouring room, a big devil of a man stood outlined, with something heavy in his fist.
'*Verzeihung!* Sorry, monsieur. I thought my friend Horst was there. *Mein Freund!* I wanted to make . . . a little joke . . .'
His speech was slow, the speech of a foreigner who has to pick out his words, with a very heavy accent. He looked a lively fellow. He stood up, and bent forward. What he was holding in his hand was a camera. He went in. He was clean-shaven, with a square jaw, high cheekbones, pale eyes, even paler than Abel's. The visitor looked at the walls and swept them with his electric lamp. Suddenly, he seemed to find what he was looking for. A signature on the wall. He put his fore-finger on it and began to shout: 'Horst! Horst!' He was exultant. He had found himself there. What luck! Of course, for them, for the defenders, it was much easier. 'Horst! Horst!' He showed Abel the name. Then, drawing himself up proudly, until his ornamental feather touched the ceiling

62

of the bunker, he pointed to his own chest. He raised his eyes
to the sky. He was miming sleep. He expressed in gestures
the surprise of the bombardment. His arms were stretched
upwards while his head went back into his shoulders. The
action which, at first was soothing, suddenly became
dramatic. The German yawned, shook himself, mimed the
alert acting in turn the parts of the sergeant, the lookout, the
loaders, the gun layer and the O.C. *Ja wohl! Heil Hitler!*
Horst! Horst! Schnell! He rushed to the machine gun, he
carefully drew away the body of a comrade. Not so good. He
sat on the gun-seat, and fired, trembling from head to foot.
He changed the magazine, burning his fingers, turned round,
opened his eyes wide at the sight of another pal knocked out,
took up the machine gun, pissed on the barrel to cool it off,
sat down again, looked for the magazines, took off his blouse,
fired again a few more sparing bursts, stood up beside the
empty weapon and flattened himself against a wall as he
protected his belly, gasping, with shining eyes.

In the other room, the door disclosed a parallelogram of
sunlight. The German, now untidy, dishevelled, wounded,
went tottering out and fell on the sand.

He did not budge.

Well! Was this really serious?

Perhaps the emotion was. Perhaps the surprise. And the
past which gripped at the throat like a bandit. Abel went over
to the German and shook him. He let himself be turned over.
He was really sick. No! He just half opened an eye in which
the light of mischief glistened. Well played! In the open air
his eyes were the colour of forget-me-not. *Vergiss mein nicht.*
He appeared stouter in the sunlight, older, more careworn, a
worthy enemy. With a long face, Fritz slowly lifted up his
arms, his hands open. Piteous. Defeated. Finished. Grief-
stricken. Ashamed. A prisoner. *Kaput.*

Yet he too had come back. Called. Summoned. Invoked.
By whom? For what ticker-tape parade, for what period of
reserve training among ghosts, for what hideous rendez-vous

had they come to the beaches of the West, invaders and defenders both?

Whose orders were they obeying?

To whose command did they belong without knowing it?

Fritz's face had grown gay once more. He mimed *joie de vivre*. The pleasures of travel. Of good food. Of the sea. Of the sun. Of sleep. He pointed out Valerie, in her swimsuit in the distance. He expressed his appreciation of the young woman's figure with eloquent gestures. Then he uncorked a bottle with a click of the tongue, poured out two glasses, and gave one to Abel. Abel could never refuse a drink, even an imaginary one! He drank, drained it carefully, showed that not a drop was left by shaking it and then threw it with all his force against the concrete. Then, without a pause, he started to dance Russian style, while the German beat his hands faster and faster. Out of breath, Abel stood up. He re-created in his turn the hugeness of the beach, the endless expanse of the sea, the planes, the countless ships, the United Kingdom behind and, still farther back, the American continent, and the immense invasion. Then, everything was reduced to the scale of an infantry man in a few feet of sand, crawling, fidgeting, twisting, firing, begging Heaven, scraping the devilish earth. Stretched on the sand, Abel fired a Bren, spraying anywhere. He pointed out his pals whom the stretcher-bearers were carrying back towards the huge armada. At last, just as the German had done, he stood up, put his hand flatly against his chest and swept it out to the sea in a musketeer's salute.

Peace slept on the beach.

The German, his heart in his mouth, holding the base of his long green waterproof between two fingers, like a skirt, began to dance the can-can, as he hummed an Offenbach gallop. His joints cracked. He burst out into uncontrollable laughter and let himself fall on his backside. Abel sat down beside him. They accentuated their breathing, laughing at themselves and at the sadness of age which was approaching. A game was reawakened from the distant memories of childhood and they squatted on their heels, face to face, with palm to palm, with bent legs, like leaping cockerels trying to push each other backwards. They danced round, turned, dodging. They were twelve years old.

Then Horst turned up. They burst into laughter at his astonished expression.

Without doubt, that was 'his' bunker. The bastards, how they had made him sweat, with his nose in the seaweed, prickled beyond endurance by the sandfleas, beneath the path of the bullets which Horst and Fritz had sent over their heads. He went up to Fritz, took his hand and shook it violently. Then he said, very quickly:

'If ever I tell Valerie about this, it's certain she's going to accuse me of drinking calvados till the cows come home. So long, blondie. Very pleased to have made your acquaintance. Bon voyage, but don't come back here again.'

'*Ja,*' said the German, put out by the speed of Abel's delivery, satisfied merely by the tone of voice and the outstretched hand. '*Ja. Gut. Ja wohl. Friede.* Peace. *Auf Wiedersehn.*'

That 'till we meet again', we can just do without that, Fritz.

The French never swim until a good three hours after lunch. They are right to do so because they are stuffed full! However, this prudence brings them out late to the beach, when the sun has lost its strength. They are not a sporty race. They are not a nature-loving race. They are not a sun-loving race. Abel stripped and showed himself, on his naked torso lot of hair which here and there had started to whiten. The tide had left behind bits of damp seaweed. Right along the shore the sea marked out its retreat in this manner. The dunes stretched out, soft and eternal. Beyond, cows munched the salt grass. Above, seagulls were screeching out cries of indignation in the tone of a maiden lady who has been shown a dirty postcard. Abel burst into laughter. I must show Valerie some dirty postcards, and call it a scientific study of sex.

'Hi!'

There she was. There was no question of showing doubtful pictures to this shimmering goddess in her white swimming cap. You couldn't see a single thing out of place. No blemish, nor pimple, no straying hair nor slack muscles, no mark anywhere. *Parfait*. An icecream.

Valerie shook water on to him.

'Coward! Come and swim.'

'It's too cold.'

She undid the chin-strap of her cap.

'I'm not shivering,' she said.

Not even goose flesh!

With studied indifference she said:

'Well, was this the place?'

Happily, he affirmed it with a nod of his head.

'Well, then. You see? You are making mountains out of molehills. You men are all the same.'

Her tone was biting. It was significant. These displays of feminine superiority had won over Canada. Even in its Catholic parts, following the United States, it had surrendered to the powerful women's societies, which rule like the matrons in those far-off matriarchal civilisations, by cant, by taboo and by the excommunication of those rare sons of Adam who dared to revolt. Nothing annoyed Abel more than these signs of a lunar servitude. For they were all daughters of the Moon. Like Diana. They were the Amazons of Diana. And men were promised the fate of Acteon.

She sat down.

'Really not? The water's fine! Right, then. I'll take off my cap.'

Her hair rolled down on to her shoulders.

'Abel, I had an odd notion while I was swimming. I got the idea that you did not want to tell me where Jacques died.'

She, who had been so infuriatingly obtuse so shortly before, now had got the message!

66

'Is that why you drink?' She asked after a moment, when he had not answered.

'I drink, I drink, don't let's make too much of it! Why I drink as much as I do, that's because I'm sick of it, Valerie. Life does not interest me. But be careful—I'm not a vulgar everyday drunk. A stupid Latin or Irish drunk. A drunkard, yes, but hygienic.'

He laughed savagely. He laughed too loudly. This play-acting threw Valerie back into her exasperation. One against the other, they were working on each other's nerves.

'The "perroquet" is for the exotic touch. Like the negress in the brothel. But in the end, it's whisky I like. Whisky is clean, plain, well brought up. You get the same drunkenness in San Francisco, Tokio or Ottawa. I like cleanliness. Because it is peace. You have to have a lot of peace to get two pennyworth of cleanliness, Valerie. So, I like whisky. There aren't any local microbes in whisky. So, Valerie, I value all of these things because they are not going to endure.'

He turned on the sand, suddenly sober.

'Ah, yes, I know your women's world. It's made up of showerbaths, tooth-cleaning and hair-washing, credit sales, central heating, chlorophyl, penicillin, vitamins, deodorised armpits. All that is not going to endure. You girls think it's all permanent. You're completely wrong, ladies. Chaos is the way of the world. The order of the world is disorder. And that's why I drink. To discover once again genuine chaos, beyond radio and TV, beyond papers and advertising and propriety and hygiene and good manners. I drink because I covet poison, war, incest, rot, I want to grow a beard and stuff my belly with mushrooms, snails, frogs and well-hung pheasant. You understand? Of course you don't. *Vive Marie Harel.* I want a well-soused life and stinking cheese.'

He was infuriating when he did this party-piece—he'd often done it before for the lads at Radio Quebec.

She was digging pensively in the sand with the palms of her

67

hands, carefully, so as not to ruin the varnish on her nails.

'Don't dig in the sand. You mustn't dig in the sand!'

His voice had completely changed and now was harsh and sincere.

She obeyed; then she stood up slowly. She stood over him, outlined against the sky, elegant in her burgundy-coloured swimsuit, a garment which carried a red and blue shield and the word:

ATLANTIC

Ah, yes, she is really a woman of Atlantis! One of those who, for so long, have imposed their law on the men. While he and his father had fought two world wars to save freedom from a deadly perversion of humanity, the women of Atlantis had taken advantage of the situation by enslaving their continent. Victors in Europe and in Japan, the men had returned home vanquished by their own women and without having noticed it. Just a little more and these peremptory matrons would have thrown them into complete subjection. All things considered, a matriarchy is as hard on the race as the Black Death.

She refastened her cap and ran towards the sea with a lithe grace.

Some little girls were fishing. The more daring played in the waves, testing it, running after it, and fleeing from it in a chattering throng as soon as it came to them. True daughters of Eve. No huntresses here. No Amazons. But all these little ones, with their awkward, coltish movements wore the same vermilion swimsuits. Little sea anemones. My God, what have You done with their fathers? Their fathers are sleeping in the sands. Now and then, a child while digging will bring to the light of day the white smile of teeth which have clenched on a dying scream. Dear God, these were my brothers.

Abel ran into a rainbow made by the sun in the foaming waves. He went imperceptibly towards the distant open sea,

68

step after step, his legs pushing powerful bow-waves ahead, his torso like the prow of a ship. It was Jacques who was the good swimmer. Luckily, he could swim, Jacques, luckily, because ... Luckily ... ? Well, then ...

CHAPTER VI

A FEW BLUE lights flickered. The invisible sea slapped the boat. They were inside a sponge.

'We bellyached about Southampton,' yelled Jacques, 'but I'd give a lot to get back there.'

'Because of Jennifer?'

'Of course, because of Jennifer. I had a date with her.'

'Me too,' said Abel.

But Jacques didn't hear.

The din increased in volume. You could have imagined yourself to be in a tunnel of iron. Jennifer was the daughter of a shopkeeper in the old town, close by the ramparts, beside the Hotel Tudor ... She was a well-developed young lady, with a milky complexion, as pretty as a picture by Reynolds. She had a weakness for young soldiers, so that her virtue was severely tried by the attentions successively of the Tommies, G.I.s, Canadians, marines, French, and Poles! She was very well guarded by her mother, in the perfect manner of the English mum. These two forces had kept the situation in balance until the handsome Jacques came on the scene. 'He really is handsome, that one.'

'She's still a virgin,' said Jacques.

'Ah-oh,' replied Abel, out of modesty.

'I've had my hands on her.'

The milky streak which announces the dawn was becoming larger. The bow was kept into the waves with short bursts of the diesel and the barge came towards the land. Jacques took from his pocket an expensive Dunhill briar pipe.

'Jennifer gave me this,' he said.

Abel took the pipe, turned it over and gave it back without a word, very pale. Jacques filled his Dunhill. No, he was not going to smoke at five in the morning! On the deck some of the tough ones were playing poker. It had been some days since the last letters had arrived. The camps were sealed, the orders had been learned by heart. Exercises for battle, for embarkation, for landing, had stretched their nerves. Now they found their justification for living only in an assertion of manliness. A fever had gripped them, the fever of the Channel.

'It's two months since I had a girl,' said one lad.

'How much older are you than me?' asked Abel, thinking of that little slut Jennifer.

'I was born in 1924. May 1924. Valerie's a year older than me.'

That's true, he's also got Valerie. What a man! They were opening their eyes wide like children who do not want to go to sleep. By the occasional lights of the bombardments and later by the dirty gleams of the dawn, they became aware of many sorts of presences, of shimmerings, of distant rumblings. The air offensive had begun when the boat had stopped. The land rose up before them, a huge surprise. The grey turned to a grey blue.

'We're really going to land in style,' said Tit-Rouge.

'Feet first, old lad.'

Siméon was afraid of dying. He avowed the fact with an openness which became a sort of courage.

'Even the sailors were seasick,' he said in disgust.

'Did you throw up?' asked Jacques, drawing ostentatiously on the pipe.

'No.'

'Well, what are you complaining about, then?'

Siméon was quite right. Even the sailors had been ill.

'We've lost Petitjean.'

Petitjean was the lieutenant, a lawyer from Quebec with the face of a girl. At twenty-five, you would have thought him the kid of the pack, and he gave his orders with a girl's voice. All round them, everyone spoke English. The Chauds were detached as a commando in liaison with a British regiment. Slowly, the sky was filled with a gleaming whiteness. You could just about make out the sea. Jacques's jaw closed firmly on his new pipe which inevitably burned his tongue. But it was he who remarked to Abel:

'You've got a long face.'

Abel did not answer. The story of Jennifer wouldn't go away. Yet Jacques had known well enough that he and Jennifer . . . Something stopped him from speaking, something other than modesty. It was the unaccustomed silence. For some moments it had been like a film with the sound cut off. The picture was still showing the peony-shaped shell bursts but all that could be heard was the vast sigh of the Channel. Rapidly the entire coastline came up, separated, broke into pieces and fell back, miraculously reassembling its pieces into a whole. The thunder started up again! With frantic cheers they greeted the bombing planes which had come to beat down the famed Atlantic Wall.

Abel, his face creased, his temples damp, took off his helmet. His uncovered forehead was unusually sensitive to the cold. They had been given new helmets, a cross between the old British soup plate and the American football. Abel swallowed a seasick pill. The boat was taking in some filthy water. They baled out; but their efforts were not enough. The British in their salad bowl helmets came to help out. The act

71

of balancing, with heads lowered, and the crush in the belly of the boat kept them on the verge of sickness all the time.

The line of fire which had been smashing on the beaches a few minutes before, started up again. The bursts were now much nearer. Splashes fell back on to the barge. A skirted tank was disgorged by a transport. It was an extraordinary animal, mounted on an absurd rubber skirt and it slid awkwardly into the thick water, with a man half-way out of the turret.

'Donald Duck,' said an Englishman, delighted, as though at a cinema show.

Breasting the waves, the amphibian tank turned into a crab. It really did resemble Donald, the old D.D. Suddenly a burst of orange fire exploded before it and burst the fragile skirt. The turret tipped forward. The man was swimming. Another popped up out of the narrow orifice, slithered down and slid into the sea. A third appeared, head and shoulders out of the hole. Making desperate efforts. With sickening gurgles the tank sank. A slick of oil spread slowly towards the boat where Abel, weeping from the salt water, vomited in the direction of the thoughtfully provided paper bag. He missed, threw up into the water, shaking his soiled hands and then bent over the water which seemed to be boiling.

Abel and Jacques were pals, in England, pals in a happy rivalry, a rivalry over the girls where Jacques always won and a rivalry in sport where Abel dominated. Then there was Jennifer. There was the pipe which the little hussy had given to Jacques. Abel stroked an identical pipe in his own pocket, a pipe he had not dared to show. Now, there was friendship in this dirty dawn light, in spite of a pipe and a little barmaid, in the presence of a burst of orange fire, a patch of oil on the sea and a sunken tank.

Low clouds came up, studded with chattering seagulls. The Canadians greeted the shells with frenzied curses. The barge heeled over, driven askew by that damned swell which never gave up. As the day approached, paradoxically, the explosions, the smoke bursts and the mists diminished the landscape. The sun shot up, red and huge, bathed in wisps of cotton wool, a sort of hospitalised sun. They all whispered, seized by a primitive emotion.

Vadboncoeur murmured, inexplicably:

'That's good, the sun, the sun . . .'

The naval guns had stopped firing. The land of Normandy stood up above this dirty sea, a narrow band cut off at the sky where clouds from the West were scudding along. There were the low houses cowering as though from fear; there were the broken trees and the sharply pointed steeple, blue amongst the pink lights of the morning sun.

'It's got a ring round it.' Vadboncoeur spoke again, he had reflected long before letting fall this sombre truth.

The coughing of the diesel slowed while the capstans dropped the chains and the sailors yelled. The barges went about, taking the swell on the beam, warping up, then turning away and grounding higher on the beach. The barge ground on the stones with an excruciating noise. The sailors threw nets out over the sides. The men jostled together, then separated and fell again against each other. They cursed. In the moments of calm they stared stupidly at the kit of the fellow in front. A megaphone yelled its orders in the asthmatic voice of a station announcer. Abel was a yard away from the green water. The fellow who went before Abel was in it up to his waist. The wave took him. The soldier got aboard again, distraught. Another wave took him off and threw him forward. The spumes of spray spat up, amid the intestinal gurglings of the submarine explosions. One persistent sound unnerved Abel, a sharp hammering at the armour plate, the homely noises of a smithy. Poised between a fear of the water and a fear of the bullets, Abel let himself slip into the oily water. He floundered about, knocked against some English who were pushing an inflatable boat in front of them. He threw his carbine with the short bayonet

73

into it, he gasped and looked for Jacques in that grey land-scape where it was impossible to discover if one were looking at steel, concrete, air or water.

'Jacques!'

The call was feeble in this din.

Abel overcame the fear in his guts of the waves and turned round, forcing foot after foot against the tide, his legs making a double wave ahead of him. Jacques must have fallen into a hole for there he was floundering about, dragged down to the bottom, his machine pistol in his fist. His lifejacket had slipped and he was bobbing this way and that. His legs were kicking grotesquely. Abel went up to him, supported by his Mae West. The wave knocked Jacques against the boat, turned him over, set him on his feet again. Then he re-appeared, coughing and spitting, half choked. He had succeeded in getting rid of the air belt.

'Forward!' shouted Petitjean. 'Leclerc! Get going. Don't bunch up.'

Abel found his feet. He walked. On the beach the waves melted into breakers. He found the inflatable boat and picked up his gun. Wasps were harassing him. The lieutenant sprawled full length on the ground. Petitjean snorted, spat, and gave furious signals. The wasps! Suddenly, Abel had flattened himself, temples throbbing. The penny had dropped!

With his nose to the ground and his chin in the sand, Abel grabbed furiously at a little transparent crustacean, a land shrimp, which jumped from his clenched fingers. This was more horrible than the bullets, a sort of rotting voracity! Nearby was a broken timber beam. He dragged himself up on his elbows. At the base of the timber, in a little dip, the shrimps were swimming. Some enormous rusty crosses, en-twined with barbed wire, barred the horizon. The Brens answered the fire of the German machine-guns. Abel fired between the crosses. The recoil thumped his shoulder. He fired again; but for no reason. Just in order to feel alive.

74

Above them were the lines of the bullets. Underneath, the mines and the barbed wire entanglements. Behind them the waves were breaking thunderously, but the sea had not surrendered Jacques. My God, where is Jacques? A sticky mass adhered to his leg. He kicked it off. There were four, five, six of them in this shelter, including Petitjean, under the slanting timbers of the remains of a breakwater.

The commando regrouped. The beach seemed all on a slant. The strong waves arrived in threes and the spray from them came up to their waists. When they had gone, Abel was still for a few moments. The soft mass hit again against his left knee. He stretched out his leg nervously. This time the icy water came right up to him. He pressed himself against the beam. The waves came constantly, and washed away. The soft mass again. He pushed it away, turned round and saw a drowned bareheaded body, with flaming red hair, a shining inflated pocket between the shoulders. Frantically, he pushed it away with his foot. The wave brought it back. This time Abel did not dare to kick because the dead man had turned and was floating on his back, his glazed eyes staring up at the sky. They were together there for hours, for years. Abel and the red-haired corpse.

Noise itself built its walls about him. Typhoons dived due south and released their rockets three thousand yards away, but all that was beyond them, it did not concern them. Abel climbed as far as a Sherman. The gurgling of a boiling kettle came out of the inside of the tank. Suddenly Jacques, very dishevelled, with his helmet on the back of his head, so soaked that the khaki of his uniform was dark brown, fell down at his side.

'Luckily, I'm a good swimmer.'

He got his breath back.

In front of them, there was still the deadly pattering of the machine-guns and the incredible shambles of the defences, a network of intercrossed rails and these damned porcelain fleas.

'We need living space,' said Jacques. 'I'm beginning to understand Hitler.'

Abel was content. His friend Jacques was there. His cheerful friend Jacques. Abel had never looked up to anyone since his uncle Jolicoeur, the huge lumberjack who would push him gently away with a hand in the back, before giving the last axe blow to a beech tree.

All about them the rifles piled up with knapsacks, a huge tyre, bottles, papers, a gas mask, a chamber pot, and still more papers, papers which flew about in the shock of the explosions. The German shells were still falling into the water lifting up little gleaming sprays, a series of little mirrors which broke into droplets, shimmering a thousand suns. Abel, who was starting to shiver, heard Jacques say:

'Next time, don't forget your swimsuit!'

CHAPTER VII

STRETCHED OUT on his back, Abel looked at the waves of the sky moving lazily towards the East. How good it would be to fall into that warm blueness! He had experienced this sensation before . . . But when? His past was eaten away by forgetfulness. He was no longer listening to Valerie. She was a sea animal. She could stay in the water for hours. The untidy sentinels dozed. The organs of communication, the posts, despatch-riders, telephones, and the numerous police forces slept. Only the *Renseignments Généraux* stayed awake, but leisurely so. *Renseignments Généraux* . . . General Intelligence. Abel loved this typically French expression because of the strange and untranslatable quality hidden in a form of words which were superficially transparent. He never thought about this watchfulness which was within him except in those words, no doubt taken from a thriller or spy story. Automatic, like heartbeats or breathing. Breathing! . . . Now, wait! There was someone . . . called . . . Grandpierre! Yes, Grandpierre. A voluble, swarthy, darkhaired man. And sometimes he would grow pale. He had a curious malady. He would forget to breathe! He used to drown in the fresh air! You had to clout him in a helpful manner. Then, he got going again. Where and when was this Grandpierre? The forgotten breathing and the desire to fall into the sky? A guardian answered with a yawn. Grandpierre, you said? A swarthy little man who would forget to breathe?

Three seagulls flew over them. The first was holding a fish in his flat beak and the other two chased him, screaming.

Sixteen years have passed since the seagulls! Jacques was really fit, when he lay there drying out in front of the barbed wire those swine of Germans had put out! You really ought to see yourself, old man! It was true enough, the only reason Jacques got clear away was that he was such a good swimmer; there would really have been something to look at if they had been able to turn over on to their backs, as Abel was doing today, and contemplate at their ease the sky and the armada, the cables, the protective nets, the shimmering aluminium balloons like Christmas-tree ornaments, a giant spider's web dumped on to Normandy, with the Germans up above—and us! There was no longer a single thing in the sky. Ah, yes, an aeroplane. An old kite. Sixteen years! I'm not married. 'He is not married.' Who is 'he'? Who is 'I'? Abel is not married. Abel Leclerc. Private Leclerc. 'Why haven't you got married?' Marie, Marie . . . I'm not married, mama, mama Marie. So today I don't have a young Abel,

77

sixteen years old, who'll come to me to say: 'I'm joining the fight on behalf of right and civilisation.' Against Barbarism, the Nazis, the Russians, the Chinese . . . Now I no longer believe in anything except the blue sky into which I'm going to fall. I'm going to swim with my brother, the little aeroplane which, a long way off, is in the process of making an S . . . No, an F . . . Or an L . . . 'My son, so you want to fight for justice and civilisation? Good. Very good. Against whom?—'Against the Barbarians, papa.'—'Just so. That's who it is always. Which Barbarians?'—'The ones who are threatening liberty.'—'Naturally. Which are they?' 'The Chinese and the Russians.'—'Really? But the Chinese and the Russians defended liberty along with us!'—'That's all changed, papa.'—'Against the Germans?'—'Of course not, papa. The Germans are our friends, papa.' My sons, I tell you true. Happily I never begot you! What could I answer you? Both my father and I got caught in the same trap. Your grandfather. My father is dead and I, Abel Leclerc, have chloresterol in the blood and boredom in the brain. Clowning and putrescence! I've not given a child to Simone in Quebec nor to any other girl and that's a good thing too, for they also would want to fight the Barbarians! I must send a postcard to Simone. That's what I'll do. She wasn't mad when I didn't marry her, when I didn't give her a child, when I left her, but would be very annoyed if I didn't send her a postcard! I'm going to send a beautiful bright card from Arromanches, showing the Museum of the Disembarkation with the tank *Vimy* in the foreground. Clowning. Clowning and putrescence.

In the centres of decision, however, something was taking shape, an urge to get up and continue the search. But it was no more than a whim, a feeling of impatience, a vague notion. The sturdy little aeroplane had just finished making the tail of a letter. From where Abel was situated, he had to twist his neck to read. But how would he be able to remain indifferent if the words written in the sky were solemn ones. *Peace*? or *Justice*? or *Love*?

'*You're fine here, but what are you doing about it*?' Bureaucrats stirred in the white offices. They passed from door to door, lifting the mosquito nets. It swarmed with movement like an awakened office block.

The clouds had ceased their procession, fairly low down in the horizon, in order to build up a distant prospect of palaces with rising terraces where the armies of the storm marched out before the Gates of War. Fanfares sounded as in a scene from Aida. '*That's not all there is to it, you must see that you don't lose the fish from the line.*' He got up on his elbow. Everything had changed. He was no longer outside the world, above himself, suspended. He was inside again. Just a little movement and he had returned to earth.

A flea jumped on to his leg and scuttled between his hairs. He picked it up between his fingers as before. And that made him see it as though for the first time. The tiny animal resembled a miniscule pig with crab-like legs. How it waved its legs! A little block of icy anguish. An answer was taking shape, laboriously fabricated by Intelligence, incomplete but, taken altogether, reasonably satisfactory: 'I'm here because I was not able to do anything else.'

He threw the flea away. General Intelligence, hotting up the pace, no longer hesitated to send out a stream of tele-grams, first priority: Danger, Danger, Danger . . .

'That's the heart of the matter,' he thought, distinctly. I forget. Forgetfulness. I recognise nothing. Even here, I am not sure that this exists. Or is it that I have changed into another? However, this really is me. Me? What do you mean by that? Explain yourself! 'Me!' This host of microscopic activities which marry up, interpenetrate, fight for supre-macy, contradict each other, this interior city, this Canada! Me? You? Him? Who? 'They?' 'They' say that the cells of the body renew themselves completely in seven years. All the living cells of Canada renew themselves every hundred years. There'll always be a Canada! Life is cellular. So, I have become more than twice a completely different being since the embarkation! Clown! Forgetfulness has taken possession of my head. And Valerie loathes me because I forget. She is going to put me on trial. Intelligence plus forgetfulness. But, damn it, remove the defences of the wartime beach, the timber beams, the iron crosses, the rails, the landmines, the barbed wire, then what would you have left? The water and the dunes!

The aeroplane did not make a single word in correct succession. It was advertising on behalf of a Parisian newspaper the opening of a beach competition.

Forgetfulness is death. You might be sure that, next year, there will be a little less concrete left in Mulberry II, gnawed, eaten away and digested by the algae and the vermin of the sea. The scavengers of the land were blanching the skeletons, turning to tatters the last identification tags, rotting the badges and the shoulder straps and the mottoes saying *Aere Perennius*. More resistant, more durable than brass. And the best of luck to you! The wonderful Jacques was just completing his disintegration in the flooded valley, near the spire with the series of slopes which came down to the gutted cemetery. Jacques was choking under eighteen inches of slime and you could still see those loathesome bubbles breaking the surface, while Benjamin was saying: 'Forward! Forward! Don't help anyone. Leclerc, go forward!' When the convoy went into the valley, General Intelligence had warned me, *This is the Valley of Death*. Jacques had told me that he knew this steeple, although he had never seen it before. At that time I did not know about General Intelligence, but they knew their business. *Attention Danger Zone*. Danger, danger, danger . . .Offensive, stinking, terrible. The primeval swamp. A womb of death. And, we, within it, abettors! Wishing to forget. So soothed. Guilty of forgetfulness. And forgetfulness in Canada. Forgetfulness pro-

80

visionally suspended, in regard to Jacques by Valerie's relentlessness. Swear that Jacques is in the way!

Yes!

I am ashamed. Friendship was not like this, was it?

The shattering steel of the Sherman was grinding away. The white star had turned to the yellow of an egg yolk. Behind its broken track, the number was still legible: X 1722 4/B; and the name could be read, *Saguenay*.

Saguenay . . . The kingdom of Saguenay and of the lumberjack uncle, Uncle Jolicoeur. Maman Jolicoeur, Mamie, Mamie, a ripe plum for Abel . . . It's true, I used always to call you Mamie, my little aunt, Mamie.

The heat of an oven rose from the tank. The beach stood up in a steep slope to the regions of the dry sand. This is the Promised Land. A clump of weeds, a sea-pink, a box of jam took on the importance of a church, a fort, a forest or a silo. Some distance off, in the disputed zone, something caught Abel's attention. It appeared to be the thigh, leg and foot of a doll of a crude pink. Flat on his belly, with the cold of the water rising up to his thighs and his shoulders and face warmed by the tank, he was disturbed by the undeveloped strength of this body pressed into the damp earth; and the sensation filled him with a proud but useless vigour. His hand came upon a chalky shell, stripped of its mother-of-pearl lining. He threw it to the legs. He hit it! The leg turned over with a kick like a can-can dancer, then fell back showing for an instant the flat section of the thigh, the bit that joins on to the pelvis and, in the middle, in the middle of the back, a row of stitches. It was, indeed, a doll.

An explosion tore the earth which continued to tremble whilst a rain of stones and sand fell back, crackling, onto the helmets. Abel listened, his nose to the ground, pushed into the seaweed. Jacques touched his shoulder. O.K., fella? Thirty yards away, phantasmal in the smoke, a bulldozer tank was working away, beating down the barbed wire, ripping up obstacles and pushing them away. The monster lurched around amid the crackling of machine-gun fire. Behind the tank, shadows plunged down and got up again. The sappers attacked the defences, cussing at the infantry who got in their way. Abel wondered if he should go forward. But he had had no orders. There were twelve of them in the liaison commando. Petitjean had given them their instructions. 'Wait on the beach. Don't move. Wait for me.' But there was no longer Petitjean to be seen, nor any member of his group! They had vanished. In front of Abel, smoke rose up from the cut grass. The tide came up to them again, announced by the infuriating profusion of sand fleas. Pinned into the barbed wire by the fire from automatic weapons, pushed on by the sea, suffocating under the yellow grass-smoke, they waited.

Abel unearthed a cockle which looked like nothing so much as an obscene backside. The mollusc resisted the twisting of his knife, then suddenly split in two, dripping with iodine. Abel swallowed it. With his mouth full of the fresh sea taste, he offered a shellfish to Jacques who made an expression of disgust. Suddenly, explosions, shouts, whistles!
'Go on! Go on!'
Soldiers flattened themselves on each side of them. They were coming from everywhere! They gathered together in the shelter of the burning tank. Abel read the name on their shoulder tabs:

17th Duke of York's Royal Canadian Hussars.

Well, some English-speaking Canadians! What the hell were they doing here? He had all the time he wanted to look at these cavalry-men without tanks or horses. The triangular badge was yellow and gold. The initials were picked out in

82

silver on a black ground. Here was also a crown and the motto:

Honi soit qui mal y pense

One of the Hussars took out a sandwich and munched it, stupidly. Their Robinson Crusoe beach had begun to swarm with people.

Fifteen yards away, a man turned round and showed a face spattered with blood. Something was hanging from his cheek, red and hairy, like a beret. Abel's eardrums started to hurt him. Orders rang out. Abel and Jacques leaped up and put themselves down again ten yards farther on, underneath a black and white sign, with lettering, a skull and cross-bones:

ACHTUNG! MINEN!

Protected by the brushwood which held back the sand of the dune, Abel breathed again. Jacques had picked up a yellowing magazine, full of beautiful laughing girls, of pot-bellied French parliamentarians, of illustrious generals and of magical Nazi ceremonies. The cover was taken up with a picture of Mae West, enormous thighs, hugely hipped with vast breasts, a parade-ground of love for a battalion. Some shouted, orders disturbed their tranquillity. One by one, the men crept towards the dunes. The noises died down. The war was going away. They were in the eye of the storm. They put their noses over the top. In the gaps of the smoke, the village was blazing. Bent and loaded men, in single file, slid forward and behind them was a sea whipped up into white horses, covered with a thousand varied marks of the landings, an immense dragon spitting out fire, tanks and men.

'I'm dying of hunger,' said Jacques. 'What's the time?'

'Eight thirty-five,' said a sergeant. 'What mob are you with?'

They told him.

'Good. Come with me, I'll take you back to your officer.'

They followed him. Suddenly an explosion threw them to

the ground once more. They turned round. The tank *Saguenay* had vanished.

Abel rolled like a dog in the warm sand. Women were knitting in the spot where once the wounded bled.

He went up to the bunkers. From there, he looked at the cropped vegetation, of a milky green. 'Newly mown grass smells fine.' Birds sang. He really did not wish to imagine the explosions, the mutilated men, the terror of the mines, nor even the tank *Saguenay*. A little later, the sergeant came up close to the last entanglement, carrying a Bangalore torpedo. He fired it but it did not work. He went and found another. When he lit this a burst of orange flame shot from the earth. There was nothing left of the heroic sergeant. There was no barbed wire, either. They themselves were in a pleasant orchard, close to a wash-house. Flak was bursting in absurd puffs of smoke.

Jacques was not quite as tall as Abel, but slimmer. He had fair curly hair, girlish features, dark thoughtful eyes, a fair complexion which the sun would bring out in freckles. His high cheekbones gave him an irresistible smile. I could have wished to be like him instead of having my bullet head.

Abel stayed stock still on the top of the dune, thoughtful, on the frontier of sea and land.

The fat land of Normandy was clouded over with an Olympus swarming with naked goddesses and their ample charms to take the place of vanished Persepolis or lost Babylon. The sky formed a travesty of Mae West in clouds, a dozen or so breasts to each of them. Mae West or Mamie! Mamie! Well, look, here she is coming out of the forgotten past! Mamie! Hi, Mamie!

Hip, hip, hurrah! After all, it was normal, they all love bosoms so much, these Americans. So badly weaned, the Yanks, fascinated by the mother-figure, worthy pleasant slobs, as naive as their strip cartoons. When'll they put the

84

Bible into cartoon? Bah, they must already have done it. Mamie. Mamie of Caen! What a surprise. Not the Caen of the trenches in the outskirts, machine-guns in the petrol stations, houses snatched up one after the other. No. This was the Caen of the dusty ruins, the capital city of the foot-sloggers and the refugees, of deserters and drunks, bridge-head of the first robbers, Caen of heaped up stones and human vermin.

What happened after the incident in the orchard? Don't count on me to write a history of the war. Night fell on the village, as in the fifth act of an Italian opera. Which village? Bernières? Verville? Courseulles? Gray-sur-Mer? For some hours, you could have described it simply as 'the' village. The smell of cows, the stink of dung and the bellowing of the animals. 'The village', that's all.

Valerie, dripping, came up to him.

'You remember the old chap with the white goatee beard, at Caen?' she said.

'The one who spoke so quickly? Of course. Now wait: "Leclair, from Loire-Inferieur". *L'éclair.* Lightning. That's clear, 'sclear. Leclere, came from Clères, in Seine-Maritime. Local name and personal name, both originating from the same stem. Obvious! *Le clair,* the clear fellow. Blond. With clear eyes. Vikings, Northman. Or even *Clair,* meaning abundant. It's all relevant, it's obvious, obvious.'

She laughed. He was a good mimic.

'In that case, it should have been Jacques who was called Leclerc. He had a clearer complexion than you.'

He pretended to be annoyed.

'Abel, let's be serious. In Quebec you said: "We can use this visit to the land of the Leclercs to rediscover the places where Jacques and I fought. We could find his grave".'

Yes. Well, she had thought about it as she swam. It's

starting all over again. Indefatigable! Abel's eyebrows arched with a sudden anger.

'No, no, no! "His grave", no! They're your words.'

Or, even, if he had used the word 'grave', it was in the sense of resting-place. Symbolical. The cliché, however, had hardened in Valerie's mind into the comforting shape of Jacques' 'grave'. 'We'll go and put some flowers on Jacques' grave.' It's true, she had said it any number of times, in Quebec, or on the boat; and he had not bothered to put the record straight. He had not made a move in time and she was coming back to the charge. But the manner of his answering was brutal enough for her to change the subject.

'The tide's still going out,' she said.

'That's the time when we used to be able to breathe.'

They crossed the dry sand, skirting the line of seaweed pullulating with sandfleas, and went down into the realm of the moist sand, soggy under the naked feet. The sea uncovered rocky outcrops among the green swamps.

'They valley of Josaphat,' he said, pointing out the shining rocks under their dressing of algae.

Some of the larger stones resembled heads shrunken by the Jivaros. He threw some of them into the sparkling water. He did not throw like a child, along the line of the shoulders with a movement like a whip, but as infantrymen throw a grenade, in a half-circle above the head. A medal of gold, on a thin chain about the neck, beat against his chest and it looked odd, this tiny jewel jumping about on his hairy skin. She smiled. He caught her expression. In his turn, he smiled shamefacedly.

'I like it when you smile, Abel. You become a little boy again, a little boy who hasn't grown up.'

'I was a little boy once, Valerie. Then a lad who was wet behind the ears. But I stopped there. At the age when I should have been dry behind the ears, the war came. When I got back, I was twenty!'

She was saddened by him, and annoyed at being so.

86

'You're not going into the water again?'

'No, too many shrimps.'

'Well, I'm going to get dressed. It's getting chilly.'

A young woman came down from the dunes, and crossed in front of her. The two women looked at each other. The newcomer was wearing a vivid yellow dress with a square neckline which opened over the gentle swelling of her breasts. She was suntanned, and wore little make-up. She spread out a sea-blue towel on the sand, then slipped off the dress with delicately intriguing movements. Abel had seen this young woman before. At Caen? At le Havre? At the newspaper reception? Ah, it was this morning. At the Gates of War. That was it. The young woman with the dress in the sailing boat design. She appeared in a royal blue bikini. She turned her back on him, showing a lightly golden skin, the shade almost of champagne. Her slender body was cut across by a thin scar, perhaps fifteen inches long. As Valerie and he went off, he turned round towards this young woman who had been cut in two and stuck together again. She was taking a sunbath. She smiled at him, as to a friend whom one is certain to see again the next day or the next, whenever fate plans it, the rose in the wood, as the old Norman song has it, the old rediscovered song which old Sebastian was playing on his mouth organ.

THE COURTYARD of the *Diable de Mer,* planted with tamarisk, gave on to a flat-roofed house, a surprising thing to find among so many gables. But the interior of the hotel was even more foreign-looking than the outside. It made one think of the inns in the Midi, a Spanish *fonda,* a Neapolitan *trattoria,* or a Franco-Oriental restaurant such as one might find in a suburb of Marseilles, Naples or Algiers. Posters displayed the tourist paradises of Sidi-Bou-Said, Hammamet and Djerba, sufficient to make Ulysses dream; and, as a counterpoint, there was the legacy of a previous owner, four well-endowed ladies in the *Quatres Saisons* by Cheret, a picture completely out of key with the surroundings. Above the bar, a Chinese fish with spines sticking up was swinging at the end of an electric cord.

The radio was relaying the news in a low tone:

'In Algiers, no untoward incident occurred during the funeral of the three . . .'

A small man, as brown as a nut, switched it off regretfully:

'Fine start to the season,' he said. 'Obviously, people here don't know how it's going to turn out. But . . . Times change . . . Like the tides . . . You don't come from round here?'

'No. And you?'

'Me? I come from Sidi-Bou-Said. I kept a restaurant there. It was paradise, monsieur.'

88

He had an accent which was harsh and lisping at the same time, full of soft sounds and spitting noises. It could be Sicilian, Maltese or Neapolitan, like his place. And he was an actor with it! He adopted the pitiful expression of an actor who was really pushing a 'heavy' role.

'We had to sell. At a loss. Because of these cheapjacks. They sold out France. Tcha!'

Abel made the vague gesture of a man who was interested, but who did not think himself in a position to give a personal opinion.

'Well, Bourguiba really did us down! When they gave him independence, he clapped his hands together . . . like that! That meant that it was us who would get it in the . . . I beg your pardon, Madame.'

Independence? Bourguiba? In Morocco? Abel was delighted at the gesture which the *patron* had used. It came from a long history of smut in the Mediterranean ports. With his right hand open, the palm flat, he beat on the left hand which had been closed into the shape of a tube and the gesture was completed with a full quarter turn of the right hand, like a lid being screwed on. The significance was not lost on Abel, even though it left Valerie perplexed.

The hairy little *patron* and his stories had ceased to interest Abel who was still smiling into emptiness. The diamond point has jumped a groove in the record of memory. Some days earlier, on the quayside at Le Havre, the newspaper *Paris-Normandie* welcomed a hundred and twenty one Canadians of whom twenty-four were Leclercs, male and female, gathered together by the *Canada-Normandie Association*. If you called out: 'Leclerc!' twenty people would turn! And there were also some natives with the name. Even the first short speech had revealed three Leclercs: the sports editor, one of the foremen and a clerk in the subscription department. The director had put a wreath on a marble plaque which bore the names of the dead of two wars. Two Leclercs were among them.

Then, later on, from the coach they saw Leclerc the pork butcher, Leclerc the bagwash, Leclerc the undertaker, so often that you might have thought it the family name of Adam himself! Abel's neighbour, a butcher from Trois Rivières, beamed when he read his name under the sign of a gilded ox head. 'Ah,' he said, 'you could have quite a time here! If I see the name once more, it's drinks all round on me!'

The trip had lasted for nearly a week when they stopped in Caen, on the third of June. At the completely new University, where an elegant abstract figure stood on a freshly cut lawn, they suffered an impromptu lecture by the amiable white-bearded man with the pince-nez to whom Valerie had referred. 'The name of the Le Clairs or the Le Clercs, which it would be erroneous to confuse with the function of a clerk in holy orders, or a clerk at law, seems to stem directly from . . .'

The little professor spoke very quickly, in order to say as much as he could in front of the portable tape-recorders of the radio reporters.

What a start to the journey! Ruins, temporary barriers, new blocks of flats, the *Avenue du 6 Juin,* the *Avenues de la Libération,* the *Place Churchill, Boulevard Eisenhower.* The arrival of the old comrades, the dancing flags of disbanded regiments, a whirlwind round of toasts interrupted by the inevitable intervals for the two minutes' silence! A festival? But on the third, in the evening, Valerie and Abel had let the coach go off to Cherbourg, carrying off its load of boisterous Leclercs. They were not to rejoin the party until the day of departure, on the boat, on the twelfth of August. The guide stayed silent, his eyebrows raised, suspecting their patriotism.

Abel acknowledged the complaints of the ex-colonial hotelkeeper with a nod of his head, until at last the speaker noticed that Abel was not paying attention. Then he went behind his bar, his face tortured by the harsh red lights which shone out from his vengeful fish.

Abel's hand was playing with the edge of the glass and his left eye displayed the fixity which always shone when he was 'elsewhere'. Three months earlier, Abel had not made up his mind how to spend his holiday. It was like that every year. He did not want to go away with the antiseptic Simone. He had no taste for anything. He did not like his life. It was, indeed, he who proposed to Valerie that they should go to Europe with his providential excursion. She had agreed, on condition that they went Dutch. Valerie was a free woman. The equal of a man. At the very least! When they landed at le Havre on that famous night, Abel genuinely thought that all that had called him to Normandy was a vague curiosity connected with his name, his origins, his roots in the family tree, an interest which drives even unimaginative men to seek out their forefathers. Then, at Caen, he had understood. He had come for quite another thing. And, at Arromanches, on the same day, something else was made clear: *a return to hell*. Then, he had beaten like a suppliant on the very Gates of War.

'Let's stop all that, Abel,' she said, in the dry tone which grated on him. 'I have been faithful to Jacques for sixteen years. I'd like to pray at his grave. It's simple. Is it too much to ask of his best friend?'

He sighed. There was a whole ocean between them. They had been drawn apart by ideas, words, facial expressions, and the tones of the voice.

'Look, Valerie,' he said, as though he were speaking to a little girl, 'you know that the army authorities haven't been able to give you an answer.'

'That's what exasperates me.'

Why was she so stupid?

'If they haven't replied to you, Valerie, it's because there was no answer to give.'

She put down her glass. She looked at him closely, without moving. He hammered away at her cruelly, because he had really had enough:

'There is no grave, Valerie. Forgive me for insisting on it: but I must. You do not wish to understand. Or, if there is a grave, it is lost, irrecoverable, ploughed under. Or anonymous.'

'Anonymous?'

'With some inscription on it like: "A Canadian Soldier".'

She was getting on his nerves and he would have liked to slap her. Still she didn't understand! He began again:

'The officials have done their work well. I let you write to the Army. I should have preferred . . . your grief to wear away. But I went to see our old colonel. Paul Mathieu.'

'You didn't tell me that.'

'Colonel Mathieu didn't think that it could be found again, either.'

The young woman's jaw hardened under her taut cheeks. Her face closed the drawbridge, let down the portcullis, drew in the chains and fastened the locks.

'For another reason also,' he said, hardened in his turn by the hostile expression of his companion, 'the circumstances of Jacques's death were so . . . exceptional that . . . he could not be buried.'

'What?'

She almost shouted it.

'But you were there!'

'Valerie, listen to me. Take a hold of yourself. I was there. I saw Jacques die. But I have only a vague idea of the place where it happened. Because his death took place in the height of battle and . . . in a situation . . . a situation in which everything is now very different. In other words, Valerie, the very place of Jacques's death has vanished.'

'That was a good job well done,' he thought. He took a

92

long pull at the perroquet and found it good. The young woman pursed her lips in scorn.

'In one of his letters, Jacques told me you were a louse.'

'What?'

'A louse. A swine.'

How could he? . . . For what reason?

'Valerie, can you show me this letter?'

'No.'

'Ah. Will you tell me, then, if the letter was sent before or after the invasion?'

'From England.'

To her surprise, she saw him take out his pipe, look at her, caress the pipe, and a smile creased his eyes.

'I see. Southampton. Imagine Southampton. Jacques and I . . .'

He stopped short. What could I tell her about it? It was true that with her cutting ways, her authority, her arrogance, he had forgotten that she was a woman. Now she was staring at him, exasperated!

'Abel, I knew that you were a layabout, a good-for-nothing. But I thought you were good-hearted. I'm seeing you for the first time. Look at your low forehead! And that salesman's gift of the gab—that appalling taste for obscenities. That bestial expression. That weak mouth.'

She bit off the words, her eyes glinting behind spectacles which reflected two angry Chinese fish.

'I wonder if Jacques would have grown like you. The war has ruined you! You believe nothing. You drink. You are a deadbeat! You are so disbelieving that you've not even got any children.'

Carried away by her anger, she knocked over his glass. The *patron* shot out from behind the counter.

'Well!' said Abel, 'same again!'

'Not for me,' she said.

'Coca Cola, then,' said Abel.

The ex-colonial said:

'That's a drink I never sold in Sidi-Bou-Said! If you're ever round here, you ought to come in for Sunday lunch. I make *cous-cous*. I've set up an Association of Old North Africans. Above all, Moroccans. People from Casablanca. But I don't know Morocco. Only Tunisia.'

'You'll get to know the Normans. Fair to your face but! ... behind your back ... !'

Then, in a lower voice, conspiratorially, he went on:

'What do they think about de Gaulle, in Belgium?'

Abel burst out laughing. 'What? Well, you know, I'm Canadian.'

The *patron* mumbled in embarrassment and slipped away.

Now, Abel thought, could he decently recount to Valerie what had happened at Southampton, with Jennifer? Clearly, it had been no more than the story of a pretty wartime flirt and a rivalry between a couple of pals in the old Hotel Tudor in the grey heart of an English winter. Then the promise of death was hanging over the boys in khaki as they kicked their heels about in the blitz. But he could no more tell that to Valerie than he could tell her what had happened in the valley of death.

Angry at the refusal, she flared up. She stood and stamped her foot.

'You are a disgusting person.'

He emptied his pipe into his hand and poured the contents into an ashtray.

'Let's go on. There are some things that I cannot tell you. I have neither the right nor the inclination. You will not understand why I can't tell you. That's normal. You've always hated me. That, at least, is clear. So, now we draw the obvious conclusion. Our trip together terminates here, in this delightfully decrepit North African cafe. Don't you think that's wise?'

What had Jacques written about Abel? She no longer knew. 'Swine' or 'louse' or 'thug'? However, she thought that she had gone too far. She should have interpreted these men's words as a woman. But that bridge was down. She looked at him. She did not recognise this sad dignity which his face now expressed.

'Even if we hadn't had this flare-up, I should have left you,' he went on. 'I get on your nerves. To be frank, it's mutual. But you make me angry. You're an obstacle. An obstacle between Jacques and me. Now do sit down, please! There's no need for us to keep on making a spectacle of ourselves. I'm going to tell you what exasperates me. You have made for yourself a screenplay about the fallen hero, carried off in the folds of the flag and buried at the foot of an oak, with his helmet on the cross. That's not reprehensible, it's only silly. No, wait! You might as well let me speak, for you don't have to see me afterwards. You will turn into a child of Mary, become a Valerie who is still so beautiful and who knows how to remain faithful to her lover who died for liberty. Well, that's fine! There's only one thing wrong and that, if you look a little more closely, is that this synopsis does not match up to reality. You've chosen this life simply because it pleases you. You've wallowed in it. Jacques died like a soldier, I swear to you. The word "hero" always makes soldiers laugh. There are no heroes. No more and no less than me. But I've committed an unforgiveable sin: I allowed myself to come back. Well, then, Abel, who returned, this disgusting person whose picture you've painted with an unforgettable malice . . .'

'Oh!'

'. . . Abel has made his decision, Valerie. I'm not now very lucid. I've told myself those travelling salesman's stories. Was that the expression? So be it, then. But I'm here. I'm cut off for a time from Quebec. From my old life. Then, in Caen, my cousins Leclerc. Now, I'm separating from you. That's logical, isn't it? After that, I don't know what else I shall have to cut away from. Probably, an appreciable part of myself. You'll leave me with the trouble of finding out which part. Well, you keep the car. I advise you to stay in

Arromanches, June is fine in Normandy. Go to Caen, to Rouen. They're full of cathedrals . . .'

Valerie's anger had abated. There was no expression on her face, only astonishment.

'You're really going away, Abel? But it's all a misunderstanding. I'm making a pilgrimage.'

'Jacques loved swimming. So do you. Go swimming. That's the best way of making a pilgrimage.'

She was alone, left dumbfounded by Abel's revolt. The other couples stared at her in disapproval. She reminded them of the fact that a man and a woman can enter a cafe together and go out separately. The juke-box was playing bogus Arab music: *Mustapha . . . When I saw you in front of the house.* She went out. The *patron* of the *Diable de Mer* bowed. The customer was always right.

Outside, it was still sunny. It was one of the longest days of the year.

Valerie sat in her little car, waited a moment with her elbows on the steering wheel and her head in her hands. Then she carefully wiped her glasses, lit a cigarette, and let in the clutch, gunning the engine like an aircraft taking off.

Part Two : The Nazi Shrimps

CHAPTER I

THE YOUNG SOLDIER was lying on his stomach. With his head turned at right angles, you could see his face, looking far too red. You might have said that he had a crick in the neck. On his mouth was a fly. A trickle of blood flowed from his lip and a fly had stuck to it. His hand was lying close to his chin as if it was going to slip beneath it. Abel did not enjoy looking at this young dead man, but his own position was such that he could not avoid it. The immobility of corpses is very upsetting.

'When this is over,' said Jacques, 'we'll go and get drunk with some girls. But of course, you only drink milk!'

Perhaps it was because Abel drank milk that Jennifer did not take him seriously. Or perhaps because Jacques was older than he. Only a year. In his pocket, Abel fondled the pipe which she had given him and which he had not yet dared to smoke. A new Dunhill, like Jacques's, marked in the same way with that high-class white spot. Wonderful! He had soaked it for three days in whisky. It still smelled of alcohol. Well, devil take it! Jacques can think what he likes. Abel took out the pipe, stuffed it with Navy Cut which had been steeped in molasses, and tried the first puffs. Surprised, Jacques had glanced out of the corner of his eye at Abel's pipe.

The gulls flew over the bunker. Abel hated these birds with their funereal cries. The bunker which was pinning them down between the dunes and the village had a dirty roof. Their stomachs were still knotted with apprehension. Not an hour had passed since the episode of the flaming German. They had thought that the bunker would surrender, but it had started up again. An acrid smoke, like cotton-wool, came from the lookout slit. At one side, someone was moving in a recess half hidden by the broom which had kept some of its flowers. It must be possible to get there, but between the recess and the hole they were in was a flat stretch of land, as smooth as a school playground. Too bad! Those who were there seemed so very peaceful! A medic, with a red cross and two ambulance men were giving a transfusion with the regular movements of insects.

Little by little, the movements lessened. One might have said that death was parting in waves from its young acolyte, the boy with the crooked neck. A desire for sleep came over Abel. Jacques did not say anything. But . . . but . . . he was snoring! A sea pink swayed gently. Abel woke up suddenly, his mouth dry and sour. A hubbub greeted him. He dived down, so violently that he bit on the soil. A human ball landed by his side. Another too-lively sergeant!

'Don't move, men.'

This one was an old hand. He listened, sniffed the air, raised himself, stayed for a minute suspended in mid-air, then fell back on to his hands.

'What're you sodding about at here,' he asked amiably, 'Oh, "liaising"? With the English? Liaison commando.

Fine, fine. So you've lost your officer, have you. It'll sort itself out.'

Camouflaged in green and yellow, a chameleon of the sands, the bunker now seemed to be nearer. It pinned them down, from its horizontal slit, crouching on its piles of sea-weed covered rocks.

'Flatten yourselves!'

The sergeant, with a movement of his right hand, took his hand back and, with all his force, tossed a grenade. At that very instant, a helmeted German shot out of the bunker. One, two, three, four . . . It was interminable. The grenade ex-ploded a few feet away from the German. The earth shook under their bellies. My God, this is the flame-thrower all over again! The German, wounded, fell. He stirred. He dragged himself towards them. The sergeant stood up, ready to dive down again. Nothing happened. You could hear the noises of the sea. The sergeant stood right up, his Bren under his arm. The wounded German raised himself, fell back, raised himself again and drew himself towards them, dragging his leg stiffly behind. A red, sticky stain was spreading out. Other Germans in tunics, with empty hands, dishevelled, came out of the manhole, one after the other, raising their hands to the sky.

Jacques danced like a Sioux singing savagely. Abel was stupefied by this show of joy. The bleeding German was ten yards away, his face dark, his eyes sparkling like bits of blue glass. One, two, three, four, five Germans followed him, heavily. Two whistle blasts sounded. The jovial sergeant and his men crossed the dune, leaving the bunker on their left, and went off clambering over the obstacles in Indian file. Nothing was left on this pleasant beach but five iron-grey men, who were lifting up their arms, three Canadians and at one side, impassive, the clean and tidy young medic, with his two aides.

'Good luck, fellas,' roared the sergeant, cupping his hands about his mouth. 'See you in Berlin.'

Ruefully, Abel gazed at Jacques, the medic, the wounded and the five Germans who were slowly lowering their hands.

'Up!' shouted Jacques. 'Hands up!'

So there they were, the Germans, with their tunics a little longer than the battledress, but coming high over the backside, and gathered at the waist with a black belt. They were in a washed out grey-green. There was a surprising contrast between the grey and khaki figures, between the skirted helmets of the Boches and the Canadians' helmets loaded with a miscellany of objects.

Abel went up to them, his carbine under his arm. That's the way for this kind of job. He signalled to Jacques. Jacques put his automatic rifle on his shoulder and patted their pockets and legs. The uniforms were mended, thin on thin bodies. The oldest man, half balding, was at least forty! Steel-rimmed spectacles gave him the appearance of a civil servant. He wore a black and red ribbon, cut diagonally, just above his waist and there was silver piping round his shoulder straps. Several times, in different tones of voice he repeated: 'Komrads, Komrads.' Apart from the injured man, they were all shorter than the two Canadians, and, except for the balding one whose scarce yellow locks were blowing in the wind, none of them was as blond as their astonished victors.

That these enemies looked so much like the people one could see in any train in Canada amazed the young soldiers. Abel scratched his head. He said a few words. They replied in German, all at once. One of them, reassured, said:

'Hitler kaputt!'

How are the mighty fallen! The wounded man, composed, stood on one leg like a stork. The bloodstain had spread to his trousers. Abel whistled in his fingers. The young doctor turned round. Abel showed him the German. He nodded. The German went towards the aid post. That was one less; four left. Abel signed to the prisoners to sit down. He knelt down in front of the young dead man. He had forgotten him.

100

His colour was still rosy. His mouth still pouted. And still the fly was there. The dead man was now of no importance. He had slipped back into everything that had gone before.

Anxiety suddenly took possession of Abel. What if there were some others, in the bunker? He would have to see. But what could he do with these?

'Keep an eye on them,' he said to Jacques.

Jacques, with his carbine in his fist, took up a pugnacious stance, his jaw set firm. Abel went inside the bunker.

Jacques moved. His gaze did not leave the prisoners. But where was Abel going off to? He was alone with his Boches, who now were slipping from the role of the warrior into the slow manner of the prisoner. Twenty yards to the bunker and back. Then the journey once again. Jacques shouted: 'Abel!' No one answered. What if the Boches escaped! Well, let them escape. Yes, but they might find their arms again. To shoot him in the back. Abel! Abel!

Abel returned, as white as a sheet.

'Go and see,' he said.

Jacques went in. There was nothing in the first room. Choked by the smell of rotten eggs, he went into the second. There were six men. Several were standing. He did not understand at once these strange motionless sentinels. Little blood was to be seen. Merely a trickle which ran from the ear of the nearest, crouched on the seat of his machine-gun. One of them was spreadeagled against a wall, his eyes, seen from below, seeming to be held in their sockets by a mere ligament.

Jacques rushed out and emptied his lungs. Heavens, Abel was talking to an officer! The officer was listening, beating his leg with his stick in little sharp smacks. Jacques came up.

'I didn't ask you to capture them, did I?' he was saying.

'But . . .'

'You're probably stragglers! Quiet! Wait for your leader! This is crazy! There must be a beachmaster. What a shambles! It's unbelievable. People have landed just anywhere.'

101

He went off without turning round, still tapping with his stick.

A newcomer brought up blankets, water and plasma to the aid post. Behind them the beach was filling up with jeeps, tanks, and bulldozers. In ten minutes, there was a mob. Some lads wearing armbands were playing traffic cops. They were blowing-up entanglements, upturned barricades, barges and landing craft grounding on the shore, the bombardment recommencing. The pearly countryside of the Channel coast became dismal with the flat sheen of steel, swarming with thousands of removal men who humped packing cases, carried arms, went forward, bustled each other, walked, fell, laughed, shouted and swore in front of the young ones who were envying with all their hearts the veteran comrades who knew what they had to do.

Abel, sitting on the dune, had pushed his helmet to the back of his head, exposing his forehead to the fresh air. The sea, now at full tide, was decorated with a fringe of white along its length, then it turned into a deep green which grew more and more dark until it changed at last into an ink-blue, at the horizon. Hunger was gnawing at his stomach. Sullen, he stared at the incongruous Germans while Jacques opened a tin of bully with the point of Abel's short bayonet. Then he stopped and laughed gaily at the anxious expression of the younger man.

ABEL HAD DEFIED the Mother Goddess, Diana. He was free. He felt weightless in this countryside whose light emerged from the interior of a pearl. As when he had gone to Mamie for the second time—oh, yes, not for the first because on the first occasion . . .—Mamie, the renowned Maja, the Anglo-Saxon shiftworker among the French *vivandières,* the Madelon of the songs, the matron who marched hand in hand with the spectre of war, *Margot l'Enragée,* Margot the Mad, who helps men to die, sometimes Mother Courage, sometimes Mother Maquerelle. Mamie, whom I knew at nineteen; Mamie! who went to work with the precision of the diorama at the Gates of War. A four-stroke engine! A pump! You could take a record of her operations and you would find that her performances number hardly less than those of the Exhibition of the Disembarkation. Abel could see in his mind's eye the beautiful woman's gorgeous dressing gown in cashmere, her anodyne gestures, her wide mouth, like Joan Crawford's, and especially her breasts, overwhelming, heavy, upturned, bursting, firm at the nipple, firm at the root, breasts fit for an invasion!

On that famous night with Mamie, like the night with the prisoners, Abel had made a leap forward in his own existence. Certain acts, however important, do not involve a man, others change him irrevocably.

After he had crossed Courseulles, Abel walked gaily in

103

the direction of Verville-sur-Mer, with its oyster beds, its many family hotels, its swing bridge and the choked debris of the barges. In place of a lunar landscape of dunes, he saw a smart little town where couples out on a spree were gobbling the milky summer oysters, washed down with Muscadet. 'It was the same when, in 1950, I went back again to the shores of the *Baie des Ha! Ha!* with Uncle Elie. He still had his leg, then. And Mamie Jolicoeur was so nice! The lake was as big as ever, but the village had become so very little!

Near the immense *Baie des Ha! Ha!,* in spite of the factories, you could still imagine the cry of admiration uttered by the first whites who had given it its name. Indeed, the decor of mountains had a Biblical rhythm, and the scent of turpentine from the resin-pines lingered amid the musty smell of frying on the banks. Indeed, every evening the mists drew out the fairies' shot-silk mantle and Hiawatha's canoe still slid between the reeds. The bark of the birches and the rough leather of the pines still sang in two voices, the complaint of Saguenay. *Saguenay!* The name of the tank which had exploded behind them. And, sixteen years later, that other tank which crouched down in front of the Gates of War like an obscene Cerberus and which said: *Vimy!* Things never ceased to talk to men, but men hardly ever heard or listened. Oh, certainly, the strawberries of Saguenay were still as flavoursome as ever, but that land, once crowded with old trappers who had their stories of legendary moose to recount, of game which ran from under your very feet in the good old days, of incredible sleigh-teams ringing their way through the snow, of hungry and crafty bears, and of lumberjacks in love with their red maples. But this land of his childhood, this vast Normandy, was later to be latticed with highways, made bare by the industrial zones, disfigured by power stations. All that remained was the trembling of the red maples beneath the wind. In Canada or Normandy, everything was changing. It is not the dead who pass quickly, but the living.

*   *   *

Beyond the dunes, and lower down, some little wartime vegetable allotments jostled together and, here and there, gleaming, the rectangular stretches of the oyster beds. He stopped in front of a mansion ornate with columns. Statues, chilly in their rain-spotted peplums, stood behind freshly painted railings. This is it! This is fine! Almost as good as leaving Valerie!

> Malurette demande à sa mère,
> Un remède pour son talon . . .
> Sa mère lui répondit : Ma fille . . .

The lost soldiers had crossed the park, glanced at the wounded nymphs and then cut across by the right wing of the house, among the rubble and the papers, the smashed furniture which was spewing out feminine underclothes. Now everything had changed! The laws of propriety rule once more. One must skirt round the estate where the box-trees had shot up again, their heads dressed in globes. A gardener looked at the walker, his secateurs in his hand.

'Hallo, friend,' said Abel.

The gardener turned his back. Two sphinxes in veined marble, faced each other, with thrusting breasts, heads like la Pompadour and la Dubarry, bewigged in rolling curls, at the beginning of a nearly gravelled avenue. He stopped, perplexed. He could not remember the sphinxes. He walked slowly round the house. *La Délivrande*. The patina on the marble plaque showed that this property had not awaited the Liberation before being given its name.

He went off into the lower land, uncertain, towards the oyster beds, the tarred beach huts, the barns and the gravel works. A dog barked furiously.

> Un oignon, ça s're-t-i bon?
> Un oignon, c'est trop rond.
> Un oignon, c'est trop rond?
> Ah, l'homme engagé . . .

He went straight to the bridge, crossing a pasture where a bath-tub with goat's feet served as a cattle trough. He was looking for linking signs, recovered ways, traces imperceptible to anyone but himself, left by the quick dashes and the filthy acts of lying face-down between the cowpats while the four Germans stuck to their heels. Not far from there was a small shed with a heart-shaped hole in its door. The violently ammoniacal stench assaulted his nostrils, the unique odour of the *cabinets* of the old continent.

He went round this wide terrace several times and stopped in front of a grassy hole, an old individual emplacement made once upon a time by a soldier digging frantically. Yes, this was indeed a foxhole, the hole of an isolated sniper. The contours were rounded. He jumped in. The bottom smelt of rotten vegetation. He leaned forward on his stomach against the cold earth, his shoulders exposed, looking at Verville, at battle height. At that level, an entirely new world appeared. It felt good, in this hole in the ground, to lift up the head without hearing the bullets whistle by. Something shone in a tuft of thistle. At arm's length he picked it up, an absurd child's pistol, with a plastic butt. Nearly as fine as Patton's pistols! Abel blew on the barrel in the way he had seen gangsters do in the cinema, spun it in the air, caught it again and stuffed it in his pocket. The church bell tolled quietly. It was probably Benediction. From the thick stubble there rose up a gentle scent of crushed grass.

'The prisoners!'

'What about them?' shouted Jacques.

Trees of fire shot up from the earth, a fugitive palm-grove. Other shells crashed on to the ground, breathless, like over-ripe pears, in a warm sigh. Abel was locked in his foxhole and Jacques only a few yards away. The embarrassing prisoners were glued to the ground like grey snails.

106

'It's their shells,' bawled Jacques, appalled. 'Let them sort it out.'

War is also a show. The arrivals of the shells came near, then went away, returned and made an incomprehensible pattern of long and short shots. The soldier is outside this movement of blind particles. It is a lattice which perhaps makes sense elsewhere, in another world. Not on this earth. Yes, these were certainly the mysteries of free particles, in a ballet immeasurably enlarged by the war. From time to time, tearing himself away from this deadening abstraction, Abel threw a glance at the Germans. They were his! He was responsible for them. Suddenly, he made up his mind:

'Hop it,' he yelled, in a moment of calm. 'Get out, go, go!'

There arose the warm, sickly smell of a dead cow. The Germans did not budge. They did not understand at all the sudden anger of their victor. Abel pointed his gun at them, fell back with his nose to the ground, and started again.

The *feldwebel* with the iron-rimmed glasses looked round him, indicated the château with his arm and shouted an order. The grey-green shapes slithered like partridges from shellhole to shellhole, up to the ditch which ran along the wall of the house. The bombardment began again. From time to time their guts were twisted by the sound of the rockets, a sound like a tortured animal. Mechanically, Abel counted the explosions, with a pain in the back of his neck caused by the pressure from his helmet pushed to the back of his head.

Abel got out of his hole. It was a good hole. Like him, it had seen better years. It had rounded off, become velvety with grass and moss, but it was a pretty good hole, for all that. Abel was talking to himself, like a shepherd. Two boys were lying in ambush for him. One, in an old-fashioned black smock, held out a catapult. The other was wearing a smart pink and white check overall. He had curly hair and the girlish air common to boys who are cossetted.

'Seen the old man?' asked the black-smocked urchin.

Abel pulled a face. He drew the toy pistol out of his pocket. 'This yours?' he asked.

The butt shone.

'It's the girl's,' said the black one, indicating the pink one, who lowered his face and shot at his companion a distracted look.

Abel held out the Patton-type pistol to its owner, who made a bow. The black smock sneered in disgust.

'Your pal?' said Abel.

'Kid from the big house; he dodges out all the time. And when he does, he always comes to me. He makes me sick. His mother's a widow.'

'And yours?'

'She's dead.'

There was a degree of irrepressible insolence on the thin, defiant face, a degree of hatred, at any event, and a lot of candour. Abel went through his pockets, found a coin, realised just in time that he had been on the point of making a mistake, took out his packet of Camels and offered it to the kid. Black Smock took hold of it and jumped back a little. He already had had a good experience of men. But as Abel continued to smile, some unexpected dimples appeared gaily on his pink cheeks.

'You've been had! He's a radio. He's transmitting to London.'

The boy from the big house, filled with his own importance, said:

'Di-di-dah-di-di, di-da-di-da-di-da.'

He cut himself short, apprehensively.

'The gardener's calling me. See you tomorrow.'

'So long, Norbert,' said the urchin.

The other boy went off running.

Abel lit the kid's cigarette. From the way the child took it, you could see it was not his first.

108

'Pretty posh fags,' said the little urchin, with respect in his tone. 'Just now, you were singing in the hole.'

Abel sang:

> L'homme engagé connaissait
> Bien l' bobo de la fille . . .

He stopped. The child's eyes were bright with curiosity, two black olives soaked in oil, with a fleck of gold in the iris. Insolent, direct, splendid. Abel whistled the tune of *Bobo d' la fille*. The kid took it up, also whistling. He had a good ear.

'It's a Canadian song. French Canadian.'

'Do they speak French in Canada?'

'Didn't anyone teach you that in school?'

'I don't go to school any more. My old man wants me to go out to work. Old swine.'

Abel sighed.

'That's the song,' he said. 'It's about a girl called Malurette. She's got a bad heel.'

'A bad what?'

'A bad heel.'

'Heel. Well!'

'Her mother suggests a heap of things to cure her heel. An onion, a sweet potato, a turnip, an eel and, lastly, a boy. Then, the girl's happy.'

'Of course.'

'Why "of course"?'

'It's always like that.'

Abel smiled. Trustingly, the boy uncovered a face which could belong to an adolescence of antiquity, a model for a statue of the Virgin. He had watched his companion out of the very depths of that medieval France from which he had emerged. Then they started to sing together, the boy's sharp voice wavering above the deep voice of the man.

> Eun' barbote, ça gigote!
> Un navot, c'est trop gros!
> Eun' pétate, c'est trop plate! . . .

109

The boy took Abel's hand. 'Here's another of them. I seek a man and I find some kids. Yet the man was a child and he is dead.'

'Thirsty? Have a pop. Lemonade.'

'You bet!'

Doubtingly, he added:

'With mint cordial?'

'With mint cordial.'

Abel walked in big steps.

'You go too fast. Your feet are too big!'

He stopped. Abel stopped too. The black eyes of the boy stared straight into his blue ones with the unswerving demand of the child.

'Tell me?'

'O.K.'

'Were you there?'

'There?'

'Down there.'

With his finger the boy pointed out the hole. He hesitated, then, with an exquisite tact, he ended:

'Were you there ... before?'

'Yes,' said Abel, he felt his throat constricted.

They sang all the way to the village.

In front of the Calvary, the Whitsun walkers saw the son of that drunk, Courchinoux, pass by with the Canadian he had caught. As for the Canuck, he had a little less of a burden on his chest—Valerie—a little rough child's hand in his and a lark in his heart.

CHAPTER III

'HALT!' YELLED ABEL.

Black silhouettes stood out against the fires of the setting sun. Jacques, flat on his belly, got hold of his machine pistol. Abel, his carbine under his arm, shouted, in a strangled voice:

'Stop, there!'

Three shadows stopped dead.

'I'm going to fire, you know, I'm going to fire . . .'

There was a gesture from one of the shadows. Abel's gun slipped from under his arm and cracked him on the leg.

'No fire, *nicht* fire! We, prisoners . . .'

Abel, appalled, recognised his sheep! You could have said they were returning to their mother. They all spoke at once. Obviously, they were trying to convince the two Canadians not to abandon them again. What about the rules of war? Well, what do you do about them then, these rules of war? These conquerors had no experience. Abel sat down on a stump, took off his helmet and mopped his brow, disgusted, while Jacques declaimed:

'My Lord, tell me where my flock has gone.'

In the devastated park, the statues spoke with each other. Without enthusiasm they stared at the water in the bowls of the fountains. A German was drinking from his hand. Abel carried the water to his lips and spat it out. They went through the same house and crossed the resounding rooms,

111

skirted again the encircling wall and set out for the little town, unbelievable in a light like stained glass, lit up by two suns, the real one which shone over the beaches of Contentin, the other the sun of war, over towards Caen. They went in a zig-zag across the barbed wire, the shell holes filled with putrid water a heap of cranes, some disembowelled tanks, a few agricultural machines and a graveyard of vehicles. Abel pushed open a door with his shoulder and entered a high room in which the electric torch picked out of the dark an unsold ovenload of bread; long loaves, round loaves, crusty brown loaves and golden rolls. The dead bakery rang to their footsteps, displaying its open oven, the mixing trough, and chocolates made with a thin crust on a white paste. Abel broke a loaf with Jacques. The Germans stuffed themselves and filled their pockets. You could only hear the jaws which champed on the bread made by the baker of Verville, bread begun before the Liberation, put into the oven under the bombardment, a good everyday bread, of a superior quality because the baker mixed black market flour with rationed flour; bread which to some extent had dried out during that interminable day of war, but which still was crisp to the bite.

Jacques looked for something to drink. Everything was locked, and he did not dare to force the doors. They came out again. The night was stirring. Some demolished houses were smoking and a smell like boiled milk came from them. A gilded horse's head shone from the first floor. Rockets floated swinging down to the ground, and brought to the night the glare of an all-night pharmacy. The bursts whistled and echoed round the walls. Abel and Jacques ran straight ahead, crossing a farm, fell down, got up again, rushed into a rubble of masonry, and slipped from side to side of an alley. A door banged open as though it would tear itself from its hinges. A violent current of air came out and blew some papers about. A crackling sound, followed by a slow, endless crumbling announced the collapse of a roof behind them. The electric torch swept round the arched passage which led downwards

112

to steps slippery with dirt. They clattered down and burst into a cellar. A young woman, in skirt and slip, her dark brown hair loose over her shoulders, looked at them wide-eyed.

'Don't worry, lady, don't worry.'

'You're French!'

'Canadians.'

Abel found his mouth dry, now that he was faced with the half naked woman. The old, old, longing seized his loins.

'But . . . what about the Boches?' she asked with lips trembling from a hope he had hitherto denied herself.

'Gone! You've been here some time?'

'I don't know. At least twenty-four hours. How's the village?'

Abel felt shame. As if he had personally smashed up the town. He turned his torch to Jacques, magnificent in his role of Liberator, his chest generously expanded beneath his battledress. The temperature rose so that at last the woman understood.

'My God! So they really have landed!'

Quickly she lit two candles which stood in camembert boxes. Jacques put out his torch. The flickering light replaced the cold mechanical light which changing shadows. The dishevelled woman had a bra strap which persisted in slipping; and she replaced it with a mechanical gesture. She went to a stove and poked it. The coals reddened. She put a cauldron on the stove from which she had removed a round lid with the aid of a poker. She turned round, her cheeks shining. The two children on the mattress stirred.

'Are they yours?' said Abel.

'The smaller one is, the other's my sister's son.'

She looked round for a garment, put her hand on her well-exposed breasts, went towards the stairs and gave a shout. Abel grabbed his carbine but stopped when Jacques yelled.

'Sod off, you pig's head. Just you wait, you son of a bitch!'

Jacques gathered up some bits of plaster and threw it.

Stupefied, the young woman glimpsed the inquisitive German with the steel-rimmed glasses redouble his excusing gestures and disappear. Certainly, she did not understand a lot about these Englishmen who spoke French with an appalling country accent, and who chased the Germans away by throwing bits of plaster at them!

'Prisoners,' explained Abel. 'We catch them with flypaper.'

The elder of the children rushed to cling to her. She repeated 'Prisoners', as she reflectively caressed the child's head. Abel went up to her. The kid had the light of admiration in his eyes.

'Show us your gun, mister.'

'Gérard!'

'The Boches have cleared off,' said Abel reassuringly.

The earth movement which shook the cellar underlined at once the limits of this assurance. She could not altogether believe him. He appeared to be too youthful. She wanted to say something. She turned back to her pot.

'I beg your pardon,' said Jacques, suddenly very proper, 'but we're very thirsty, madam...'

She went to a barrel and held out to them a couple of mustard pots.

'To the liberation of Normandy and the Normans,' said Jacques.

She was getting something of a feeling for him, with his white skin, his dark blue eyes, his good voice and his boyish laugh.

Abel tasted the liquid which tasted so strongly of apples and choked on it.

'Is it really true that you're Canadians?'

Jacques laughed easily. She laughed a little more loudly, then openly. Certainty poured into her. She was suddenly convinced, for no other reason than this youthful laughter which melted her, raised up her chest, so that she just had to shout for joy and throw herself into Jacques' arms, hug him with all her strength, push him away, devour him with her

114

eyes, start again, leave him, seize Abel by the shoulders, embrace him with smacking kisses like a nurse, with damp cheeks, then she burst into tears. Abel put his arms round her round, naked shoulders, grief-stricken, saddened, then he gently pushed the perspiring woman away.

'My soup!'

Here were the Allies. And the children were alive. Thank you, God! But how better to thank God than to prevent the soup from burning?

Arranged on a dresser were yellowing photographs of women with heavy eyes and wide bony faces, of men encased in their hideous Sunday suits. Those faces, marked with a cold buried passion which became evident in the creases of the mouth and the wide nostrils, seemed alive in the candle-light. Near the stove was a Sacred Heart shining in crimson velvet.

Abel sat down on a stool and took the elder child on his knee.

'I'm Lucette,' said the woman.

They exchanged names. 'Lucette,' 'Abel, Jacques.' Jacques, well, that's ordinary. It would be better to be called Abel. There was a smell of bacon and peas in the soup and *croûtons*.

'That means "little light", Lucette,' said Abel.

Jacques laughed. Abel could have hit him.

'Well,' said Abel, 'we must wait for daylight. Madame . . . I'm sorry, Lucette, do you have any water? I come from cider country, but I don't like cider. Or perhaps you have some milk?'

'The children have drunk it all. If you want water, you'll find it in the courtyard on the right. Take a bucket.'

How things change in war! A few minutes ago the thunder of the gods and now, this cellar, this gay woman who is cooking soup, breaking eggs and holding out a bucket to the

115

Liberator. Abel took the lamp, went up the stairs, and out into the yard. A dim light burst over the village. The sky groaned, swept by the brush strokes of the flak. A house in flames lit up a fountain like a theatrical set. At that moment he was only aware of the soggy state of his hobnailed boots and his trousers. There was a gurgling sound and the water spurted out. He drank in long draughts. Straight away, he stripped to the waist and splashed the chill water liberally on his face, his powerful shoulders and his wide chest. The golden medallion danced. His mother had hung it round his neck because she was called Marie and because the medallion showed the Mother of Christ. He snorted under the shock of the cold water. He stood up, rubbed his aching neck, felt the tensed muscles relaxing under his finger. Then suddenly he stopped. He jumped back behind the fountain and slid into the door. There was a man whose legs were inflated by packed pockets, with a grenade fixed to the right leg. His face was black and glistened with a matt sheen.

'Damn it!' the man swore as he tottered in.

American or English! The face had been blackened with soot and his white eyes glared out. Abel came out of the porch. The other lad leaped back.

'Don't fire,' shouted Abel.

He was a British parachutist, a pathfinder. For twenty hours he had been wandering in search of his group. 'Good. I'm not alone,' he said. It was humiliating. To be lost. Wandering. Not to know what to do, when the rest did know it. He did not know. Abel suggested to this man, a Cockney from Whitechapel, that he should share their shelter. The soldier, exhausted, could not make up his mind. He was a professional soldier. Abel returned to the pump, dried himself as best he could with a handkerchief, quietly filled the bucket—how he loved the sound of water!—took up his shirt, his sweater and his battledress under his arm and went back towards the cellar, still inviting the paratrooper who . . .

The night burst into fragments.

116

It took an unconscionable time for the debris to finish falling. Abel opened his eyes. Nothing. Nothing any more. The smashed house breathed out a puff of plaster. At the back, the fountain had disappeared with the paratrooper of the blackened face. Abel slid underneath the collapsed beams and called out. Nothing. He looked for the staircase. Nothing. With his face creased in anguish, Abel saw Jacques emerge placidly from the neighbouring house, unharmed.

'Well, now, you might have taken the kids for a bit of a walk! That farmer's wife is nice!'

He had the same fatuous expression as when he was speaking of Jennifer. For a moment, Abel loathed him. They dived back into the cellar, not before time, for a new chain of explosions threw them to the foot of the stairs, twisted the candle flames and threw the boys against Lucette who lay couched flat on her belly. She raised herself fearfully on her forearms. She breathed deeply and tremblingly between the two males gathered at her sides, these two young men who had come from the other side of the sea.

CHAPTER IV

THE SUN was bleaching the coastline. Abel came across the boats once again which just hours ago were proudly afloat and now were stuck in the mud. In the middle of the channel, a thin, clear trickle of water flowed, glistening beside the cloudy sheen of the mud.

'There's seaweed there,' said the boy in the black smock.

117

The mud was laden with weeds which looked like the very entrails of the sea, the colour of raw liver, a wet brown shadowing into violet, according on the way the light took it. The seagulls walked around insolently, leaving behind them slender stars from their claws. On the other side of the channel, the village was heaped up into a grey wall of houses. At each step, golden reflections flashed in the windows.

At the lock, the boy let the Canadian's hand go, and Abel smiled because he had wondered when the little lad would do this.

'Where are you taking me?'

'To the *Père Magloire*. They've got t.v. there.'

They left the sea front. The road had a pretty name: *The Rising Sun,* and ran east-west. Just so was the road in that dead village, the spot where the high cellar had been, the plump white Lucette and the engulfed fountain.

The hotel-restaurant *Père Magloire,* offering 'gardens, games, weddings and banquets' hit the eye. It was very new, with creamy walls, with varnished half-timbering. Abel loved the houses of Normandy, with the plasterwork bulging out between the beams, underneath a menacing overhang. Houses which the centuries had knocked about without destroying, with ornate timbers and sculpted masks of drunkards, demons, lascivious monks, washerwomen and cheerful workmen. This hotel was merely a copy for tourists. In the side of the outrageously new house was a dumpy wing perhaps a hundred years old. On the front of the old inn, the recent paintwork, now attacked by the acidity of the winter rains and fogs, had let the previous sign show through:

A LA LIBERATION

Already! Already the landlord of the hotel—no doubt re-built out of war damage funds—had reverted to the old name of the coaching inn, the name of the old bonneted Père Magloire. Well, he hadn't been slothful about it.

'Is it a long time since they called it the Liberation?'

118

'They changed the name when they made the place bigger. Two years ago. But I prefer *Père Magloire*. It's not so stupid.'

At the door, a peasant cut out of painted wood invited him in, obsequious, a napkin on his arm, in a blue beret, pompom and blouse, with a red tie and a red drunkard's face.

Abel went in behind the boy. Suddenly he was overwhelmed by the din.

'It's the wedding of the Lemaresquier girl,' the child explained. 'They're still at it. They went to the mayor and the priest on Saturday morning, but they stopped the wedding after lunch. The husband's aunt kicked the bucket. She had eaten like a pig. Went purple all over! They stopped and started again today. The funeral's going to be the day after tomorrow. They've not been sober for a week now.'

The revellers were raising a deafening uproar which was being made worse by a whining accordionist and a drummer, who was content merely to mark the tonic beats with a peculiar, monotonous boom-boom. At six in the evening, the wedding breakfast had only reached the dessert. A big blonde in royal blue, with a very thin figure and big hips, was singing.

Abel, dazed by the din, heard only a few of the words because he was in range of the juke-box. Here, four skinny youths, their backsides squeezed into blue-jeans, were shaking a pintable which was decorated with bathing-suited pin-ups. The name shone forth: FLORIDA. The juke-box was giving out a tune called *Mustapha*, a tune made of Turkish delight, about as oriental as *The Snake Charmer of Old Bagdad*.

> Ali, je t'aime
> Ali, je t'honore
> Comme la salsa
> Del pommodore.

Behind the counter a hatchet-faced brunette, with dark, darting eyes, was doing a belly dance. Abel decided to give his attention to the wedding. The 'oriental' music faded to allow the voice of the blonde in blue to boom out. Before Abel had even sat down, he recognised the tune which Sebastian had been playing on the mouth organ, on the quay at Bernières. The whole wedding group took up the refrain, in a clatter of false notes.

Abel ordered mussels for the harum-scarum child. An expression of trusting friendship came into the boy's eyes.

'A *perroquet* in a tumbler for me, my love,' said Abel.

His 'love' laughed right in his face and went off to the kitchen.

'She's called Annette,' said the boy.

And, as though he were giving a present, he added :

'She's a tart, that one.'

What a mob of them there were! And all of them had once been liberated. This fact gave him pleasure. They all talked at once. Like a market. A fairground. A fisherman was chaffing the *patronne* who was seated at the counter, huge, as fat as her mussels, dignified, indifferent to the din.

'If I get my teeth into any little thing, I'm hooked. Ah, don't you have a fine life, Marie-France? Just sitting there doing nothing.'

He pulled an enormous oyster out of his bag.

'Now that's a beauty! A monster! There's a lot more like that!'

He made a gesture, cutting the middle of his forearm with his outstretched hand. The oyster went round the company.

The bridesmaid, blonde and blotchy, continued the bogus song, standing with her hands on her hips, putting on an accent, perhaps for the fun of it, perhaps because she wanted to lay claim to some individuality of which she was proud, such as an allegiance to some ancient and distinctive region. She set herself to it brazenly, the big tart.

> Mon père ainsi qu' ma mère
> n'avaient d'éfant que mê

N'avaient d'éfant que mê.
La destinée
La rose au boué
N'avaient d'éfant que mê.

At the side of the bride, who was delicately blushing, a big moustached woman in clerical purple was weeping copious tears. The uproar from the wedding party, enlivened as it was by muscadet, calvados, cider, champagne, dubious jokes, and the booming of the drum, cut the conversation of the other customers into pieces. They had to yell to make themselves understood and started *Mustapha* again. The son of the *Patron,* dressed in a light petrol-blue jacket over a thin roll-necked sweater, switched off, beaten by these old-fashioned jollifications. He took the oyster, considered it with indifference and handed it back to its owner. Someone shouted happily:

'Look into an empty bottle through the hole in the neck. It's as though you looked into a church.'

The bride lit a cigarette. The big blonde with the light blue eyes climbed on to a table, while her companions clapped their hands. She stressed the more obscene expressions with gesture and posture, shouting the magic words into the smoky atmosphere: the school at Rouet, the schoolmaster who loves me . . .

'Everybody join in the chorus!' shouted the old lady, cheering them on, and laughingly showing a bright set of dentures.

'The other day. Can't remember when. I've lost me memory.'

'You drink too much.'

'You're not paying, Marie-France!'

'Your ducks are as skinny as vultures . . .'

People circulated, sat down, drank, yelled, called the waitresses. The little boy with Abel ate seriously. He took an

121

opened shell whose two valves were still linked by the ligament and used it as a pair of pincers to pick up the fat shellfish, shining in their juices, spotted with cream. Abel did the same as the boy, and his eyes lit up.

'Want some?' he said.

'No. Just tasting. Eat up, old man.'

His voice shook slightly when he said 'old man'. The unexpected gravity of the child confronting his food had touched him.

'Goddam and blast to hell in damnation . . . !'

Abel jumped. The blasphemer was a thin, red-headed man with a darting eye and a pock-marked face.

'He's la Luzerne,' the child informed him with a full mouth. 'He's a funny fellow.'

La Luzerne was not swearing on his own behalf but he was imitating the sort of peasant who swears like a trooper, in a torrent of words, always the same, dozens of words, becoming more and more misshapen.

'Goddam twenty damn goddam to hell's bells and good God! that dirty swine of a cow belonging to Ferdinand, has broken the fence and smashed up my lucerne, the goddam and blast and damn to hell and goddam cows!'

Arnaud, the complacent middle-aged *patron* whose belly pushed out his red-checked shirt, stopped laughing to tell the servants off; then started up again. When Annette passed, he smacked her behind. The *Père Magloire* spun like a merry-go-round about the beaming Canadian. Three other young fishermen had joined the man with the oyster, and were chaffing the fat, heavily made-up *patronne,* the smiling goddess of this Olympus.

'Have you performed your conjugal duties?'

'Mind your own business!'

She spoke poshly, in a manner to suit her rank, her mouth round and small.

'The little woman in the grocer's doesn't wear any pants.'

122

'Well, it's none of your business. As for me, I'm pretty worried. I'm getting thin. My skirt's dropping off.'

She weighed at least thirteen stone.

'I'm going fishing tomorrow morning, Marcel.'

'How do you expect him to catch any fish when he has moustaches like racing handlebars? He'll frighten them off.'

Laughter burst out.

'You really are terrible.'

'De Gaulle is running us to hell,' said one wit, who was as apoplectic-looking as the landlord, with a huge, aubergine-coloured nose, marked with black spots, bursting out of his close-cut ready-made suit. 'My apples belong to me. If I like to make a purée of them, I'll make a purée. If I want to make them into calva, I'll make them into calva.'

'You're right, Blondel! It's a free country,' the eldest of them said decidedly, throwing his cards down on a Byrrh tablecloth.

There was a red tint beneath the white hair, cut *en brosse*, moustache of copper, and eyes of oyster green. He was wearing a soft shirt knotted with a bright red cord, and a waistcoat trimmed with beige velour. Damn it, they were well fed, these liberated ones. Bubbling with health! Stuffed with cholesterol! The old man's eyes were sharp, with a hooked nose pinched at the bridge and with widely dilated nostrils above a mouth which looked like a sabre slash.

'Liberty be damned. They've poisoned us with liberty! After all, liberty's not all one-way! The French economic control is worse than the Germans.'

The giant oyster came into his hands. He felt its weight, turned it over, sniffed it, suddenly very serious.

'It's a long time since we've seen them like this,' he said. 'Where did you pick it up?'

'I was sweeping beside la Vielle, monsieur Jaouen.'

'Ah, here's the doctor. The public poisoner! Oh, sorry doctor, I thought you were listening.'

'Marie-France, you're a witness. You know, gentlemen,

that you must give me the respect due to my profession.'

In the second room, in front of the table which was groaning under the set piece, in the place of honour, a big bent man, with a suntanned face, and fringed grey hair which fell over his forehead, dressed in a black frock coat of an ancient pattern, opened a toothless mouth like a baker's oven.

'That's the bride's grandad,' the boy explained. 'He's been in Algeria and in Tonkin. He's eighty-five. He's a blacksmith.'

The boy took great pleasure in showing off his little world. The wedding celebration had reached the stage at which the venerable bottles had been brought out, twisted bottles without labels, stoppered with wax and covered with dust. Abel could hardly hear the singer any more.

> C'est pas la mod' des filles
> D'embrachi les garçons . . .

With one movement the young men got up, staggering, accusing each other of being drunk. They pushed the table away with high-pitched shrieks and started to kiss the girls. 'Oh, my dress. Hop it!' They began to dance in a party of six, three boys, three girls, face to face, mimicking the amorous schoolmaster, the tailor who made the dress, the girl who tried it on, the smart aleck who wanted to kiss her. The boom of the drum took up a more rapid beat, accompanied by the panting of narrow chests and the sour stink of armpits. The huge room of the Père Magloire, which had been built out of the proceeds of uproar, rediscovered its ancient overwhelming din, the wedding feasts of former times, when the admirable forefathers stayed at table for a week at a stretch and when they 'really and truly' unfastened the bride's garter.

The conversations diminished, carried away on the alcoholic flood.

Nevertheless, someone near to Abel said once again, in a tone of deafening conviction:

'The calves aren't coming on. It's the season.'

> Mais c'est la mod' des filles
> De ballier les maisons . . .

And every one of the girls pretended to wash, to polish, to sweep, then, laying their hands on some real brooms, they started to sweep in earnest, the room, the table, the peaceful chortling drinkers, the holidaymakers, the drunks, the card players, the women who were laughing so shrilly they peed their knickers, even the old grandfathers braying like young deer. One of the ushers carried off a whole camembert, spreading it on a loaf. The fun of this outrageous song, and the primeval shouts which it engendered, the temporary victories and delicious defeats of Adam and Eve, all this happy jostling started to go from house to house. Now, the six dancers found themselves carried away in a spin which turned into a farandole.

The boy, his blue eyes deep set, dunked his bread in the sauce and deigned to smile. Abel lifted up his head and looked into the mirror. Reflected askew in the glass, a young woman had just come in. He recognised her at once. She had done her hair. She had a bouffant hair style raised up over the forehead. It was none other than the blonde whose back was crossed by the thin thread of scar tissue, the one he'd seen on the beach and with whom he'd spoken, that morning, oh, a long time ago, in front of the Gates of War.

She laughed at him with her eyes, but she allowed herself to be gathered up by a dancer and disappeared from the company. Abel turned round. She was there before him, led round like a skater by the man :

> Quand les maisons sont propres
> Les amoureux y vont
> La destinée
> La rose au bouê . . .

This young woman wore a yellow rose, the golden rose on

a dress made in the design of sailing ships: and, in spite of the turmoil, still held by the oafish dancer, she wove her way through the tables, holding out her hand to Abel.

'Come on!'

When his hand was in hers, she spoke to him seriously.

'You must not stay alone.'

The aunt with the bishop's face in a stained glass window was dancing and whimpering. Abel followed heavily, working out the steps, sure that he had danced the same dance to other tunes at home, at festivals. He was not alone: the young woman's hand had just changed into a child's hand.

The whirl of the farandole snatched up Annette, untied her apron, bundled it up and, screaming, seized Arnaud who was choking behind his bar. It just missed bumping the *patronne* from her seat, overcome with indignation. It crossed the counter behind her, shaking the bottles, swallowed up the fishermen, encircled the notables, snapped fingers at the holidaymakers, and finally absorbed the rioting youths who tried a few modish dance steps in vain and ended up by letting them pass.

I' z'y quat' par quat'
En tapant du talon . . .

And, with their heels they stamped out destiny, the rose in the mud, stamping, stamping with their heels. They dragged the wooden Père Magloire along, went down the steps, went round the trees, went to the baker's, made his little bell ring, and scoffed up the tartlets in great mouthfuls. Perhaps it was the same baker's he had met on the first day of the war? Damn the war. Abel laughed at his two companions, the young, slender woman and the other one, a great big beautiful fat girl with white skin, heavily made up, taller even than Valerie; this girl enjoying herself without missing a single crumb, in the way one does eat at wedding feasts when you're not paying for it yourself, no matter how rich you are.

126

The majestic grandfather appeared at the inn door and he tried out a trembling entrechat.

'Go back, grandad.'

A sour young man interposed himself. Leaning on his stick, the old man started to storm out an abuse in patois, very fast. The little young man, furious at being resisted by the old one, pushed him inside. A plump girl in sickly pink, leaped on the boy with her claws out.

'At his age he's earned the right to do as he pleases, hasn't he?'

'Go and get stuffed, Leontine. It's my grandfather.'

'Well, he's my great uncle. Let him go, pig.'

He held her at arm's length, jammed between the young fury and the old man who was raising a knotty fist.

'He's going to fall, like he did at Béclu's funeral.'

The wedding of the daughter of Lemaresquier! Another cousin, as wide as a cupboard, joined in, accusing the skinny little man of being brutal to Léontine. Those who had come up to separate them started to collect blows, while the heaped-up reproaches of four generations gushed out, from the inheritance of Uncle Alphonse in Mexico to the pillage of Victor's house in 1944.

'Why, we even found Charlotte's dinner service with the gold band in your Henri II sideboard!'

'Oh! That I should live to hear such things! The daughter of the pork butcher in Ver was seduced by that great pig! He jumped on her when she was still going to school . . .'

'You bitch! Saying that about a child!'

The matron in violet bawled out: 'If the cap fits, wear it!'

'Leah was a slut! It wasn't Marcel's fault. They've all of them had a go at her, beginning with the schoolmaster.'

It built up into a huge pile of insults, like the King of the Rats, a vast load of loathsome little animals all joined together by their tails, built up into juicy slanders, stale animosities, floods of poison. That little tart had made the schoolie so hot for her that he could not eat, the poor chap! And then one day she herself went into the class and the master was in the act of giving this Leah a very curious form of punishment! Inevitably the parents got their compensation, seeing that he was secretary to the town council! No, no! It's just not possible to listen to this in cold blood! Why, if your father could hear you now, he'd turn in his grave. That's how they got their war damages settled, through Leah's little hot pants! Oh, the swine! And the notary was mixed up in it all. He certainly was! He'd do better to shut his big mouth, that little rogue. He'd had little enough to say for himself in 1926, indeed, but had messed about more than most with all those fiddles on the resale of war damage claims! It was the scandal of the district. Even if there had been an inquiry, without taking into account the life assurance paid out on a couple of gamekeepers both dead only eight months after the signature was dry. There was not one death, but two! Ah, it's a lousy world.

'You can talk, codface! As for your daughter, they cut her hair off at the Liberation. She'd open her legs to anyone for five hundred francs.'

'At any rate, she didn't suck up to collaborators to steal their savings!'

'Don't forget the laws of slander, you cow! Bigamist! National disgrace! Sleeping partner for the Fritzes! Moonshine maker! Cuckold! Poujadiste!'

'Are all weddings like this around here?' Abel asked the young woman.

'Since the time of General Gouraud . . .' mumbled the old grandfather.

Two scarlet-faced men squared up to each other. The grandad stamped his foot.

'I'm going home. I've had enough of this menagerie of a wedding . . .'

And he did what he said. He went down the stone steps. Trembling with anger, and leaning on his cane, he went off. Without turning round, Booz fled the camp. The Viking Lot denied his descendants. But, look here, this mustn't go any farther! It'll bring bad luck. He crossed the road. The dignified old man executed a splendid run of faltering steps, staggered into a dog who had rushed howling from the butcher's, and went off towards the sea, brandishing his stick, leaving behind him an immense shadow.

There was an astounded silence.

Straight away, the gentle bride stood up and went out into the open air. You could see clearly that she was more than normally plump under her white dress! They rushed out together in pursuit of the patriarch. They surrounded him. They begged him. They demanded his pardon. They abased themselves. They had been impossible, good-for-nothings, loathsome creatures, stupid, unmanly, the worst that one could say and more beside. With the whole wedding party on their heels, the noble octogenarian continued his descent towards the door.

The girl in the yellow dress smiled:

'Doesn't that ever happen in Canada?'

'It does. Have a drink with me.'

'Why not!'

'Please excuse me, I've picked up a kid.'

'He's the little Courchinoux boy. It's a holiday, so his father has taken a load on board. The boy doesn't want to go back home.'

The conversations had started up again. The accordionist sorted out his tinselled instrument.

'The truth, I say! The complete truth. The naked truth, eh? Naked like the moon. Good God!'

There was a burst of laughter and giggles! What a card Luzerne is! What a wit!

'Ah me! All these young people!' said Marie-France, looking dreamily at this upset in her house which never reached her.

The wedding party split up, dissolved into a cloud of steam, vapour, illusion, just a memory. The waitresses stripped the tables under the orders of the elder Arnaud. At the other end of the counter, the boys with the skinny haunches encircled the reconquered juke-box and *Mustapha* began again.

Ali, je t'aime,
Ali, je t'honore . . .
Comme la salsa
Del pommodore

They envisioned an Orient out of the wide screen cinema, dominated by a magnificent Commodore with a seraglio of naked sultanas at his disposal. They did not think for a moment that the song was about tomato sauce! Now, with the night, the chins of the older men bristled with short white stubble like pig's bristle. The boy finished off his mussels. He nodded and, with a full mouth, said:

'So long, Bébé!'

'My name's Bérangère,' the young woman told Abel. 'And I drink pastis when anyone offers me it.'

Her caressing laughter trickled down Abel's spine. He blushed inexplicably.

It contented Abel to see these moustaches sticky with Vermouth, these shocks of stiff hair, these chicken necks swimming inside collars of a dead whiteness.

'Until the landings, we had too much of everything,' one of the companions of the man they called Jauoen, stated with conviction.

This same Jaouen, drawing on a pipe clamped between his heavy jaws, was glancing at Bérangère.

'Too much of everything. Too much milk. Too much butter. Too much meat. Too many pigs. To be sure, you had to pay the price. But who was there to buy petrol and tyres? Then the day Paris was liberated—all finished.'

This lively fellow, crammed into a brown suit, was the

130

garage proprietor, Blondel. He turned to the couple, touched his beret and, indicating Abel, said in a friendly tone:

'Is monsieur Belgian?'

'No,' said Bérangère, 'Canadian.'

The big red-faced man greeted him, with a movement of the head which was copied by all the others except Jaouen. The eyes of each of them were the colours of oysters: Portuguese, Marennes, Courseulles, Claires, Belons!

'The Canadians were good,' said the big man. 'They got stuck on the ground, but they cleared out the Boches. It was wonderful not to have to look at those dungheaps any more, with their *"los"*, their *"schnell"*, their *"raus"* and their *"achtung"*.'

This was the same man who'd spoken of the Germans being 'less severe than the Economic Control.'

'Remember the Atlantic Wall, Jaouen? And that lad who couldn't pass a bunker without pissing on it?'

'Ah yes, Trinquer. Gustave Trinquer,' asserted the thin, dry man with the look of a lawyer.

'Good old Gustave! The Boches ended up by shoving him inside. When he was completely tight, he used to say "That Atlantic Wall is me".'

'That didn't stop him dying in Dachau, like a good member of the resistance,' Jaouen cut in.

Abel tried to imagine the life story, so briefly outlined, of this drunkard, the fishmonger Gustave Trinquer, who could not stand the Germans, but who would sell them his sardines, mackerel, and his lobsters, the man who pissed on the Wall of China, the slanderer of the New Order in Europe, the 'saboteur' of the Thousand Years' Peace, the son of a whore who defied these flaxen-haired dolichocephalics with his golden urine!

'Is he on the memorial to the dead?' asked Bérangère.

'Certainly he is,' said Jaouen. 'A hero.'

'Heavens, where's the kid gone?'

The boy had gone away, without a word. Abel felt a little

131

stab in his heart. He wouldn't have done that when he was a child. But then, as a child, he had never been hungry.

The sun, which was descending slowly towards the sea, cut across the road in horizontal strips of light.

'About what time did the fighting stop here on D-Day?' asked Abel.

'On the 6th of June? Well, about midday or one o'clock.'

That started a row! The problem was not so easy! Just a minute! Just a minute! They sorted out incidents, anecdotes and stories of survival. What did he mean, 'about midday or one o'clock'? Towards four in the afternoon there was still shooting beside the Bertrand's barns? They were all talking at once.

'Come along, let's hear your view, Sebastian,' said the thin man to the old fellow with the harmonica, who Abel had noticed come in an hour before with the farandole dancers.

Sebastian screwed up one eye.

'Let's see,' he said. 'I was at Bernières that day, but I had my sister here and I came back to pick her up about midday. By that time it was all over around the cafe, that's for sure.'

'He's right,' said Blondel, the big red-faced garage man. 'Two at the latest...'

Abel's house of cards crumbled! So he could no longer think it was at Verville that he had landed. Damn, damn, damn! But what about the foxhole? the château? and the statues? everything that Abel had just recognised? False memories, tricks of memory, unnatural perspectives, tricks of time!

'Anette, set them up again, love,' said Bérangère.

Obstinate, with a creased brow, Sebastian asserted:

'Sure, it ended round midday. It was a circus, a real circus.'

'That it was,' said Jaouen. 'A real circus. Listen, my Canadian friend.'

'That's right, a circus. Long live France and chipped potatoes! All those civilians who were in the village, well, they brought out their flags. You should've seen it! It was raining,

132

you know and then, well, we heard a hell of a noise! The tanks! The Boches had woken up! They were coming back, the swine. Ah, that was, now that was . . .'

Sebastian was reliving the scene.

'Ah, it was, it was . . . I just can't tell. They started to whip the flags in like women with the washing when there's going to be a storm! No more flags! Not a flag to be seen. And the Canadian, English and Americans? Nowhere in sight. *Nicht. Kein.* Good. Everyone at home. And here's the joke. Here come the Canadians. Fly away, Peter, fly away, Paul. Now you see me, now you don't. The Germans go off again. So, we all get out the flags again. Ah, yes, a real circus, that was. My sister was singing the Marseillaise.'

'It's what they call the Epic of the Liberation,' said Jaouen.

He puffed out a cloud of blue smoke and went on:

'That's not the only story! There was Maxime's commando . . . The Fifis! You remember them, Maxime's Fifis?'

That must have been a funny story, Maxime's Fifis, for they all choked with laughter. But Abel wasn't listening to them. Late in the afternoon of the sixth of June, 1944, he had been pinned to the ground, with Jacques. Of that, he was certain. So this was not the place. Or, if this had been the place, it was on another day. And it was not his foxhole in the meadow. It was not the oysterbeds of Verville he remembered. Nor even Lucette's bakery and cellar. Or perhaps, he had come back to Verville later and his memory had mixed it all up. He had made several trips back to the beaches when they had at last rejoined the Chauds. Now where the devil could he have disembarked?

'Goodbye, messieurs. Thank you. Goodnight to Charlotte, *monsieur le maire.*'

'I know very well whom you're thinking about. I was there myself. I had five shots. Five, not six in the magazine. And not the right to kill.'

The voices were becoming thick. Arnaud with a note of scorn as marked as that of Jaouen, remarked:

133

'What the hell does it matter to you whether Verville was liberated at midday or at five in the afternoon?'

He switched on the television.

'Now it's the sixth of June 1960. I'm living in the present.'

The small milky screen showed the shaven head and wrinkled eyes of Jean Nohain. His delivery was larded with adjectives. Jean Nohain spoke properly about our good friends the Canadians, the fine Canadians who had liberated us, while his announcer began a story which started quite naturally with the phrase: 'Damn, I who am a died-in-the-wool Canadian . . .' Abel had left his national susceptibilities somewhere on the Sargasso sea . . . He enjoyed himself, smiling at the Blue Bell Girls and laughing with Bérangère, letting himself be carried along on the easy stream of narrative by the commentator who related the liberation story in his own way, repressing a tendency to gravity behind these two streams of wholesome thoughts.

'Do the people round here like this commentator, this Jean Nohain?'

'They do.'

'What's the name of the other one?'

'Leclerc.'

'My name's Leclerc,' he said. 'Abel Leclerc.'

Then, because they felt it was necessary to do something, they raised their glasses ceremoniously and knocked back a ritual swig of *perroquet* and pastis 'down the hatch,' as Abel said, to indicate that he was well acquainted with the niceties of the French spoken in France. He drank the health of all good Frenchmen, and Canadians, Jean Nohain and all the good Norman-Canadian Leclercs who are all very much at home in either country—dead or alive.

LONG AVENUES of orange light floated over the Channel, towards Cotentin. The town did not wish to go to bed. Young men were engaged in a slow bicycle race, girls passed by in chattering bands and the peaceful citizens sipped their drinks interminably between the trees on the terraces. The village smelled of iodine, cider and the hay.

Suddenly, in the town centre, something stirred.

'That's the procession,' said Bérangère. 'After, there'll be fireworks and dancing.'

Preceded by a gang of children holding their multi-coloured lamps on the ends of sticks, the brass band played loudly, with the drums beating loudly, the firemen in blue and gold shoving and hauling a vehicle itself as red as fire, as blood and as war. Abel never failed to admire those moustachioed men puffing fit to burst into the mouthpieces, with bushy eyebrows, and helmets thrown back or balanced on their noses. The flags displayed letters of gold, counterparts of those makeshift flags which came out of the ruins on the sixth of June 1944, then went back and came out again. And now, that adventure no longer seemed to him to be so funny —'a real circus'—but simply a moving tale of fear and heroism intermingled. Since 'heroes' harbour fear and courage at the same time, why should it not be the same with crowds, taking the good with the bad, writing history with smudges, false starts, contradictions, and blunders; but writing it, all the same.

The warm hand laid on the Canadian's arm seized his fist, caressed it where the veins stood out blue, travelled up the little valley which goes into the palm, in the very spot where fortune tellers look for life and death. It forced the fist closed and slowly reopened the fingers.

'Buy me an ice,' she said. 'Oh, no! Not at the cafe. Here, from the trolley.'

She was carefree and roguish. 'Bérangère is life itself.' The woman selling ice cream, with cheeks wrinkled like a winter apple, waited for them.

'Hallo, out for the fun, Bérangère? That's right, you have to enjoy yourself while you can. Vanilla and pistachio?'

'Yes, please. And you?'

She spoke familiarly to him, to this man whom she had known for a day, for a hundred years. Behind the curtain which festooned the little vehicle, covered with mirrors, the ice-cream seller could hardly see Bébé's companion.

'Chocolate,' he said.

'Sweet tooth, said Bébé.

The old lady bent lower down than was necessary to dig into her scoop and regarded the man with a lively eye.

With a warlike din, the procession returned. Among the kids, the little boy Abel had met that morning was holding the highest of the lanterns on the end of a slender pole. He stared at its light, blue, yellow and red. His pert face was lit up. This was why the child had slipped off. Suddenly, there were some shouts. One lantern had caught fire. The boy who was carrying it took fright and started to run. He ran for about twenty yards, amid an anxious buzz. Abel's jaw hardened. In smaller compass, the way of the man-torch from the bunker, the German long ago burned by the flame-throwing tank. The lantern went out in a shower of sparks. Abel's eyes were riveted in the night towards the corner where the child had taken shelter. It was an inky night. In the darkness, the dead of the sixth of June were reassembled. They were present at the celebration and only the misfortune

136

of the child had revealed their presence. Jacques was in the middle of them. But Abel could see nothing of Jacques's face. Abel merely knew that Jacques was there and was looking at him.

They wandered towards the sea, leaving the village to play at war, begging it not to return, just as animists mime the King of the Tigers to ensure that he will seek his victims elsewhere!

They went slowly along, she moving to his step. Night came from in front of them, in the dull sound of the sea. This was not the same night as sixteen years earlier. This was a huge block of dark glass sparkling with tiny fires. But here, indeed was the same proportion of water, land and beach, the same proportion of land to sky, the same littleness of the human animal. Good! This is how I best remember Normandy, by night rather than by day!

Their steps sank in to the sand. The domain of dry sand. The foreign country, the Promised Land.

'It must be an odd effect,' she said, guessing his thoughts.

Heady with joy, the Canadian seized his companion by the waist, lifted her up against himself, his mouth at the level of her breasts. And he plunged his burning forehead against the young woman's bosom. She unwound herself, bent her body against him and dropped her hair like a spray over him. It was splendid, like the fountain in that village when he had trickled the water on his naked torso. He shook her again, shook her enough to stifle her, while her legs beat gently against his thighs. Then he raised her even higher so that his forehead was rubbing against the crisp thin fabric, at the level of her belly. Then she was on his shoulder like a broken doll.

He showed Bérangère to the night, to the war, to Jacques, as his prize, warm and heavy; then he let her slip down towards him, slowly, slowly. His mouth open on the silk, then tasting her naked flesh, pressing with his leonine nose into the

137

valley between her breasts. She was still not touching the ground. His lips mounted once again and found the tip of her pointed chin. She uttered little moans, their lips met and did not part. All his strength flowed into the centre of his body. Bérangère had come down to earth. She grasped his neck in her clasped hands and drew him to her. 'You're strong, little girl,' with all her will, with all her abandon, Bérangère drew him down into the sand. With her mouth hard against the man's mouth, she gasped: 'Come, come, come!' He fell to his knees. She twisted under him. 'Come, come, come.' He felt her stretching out, her shoulders raised and still she drew him to her. 'Come, come, come.' Whilst he pressed down on her with his body, whilst she, with the frankness of nature, snatched furiously at Abel's shirt.

The sea returned. A distant crackling drew them out of their fragile isolation. At Verville, they were letting off fireworks. He caressed the roundness of the warm calf muscle bent back under the thigh.

'Tonight I saw the patterns of love,' he said in a strange voice.

She smiled. He smiled. There was just enough light at intervals to light up their smiles.

'Patterns of fire. The carpet patterns of the Caliph. Great carpets of rubies and emeralds, with golden thread. When I was little I used to press on my closed eyes to make some immense carpets. I'd look at them for hours. Did you do that?'

'Yes.'

'All children make carpet patterns. I've just seen the patterns of heaven once again.'

There was a pause.

'Just now?'

'Yes.'

It was she who asked him. But then had she not taken

138

charge of him? Did she not have to justify it? She pressed her hand on the hard muscles of his arm. A joyful laugh shook him and he threw himself backwards.

'The patterns of heaven! I've not often seen them since. By no means. Decidely not. In fact, I don't ever remember seeing them—I mean it—since the war ended. You as well?'

'Me, as well.'

'However, you . . .'

She put her hand on Abel's mouth. The wind pricked them with a million needles of sand. Clearly, he was right, but he should not have said, 'However, you . . .' There was a violent odour of seaweed . . . The rolling of the drums which were beating into their very bodies through the ground . . . the distant fête . . . the fête beneath the marquee . . . a party held on top of the dead. However, Bérangère did not withdraw. The body of the young woman held no reproach. He slid his hand under her sweater and his fingers met the thin thread of hardened flesh which cut the body of Bébé in two. Gently the finger followed the wound, climbing up to the shoulder blade, reading blindly the young woman's grievous history. He felt her shiver. He drew her towards him. She did not prevent it. She murmured: 'Abel! Abel! If you only knew! If you only knew!' He murmured back: 'Pardon, pardon, pardon!' Then he turned her over, crushed her with all his weight into the sand and possessed her furiously this time, violently, his shoulders and neck whipped by the wind, enveloped quickly in the immense mantle of a shimmering sea where flowers of the fireworks and the stars were spinning, all in the patterns of heaven.

'Where would you have slept?'

'In a boat!'

'Do you often sleep in boats?'

'Around here, it's usual to sleep in boats.'

'Haven't you left the war behind?'

She bent under him, her hand clutching the heavy mass of his shoulders. A group of boys and girls passed by, singing.

'That's little Yvonne. The daughter of the *épicière*. She's not sixteen yet! I don't know if she sees patterns every time, but if she did, she'd think she was in a big store! And there's fat Raymonde with her. Fifteen years old! Anyway, she'll make up for the bride's virginity.'

'Wasn't the bride a virgin, then?'

'Virgin, my foot! What's the time?'

Once before he had consulted this same watch, either here or a few kilometres away.

'Two twenty.'

'The aunts are sleeping. Can you keep quiet?'

'I'd hope so.'

'I warn you, my aunts are a couple of old girls who are screwed up by the demon of the flesh. If ever they ran into you, they'd pop you in the pot! You'd not amount to a row of beans between Barthe and Merthe!'

Bérangère's room was located in a wing of a high villa in the astonishing Gothic of the 1880s. A half-erased sign at the top of the steps said:

> Pension de famille
> Les Embruns

The garden was planted with massive hydrangeas, the pride of 'Merthe-and-Barthe'. The door screeched with a sea-gull's cry. The house smelt of polish. They went down a corridor swept by the pale gleams of the lighthouse, then he followed her up a waxed staircase, the walls of which were hung with fabric. At a right angle, they took a corridor cluttered with mildewed suitcases. He had to lower his head to enter a room decorated with pictures framed in gilded leaves, all showing the same subject: opulent Roman matrons displaying their ample breasts to hoary old beggars. He glimpsed the chandeliers on which the trickles of once

140

molten wax bore witness to recent electric failures; and showed him a huge four-poster bed.

Everything was decorated in dark red and brown, outlined in faded gold. A Regency chair showed entwined lovers in a heavy stitch. A glass case contained sleeping turtle doves, and, near the window, was an elephant in papier maché.

'Good evening, Babar! I bought him from a photographer in Arromanches. Before he left for the asylum. Not Babar, you understand, the photographer. He was a satyr! The photographer. Not Babar. All the little girls of the country-side around have sat their little buttocks on Babar. You'll see that I was beautiful when I was a little girl. As beautiful as my daughter.'

An amber light filtered out from the folds in the lamp-shades.

'I don't know what's the matter with me. I'm talking to you as though I've known you . . .'

'For a hundred years!'

'I'm telling you things that you can't understand, and I'm sure that you do understand.'

'I do. You've got a daughter. She's seven years old.'

'Seven and a half. You're talking too loud! Merthe and Barthe will hear you.'

She had a clear laugh which made her astonishingly young.

'You look like a cat who's just eaten a mouse,' he said.

'Well, you see, Merthe and Barthe are as deaf as posts. The deafest people in Normandy.'

'Why then are you making me talk to you as though you're going to be surprised by your husband?'

She reddened.

'It's so as not to spoil your fun. I'm sleepy, you ape.'

She put out the light. The lights from the dance illuminated the mad Gothic window. They were bathed in a milky light. Her hands went to the waistband of her skirt; the cloth fluttered down and she appeared to him naked.

'Go to sleep.'

'Is there any particular method for four posters?'
She disappeared. The sea was singing.
'Of course I've been married,' she said.

He was naked. Too much muscle, too hairy, too much belly and, shining on his massive chest, the thin golden medal which represented Mary. '*Mary, Mary, maman.*' *Marie. Married.* Bébé badly married. A tap groaned. Well, if the aunts didn't waken then! . . . over the noises of the water, her voice got louder:

'You're not saying anything. Oh, you know, it's the old, old story. We haven't been together for a long time.'

There was a swishing sound, a white flash and the living freshness of Bérangère beside him.

'Switch on. At your left. The pear.'

'What pear?'

'That pear.'

'A pear?'

'A switch at the end of a wire.'

He looked.

The object really had the form of a pear! At the bottom he found a button and pressed it. The lamp lighted, hidden by an orange skirt. He switched it off and on several times again.

'That must date from the time of Methusela,' he said.

There was a very long tranquil silence, in which one could pick out the blasts of the wind and the deafening noise of the breakers.

The enduring echoes of a pleasure as sharp as a pain did not cease beating within him.

He emerged from it slowly.

The bérangère is a witch's herb from the heavy orchards of Normandy, a summer colchicum which puts out its mauve eyes and, for those who eat too much of it, affects the vision and the ear, in a similar way to the effects which the Mexican peyotl brings on.

142

The cage of sleeping turtle doves, a monumental marble clock ornamented with beautiful Renaissance figures out of which flowed an interminable stream which symbolised time passing, the gilded pictures of the tender-hearted Roman ladies, Babar and the window open to the stars. Abel slipped and slipped and slipped towards sleep. He tried to take hold of himself, but the room moved always in the same direction; and the odd thing was that these objects and items of furniture never made a complete turn. They continued to turn in the one direction yet never returned to their starting point! He put his hand on his heart. Could this be death? It would be O.K. then. I should pass to the other side of the mirror. I should go into the reflection. I should walk for eternity into the world below. One slipped. One has gone. Hallo, Jacques. This must be it, Pascal's abysm of the left!

'Bébé, you're always happy.'
'Since the war. If you'd known what it was like here.'
'I was here.'
'No.'
'How not?'
'You were opposite. On one side or the other side. You understand?'
'No.'
'Have you ever seen a frightened mouse? His eyes go like pinheads, his muzzle trembles and his ears grow huge. That's how we were. On D-Day, I was in the Cathedral of St. Etienne. I was playing with some other kids between the pillars which were shaking and my mother gave me a clout. Then, afterwards, I was in a cellar.'
She shivered.
'You cold?'
'I always get cold when the sea comes up.'
'When the sea comes up, memories return.'

A light of admiration glinted in Bérangère's eyes.

He drew the sheet over his companion's pearly body. They were even more alone beneath the white covers.

'Tell me, tell me about it.'

'There's nothing to say. The bombardment went on. Everything became dark. My mother was no longer there. I heard my sister shout. And then, as in a tank of water, there was water. A cascade. I lived. I was not wounded, I was not ill, but the water threatened to drown us. I did not have a moment's fear. I called my sister. I called a hundred times. In the end, I called inside myself. I wanted to raise myself up, but I couldn't. When I awakened, it was the twelfth of June. Yes, the twelfth! Nothing was found of my sister, nor of the sixteen other people who were with us. Nothing was found, not even the road! The *rue de la Grange-aux-Herbes*. There must still be some old postmen who look for it from time to time.'

He lit the young woman's cigarette. An Old Gold.

'Gold! There was a landing beach called Gold.'

'You are my very lovely Bérangère. But you are wrong in thinking that the soldiers were on the other side. Anyway, why are we talking about that?'

'Because you were thinking. What do you do with your life, when you're not thinking?'

'I'm an announcer on Radio Quebec. I sell hot air. However I never talk. Never. There are some days when I'd like to talk about God, and the war and death. About the Gates of War. And of the Towers of Silence, as well. You know them? They're the transformers you see close to military camps. They are square, squat, infinitely sad. I've wanted to talk about forgiveness, little girl. About the Virgin. About Marx. About the Dionne quins. About everything. I've had fourteen years of silence on my chest, broken down by the fourteen years of stupidities which I've spoken into the mike.'

She played with the hair on his chest.

'That's nice.'

She brought the red tip of the cigarette nearer. The hairs sizzled.

'That smells like the war. Fourteen years, you say. I was fourteen in 1944. That makes me thirty, near enough. My mother died here under the town of Verville. There is a town under the town. A town of the dead. You wall up the corridors and the cellars and the wells so that they can't get out. You never dig here. You build on top. We've built a living town on top of a dead one. My mother is underneath.'

'They've been rebuilt with the war damage money?'

'Oh! Bravo, bravo, Canada! You very clever, Canada! You're more intelligent than the others.'

This time it was she who had said two words too many. Very quickly, she added:

'If you want to understand Normandy, Abel, don't forget that, under each town, under each village, there is a town and village buried, with its dogs crying at the moon, its cats stealing chicken bones, its children who wished to see and its blind grandmothers. Underneath Caen, there's another Caen, with its Vaugueux, its streets of girls, and prisoners on the run . . .'

'I'd like to see Caen again, Bébé, with you.'

'Yes, Abel; but you'll never see Caen again. I tell you, what you see is where it *was*. You see?'

'I see.'

'No. These are only words. There was a little girl. "Bérangère . . . Bérangère . . . Where are you? Malvina, have you seen Bérangère?" She must still be dragging behind. She's got a fire inside her, has your Bérangère. Yes, indeed, I'm going to cool her down. Bérangère, where have you been? From the Abbaye aux Hommes, maman.' That's the story of Bérangère. There was a little girl, there was her mother, Laurence, who wore out her eyes. Home dressmaker. To send Bérangère to school. So that she could get her *brevet supérieur*. Like the tarts.'

'Why?'

'The tarts are all officers' daughters and they all have their *brevet supérieur*. Didn't you know that, Canada?'

'No.'

'Poor Canada. With your ninety kilos . . .'

'Ninety two.'

'You, with your chest like the top of a sea-chest, and your belief that once you were an ingenuous kind of assassin, you'll never be more than a kid. We, Abel, are a hundred thousand years old. Our land is full of dead towns. We talk and dance and work and make love on them. That's why we're not so hygienic. Nothing is covered with cellophane! As for me, now you know why I'm a sewn-up doll who says "Mama" when you lay her down. You know Brassens?'

He shook her, trembling from this half-uttered complaint which she whispered between waking and sleeping, in the twisted apple orchard of her upbringing. Tenderness flowed out of Abel's fingers, from his body, from his eyes, from his polished skull which shone beneath the lamp. His hand ran slowly along the scar, along the planes, along the slopes, along the hills of her back. A bell rang spasmodically with a cracked sound, a little bell which no hand moved. Underneath was this mixture of cellars, of wells, of half-buried corridors, of cracked houses; the town of the liberated dead.

CHAPTER VI

HE OPENED the window on to the swan's-neck balcony. The tide was out. An elderly woman was feeding the chickens. One of the aunts, no doubt. There was not a cloud and the young day gave up an innocent freshness.

'You're freezing me!'

'It'll wake you up.'

'Wretch! Beast! Gorilla! Canadian!'

He consulted the clock which had intrigued him the day before with its false stream of water. But no! Not the day before! The day before that! Yesterday, they had only gone out to bathe. One whole day, idle, replete. Among the rocks, they had celebrated the anniversary of their first twenty-four hours, consuming a picnic of bread and pâté, tomatoes and a soft golden camembert washed down with a rosé *Cuisse de Bergère*. Time, time! In the clear morning, it was only a bourgeois clock on which two nymphs were leaning on columns and holding up the triangular front of the temple. At the top, the old bearded man stretched himself out. He had put down his scythe. Below, in a rocky fountain, a glass tube simulated a stream of water in which bubbles followed one another without ceasing, giving the illusion of flowing water. The turtle-doves shimmered gently.

Abel jumped on to the bed which nearly collapsed under

147

him. The hangings, of green and red palm leaves, shook with the movements. The canopy leaned down. She noticed something on Abel's neck which had been dancing on his chest. This was the moment of full richness for the lovers, when each of them possessed untold wealth in unknown banks.

'So, then, we were in Caen together.'

'Yes.'

'In August?'

'Yes.'

'How old were you?'

'Nineteen.'

'We could have made love.'

'Was that when you got your scar?'

'No.'

She laughed.

'Ah, I've had some misfortunes. That's why I'm so gay.'

He pressed her to his chest and his powerful thighs entrapped her legs. He murmured: *'Tu es mon petit bonheur.'* He loved the song by Felix Leclerc (Another of the tribe!) She did not answer.

'You're my glass of Scotch, my pipe, my sleek little cat! You're my princess from the sea, my little wound. You're my everything. You're . . . you're . . .'

She purred. He smacked her bottom. She said: 'Do it again.'

'How did you get your scar?'

'Thoracoplasty. Eighteen months in a special sanatorium in Ain. Tuberculosis! Moth-eaten lungs! Everyone had moth-eaten lungs there, the dustmen, the doctors and the pimps.'

There was defiance in her answer. She went on:

'Fortunately, you brought me streptomycin. All I've got now is the scar as a souvenir. A real artist, my surgeon!'

She watched him with a residual fear. The Canadian was so very hygienic!

'What are you doing? Oh, Abel . . .'

148

Abel jumped naked out on to the floor, and went quickly to the window, closed it; then passing before the clock with the bubbling time, he caressed Babar's trunk and tenderly drew the covers over Bérangère.

'I didn't know. I should have paid attention . . .'

'To what?'

'To stopping you from catching cold.'

Behind the windows the angry seagulls screeched.

'What's the time?'

'Nine, according to the fountain.'

She yawned. Even in everyday movements she was lovely.

'Want to come with me? On an outing? Well, an outing for you. There's a school in Graye. My girl's there. My little darling gets unhappy if I don't go to see her. She's called Christine and she's nearly eight.'

Eight! Born in 1952. Her mother must have known her father at the latest in 1951. Then she was twenty-one. In '51? Before the sanatorium.

'You're counting!'

'Yes.'

'That's mad. You'll do yourself an injury.'

'Yes.'

'Yes?'

'Yes.'

'Well, that's fine, then.'

'Certainly. I'm going with you. But the father . . . ?'

'Oh, her father.'

He began to walk about, still naked. She followed this stupendous animal with her eyes, lying on her front on the bed, completely covered up, with her nose in the bolster, the sheet moulding itself to her curving body.

'Bébé? Have you got a job?

She trailed the sheet round her like a peplum, a pantomime Tanagra, and went to the toilet. The pinch returned to his heart. But she did not go into the toilet. Instead she pretended she was a ghost, beating about with her arms. In this movement of wings her slender rounded body, so enchanting in its golden pallor, appeared and vanished. He desired her savagely; in front of the door she stopped and said gravely:

'I am a teacher.'

She covered herself up quickly.

At once he put on his trunks! Bébé a teacher! He went up to the door and from within came furious sounds from the plumbing.

'Bébé?'

'What d'you want?'

'You really said "teacher"?'

'Yes, at Bondeville, near Caen. I'm on sick leave and a temporary is taking my place. She's stupid!'

A teacher! . . . like Valerie! Well, nearly. She turned off the taps and listened to him humming:

> Ah, l'homme engagé
> Connaissait bien l' bobo d' la fille . . .

She smiled a mocking smile into the faded glass which powdered the face with a fine golden mist.

The bus was full when Bérangère signalled to the driver. He stopped, nevertheless, in spite of protests from the passengers.

'Shove up!' he said. 'There's room at the back,' said the white-shirted driver. 'Going to Graye, Bébé?'

'Yes, Etienne. How're things with you?'

Etienne was a fat little man who laughed beneath a moustache streaked with copper.

'Have you seen what they found at Jaouen's place?'

'That pig? What's happened?'

'Didn't happen to him,' said Etienne. 'But what do you think? They found a stiff in the oyster beds!'

Etienne let in the clutch, jolting his mixed cargo. Some kids were going swimming, farmworkers were going to

150

market. There were fishermen the colour of brick, with huge scarred hands, some white-collar workers and a few tourists. At the Verville lock, Etienne slowed down before crossing the wooden bridge.

'Jaouen,' she said, 'was one of the old men who were in the party at the Père Magloire. You saw him the other night. They call him "King" Jaouen. He's a lousy specimen.'

After the bridge, the bus passed by the oyster beds. Sixty curious eyes stared at two workmen dressed in musketeers' boots of yellow rubber, stirring up the mud. Etienne, his cap on the back of his head, stood up in his place and, still holding the wheel, drove slowly on. The passengers leaned over to the right. The waitress from the bistro made a sign with her hand, shaking her fingers vigorously, as though she was trying to shake them dry.

'Lucie saw him first,' Etienne explained. 'Well, it's not so good. The crabs had already started to get at him.'

'He had his mouth in the mud,' said one of the cloth-capped farmworkers, 'his mouth in the mud and his arse in the air.'

The gendarmes with two men in raincoats were talking to a weeping woman.

Jaouen! Yes, Jaouen was indeed with them at the Père Magloire. Abel recalled him now. There you are one night in the café, drinking with your friends, talking, dropping the odd profundity about liberty, government, or war and then, a couple of days later, you find a corpse on your property, 'with his mouth in the mud.'

'Jaouen,' said Abel, 'Wasn't he the white-haired man with a velvet jacket? Is he a communist?'

'What?' said Bérangère, amazed.

'Well, isn't he? He doesn't like the English. He doesn't like the Americans. He doesn't like General de Gaulle. Isn't he a communist?'

'Like hell he is. He's a Breton. A separationist. He used to live at Cancale. He came to Normandy in 1935. He demonstrated against La Roque. Doesn't that tell you anything? Then he was a *Pétainiste*. You know what that meant. At the Liberation he was chucked into prison at Caen for a month until an English major came to get him out, breathing fire and brimstone at a time when even the most generous were talking about twenty years inside for him! It then appeared that King Jaouen had been getting intelligence to the British and.that he had been amusing himself by stuffing sugar into the concrete for the Atlantic Wall.'

'Sugar in the concrete?'

'That's war! Everyone knows that a handful of sugar in the cement mixer is enough to prevent it setting. Didn't you know? Well, someone told me.'

She caressed his hair from behind, gently stroking his head; and the tenderness of her gestures conflicted with the harsh realism of her statement.

At Ver-sur-Mer, the market was bursting with fish, shell-fish, meat, fruit and multi-coloured fabrics. The butcher sounded his car horn until Bébé paid attention to him. He was smiling broadly.

'They think a lot of you round here,' said Abel.

This familiarity of Bérangère with the people of the locality rather irked him.

'Can't help it,' she said. 'It's belonging to the teaching profession.'

'This is your stop, Bébé,' shouted Etienne, a few kilometres further on.

'So long, Etienne, I'll give you a kiss next time.'

Etienne gave the young woman a gleaming smile, ignoring her companion, and the bus went off in a cloud of dust.

You could sense that the sea was on the other side of the row of dunes. On slightly rising ground, pinned to the ground by its belltower, Graye was outlined. On the left, a château-farmhouse stood up, linked to the shore by an earth road. On

152

top of the dune, children were running against the backdrop of an anemone-coloured sky.

'These are the boys. The girls go to the beach later. Forgive me, but I can't show you my little girl.'

'While you're with her, I'm going to have a swim. But I'll go along with you now, though.'

Birds sang in the brambles where the blackberries were ripening. The sun was now shining more strongly. Yet Abel's entire private country was once again mobilised, with its posts, its guards, its watchmen, its radar sets. It was not only the death of an unknown man, however frightful, nor the smiling friendliness of Bérangère which were the cause of it. Quite another thing was stirring. *State of alert. The most rigorous watch is ordered.* He had to pay attention to the blackberries, particularly to the blackberries. To the apples. And to the birds. This anxiety had begun among the curious sightseers by the edge of the oyster bed, became worse in the crowded bus and was now apparent as soon as he set foot on the ground again.

Behind the white barriers, the friendly meadows stretched out. The apples were still small, and of a crude green. They came to the side of a peaceful stream, dark brown in colour, covered with spots and humming with insects. Then, at another angle the mossy walls of a windbreak roof appeared, repaired in a vermilion which stained the greenery with the red of fresh blood.

Abel stopped, struck in the pit of the stomach.

'Bébé! Bébé, it's here!'

He was pale.

'I swear. It's here!'

He looked around him as if he was waking up. Near the rusty grill, a gate of overgrown masonry opened a way. They went in by the rear of the house, passed in front of a round dovecote loud with wings, and came out in front of the old summer house, with its barred windows and thick creepers. One unaccountable detail was that between the two sides of

153

the house there lay a bridge over which had been built a stage and a granary out of which a pulley-hoist extended. Abel changed from dead white to a vivid red. The blood returned to his face in great joyful waves.

'Oh, Bébé, you're really my little good luck charm. Bébé, without you, I'd never have come here. I'd have gone around until the end of the world. I have been looking for this for days. You can't understand. This is the place I scrambled down on the night of the sixth of June 1944! This time, it's really right. I've looked for such a time! I finished up by wondering if this was indeed the same planet! Ah, now this is fine! Everything's turning out right, Bébé, everything. Will you stay long with your girl?'

'An hour. An hour and a quarter.'

'Good. You'll find me on the beach.'

She felt deeply touched by the bursting joy of the man.

'On the beach,' he said, 'in front of the holiday home where we saw the boys playing, there's a jetty which sticks out into the sea. Two or three hundred yards to the right.'

He closed his eyes.

'To the left, still coming from here, you find some sort of building, a bunker, or some ruins. Isn't that so?'

'It is.'

'You say "Yes"?'

'Yes. Yes.'

'A big building?'

'Yes.'

'Bébé, Bébé, my dove, my good luck charm.'

He went away, drunken, mad, mad with relief, running in long strides like an athlete who was doing his training, then, with lowered head, boxing against his shadow, turning round, laughing and setting off again. She quietly blew a kiss to him but he did not see it.

On the highway, cars went by like the wind. Abel found

again the place where the driver had put them down, crossed the road and went on to the dunes, intoxicated by the wind and the past. The vegetation was sparse, blue thistles, lichens and sea pinks. The shouts of the children got louder. He sat on the ground, took off his shoes, knotted the laces and smiled sadly at the memory of Jacques which this gesture re-awakened. He rolled up his jeans and set off again. The wind blew more strongly. The tide was half way in.

The countryside was divided into horizontal bands: the sea, with its changing blue, outlined by the white border of the distant waves; then the white and green band of the beach stretching away to the horizon; and, finally, above him, the band of the pale sky. On the left, the famous jetty stretched out into the sea, the colour of tar and caramel, covered with chalky accretions and the shells of molluscs. In the midst of the broom, he saw the bunker. He stopped. This was his bunker. This was the bunker of the flame-thrower, of the insensible Germans, and the young dead unfulfilled man. His lips trembled. But he was not thinking of the dead. He was comforted. He was twelve years old. He bent down on his hands, stood up balancing on his hands, curving from the hips, his legs bent before him and he walked. He was just forming the notion that, after all, he was not so rusty, when he overbalanced, fell and found himself again on his back with four or five kids around him. He rubbed his nose. And the kids laughed! He rubbed his backside again. And the kids laughed more loudly. Then, he started to spin around, using his right arm as a pivot, raising the left with each passage. Then he missed on purpose, made a grimace and stopped dead, groaning as though crippled with rheumatism; and he ended up by sitting cross-legged, scratching his bald head and going cross-eyed. The children were beside themselves! The smallest was clapping his hands. A severe-looking woman called to them. They scampered off regretfully, all identical in swimming trunks of the same sea blue.

Abel had arrived. He was truly at his destination. The past

155

was finally taking on a few recognisable features: the only difference was that, in his memory, everything was flatter, more stretched out, under a vaster sky.

A cart carrying seaweed rolled along the damp sand, drawn by a dirty white horse. A few women gathering cockles, reflected in the puddles, retreated step by step, pushed up the beach by the rising tide.

Abel took off his jeans. He went down to the water when a dozen young girls appeared, also in blue. Bébé was holding by the hand one slim youngster with her hair in plaits. The girls undressed in the shelter, then came bubbling out like corks from cider-bottles. Bébé gave Abel a friendly sign. The little girl came up to the man, in the belief that she already knew him, for she called out: 'Simon! Uncle Simon!' She stopped dead a few paces from Abel and put her finger in her mouth. In her swimsuit with its little skirt bordered in white, with a scarcely functional brassière, she resembled her mother. Abel smiled to her. She did not budge. She looked behind her, but Bérangère was chatting with a dark young woman, no doubt the supervisor. The boys yelled out: 'The girls! The girls!' Abel, still sitting cross-legged, called to Christine, banged his thighs with his hands, then crossed his arms, pinching his nose with his right hand and his ear with his left; then, reversing the movement, did it again, getting faster and faster. Christine had the same clear laugh as her mother and the same impudent expression. Freckles spotted her nose and her cheeks, contrasting with the strong blue of her eyes.

'Come and say "hallo" to me, Christine.'

She seemed surprised that the man knew her name, advanced a few steps and stopped.

'Have you been staring at the sun through a net?' he asked.

She pursed up her lips.

'It looks very pretty.'

She bent her head, coyly. He stretched out to search through his pockets. He only had chewing-gum. He held it

156

out to her. She put out her hand and made a curtsy. Her eyes were really very big, wider than Bébé's, almost violet, eyes which recalled Jacques's. Salt-cellars were scooped out of her neck; and the thinness of this little girl who had grown too quickly inspired anxiety; but the pink which tinted her cheeks was real enough and a gentle roundness softened her shoulders, her arms and her thighs.

'What a fine bra you've got!'

She shrugged her shoulder, very womanly.

'Don't be afraid. My name's . . .'

He hesitated.

'My name's "Uncle Abel".'

Bérangère came up.

The little girl lowered her head, pretending to be over-whelmed, and said:

'I'm going to play with Monette.'

'So you know this gentleman already, Christine.'

Christine assented with a vigorous movement of her head.

'I told her I'm called "Uncle Abel".'

A shadow passed over Bébé's face.

'Can I, maman?'

'Of course, go to Monette.'

The little girl went dancing off, counting her steps. What sort of uncle could the father have been?

'You came to have a swim, Uncle Abel,' said Bérangère.

He was full of admiration for the brave face she put on her past.

'Christine is as untamed as a seagull. You've won her over. You're a magician, you know.'

In the crystalline clarity of the young summer's day, he saw her more surely than when she was naked, in the bed-room with the complaisant Roman ladies. He understood her better than when he was making love to her. She was small, but not too small. Five foot two or three. She did not seem small to him because he himself was so big. There was no over-abundance in her figure, nothing Rubensesque about her, not even the usual Norman generosity of figure. But the slenderness of her body proclaimed a provoking femininity, especially in the curve of her hips. Well aware of the effect she was producing, she played ball with Christine and the supervisor. Of course, like all women, Bébé had suntanned. But the year before she must have worn a one-piece swimsuit, while now she had on a bikini. Her skin was of two tones, white as a dove under her breasts, tanned on her shoulders, in the small of her back and golden everywhere else. Across her back, the trace of the scar could be seen, sometimes pink, sometimes white. He retraced with the tip of his finger the slightly coarsened skin of the wound, which had not exactly rejoined, lip to lip. The scar showed the history of Bébé. At first the cutting of her body in two, then the fight to regain her fitness and strength, over a number of years. When her body was cured, and the right to sea and sun had been restored to the young woman, she had not ventured beyond a one-piece suit, of the same style which Valerie preferred. Bébé had not chosen this style out of shame of her body but through shame of her wound. At last, this very year, the desire to regain her complete freedom had overtaken her. She had dominated the last obstacle: shame. Without doubt, she was relying on a tan to remove the last traces. You're a fighter, little one! One can learn a lesson from you, Bérangère!

Then an extraordinary idea came to the Canadian! The aerium was equivalent to the field of battle. The chattering children were the offspring of the dead town. Abel was present at a huge thoracoplasty of the earth in which Bébé was an airy spirit, a Tanagra broken in two and then joined together again. This was the true Normandy, lush, fertile, obstinate, natural, the Normandy of the odoriferous decay of the cider press. Bérangère was the most desirable fruit of this land, by virtue of her very wounds.

I've fallen in love with your whole country, Bérangère.

Christine, Bérangère and the children went off in the direction of the aerium. Bébé had to see a doctor. Abel dozed. The tide was coming in again. With the passage of a shadow, he felt the presence of someone near him. He raised himself on to one elbow, and saw a fisherman, in canvas shoes, trousers of washed-out blue, patched in contrasting colours, and a faded shirt. He had a strong jaw and little eyes, a forehead which sloped away from above thick eyebrows. The man displayed yellow teeth when he spoke:

'Seems you're a Canadian.'

Unsmiling and fixed of purpose, he carried a cane basket crammed with shrimps. Some violet seaweed glistened under the handle. He put down his awkward semi-circular net, a net into which he could have put his whole body.

'Just come to pass the time of day,' he said. 'These kids have told me that you're a Canadian. Is that so, do you come from Canada?'

He moved his weight from foot to foot. He was thinking deeply, and it was an effort.

'There're lots of shrimps but hardly any prawns.'

He made a vague gesture towards the sea. Then he picked up a handful of grey shrimps.

'In '44 there was a lot of 'em, a lot of shrimps.'

The fishermen of Tiberias must have resembled him. Wolfish of expression, wrinkled, with wild hair. Thought moved with difficulty beneath a bony forehead.

'Ah, shrimps! There were some shrimps, then! Well, they had so much to stuff themselves with. All that flesh: American, English, Canadian, French, Polish. Something for every taste, for the shrimps, eh?'

'Hitler's shrimps! Nazi shrimps!'

Horror invaded Abel, since the man had just put into halting words what he himself had had in mind. His adolescent fear of being eaten up next day. But this was what had struck him so deeply and darkly in the story of the corpse in Jaouen's oyster beds. Consumed by the beasts of the sea!

159

Knowing, in short, in advance, the promised fate of Rifleman Leclerc.

The fisherman pressed relentlessly on, digging into the murkiness with his muddy thoughts:

'The grey ones were swarming and the pink ones, the prawns, they were as big as crayfish! They were crammed full. But you couldn't collect them because of the mines. Anyhow, I couldn't have eaten them. But I could have sold them.'

He wiped his mouth.

'I really needed my son who was a prisoner far away in Prussia. Ah, well, that's over, that's past.'

He took out of his pocket a piece of strong paper, fell on his knees, facing the sea and put the paper down in front of him. He spread it out with the flat of his hand, placed in it a layer of seaweed, laid out on it the largest shrimps, carefully, one by one, while Abel's eyes opened wide in an effort to understand. Then, the man from Tiberias covered the shrimps with more seaweed, twisted the paper adroitly and held it out to Abel. He insisted, put it forcibly into his hands saying: 'Ah, well, there you are. There you are. There.'

He put his net back on his shoulder and his basket on his arm; then went off at a regular pace towards the dunes, without turning back.

CHAPTER VII

BERANGERE WAS wearing black slacks, fitting close to her body, and a brilliant red and black blouse. She had taken up her hair in a chignon and the boyish style gave her an equivocal charm. He picked up the paper and read aloud from it, as though into a mike: 'Wearing trousers alters the psychology of woman and tends to modify the relations between man and woman.'

'What imbecile said that?'

'The Bishop of Gênes.'

'Oh pardon, monseigneur. Anyhow, do you know who has been killed in Jaouen's oyster beds? No? La Luzerne! Ratier! The man who used to swear so elaborately. Poor fellow.'

Abel saw La Luzerne again and his somewhat scornful manner of imitating the locals. La Luzerne always played the country bumpkin. But his death was present in the room with the wedding party and his fate awaited for him, like a rose in the mud.

Coming out of a little alley which gave on to the *rue du Soleil-Levant*, was a tall distinguished-looking man, with a golden tan and whitening temples.

'Have a drink with us, Monsieur le Maire.'

'How could I refuse, my dear? You look like a page. What a business! Really, what business! A half of Muscadet, Annette!'

161

All the men knew Bébé, all spoke familiarly to her. However, none of them seemed to lack respect for her.

'Do they know anything about Ratier?' she asked.

Someone had seen a light, at about two in the morning, in Jaouen's house. Jaouen heard nothing. His wife had a raging fever, and was in bed.'

'La Luzerne was full of fun.'

'He was lucky 'cause his relatives had money,' said another citizen of Verville as he sat down. He was a big bony man, with a creased face.

'Hallo, le Dernier,' said the jovial mayor.

'My name's Vauthier,' the newcomer explained pacifically when he had finished sorting out his limbs. 'However, they all call me "le Dernier". "The last what?" you ask. Well, the last member of the Resistance. That's just to put you straight.'

Vauthier's right hand was like a lobster's claw. The three middle fingers were missing.

'You've been here for some time,' said Vauthier. 'I've seen you about with Bérangère. Our little Normandy is hard to understand. Listen, I'll explain to you . . . Do you mind, monsieur le Maire?'

'It's a free country.'

'Verville is half farming and half fishing. Conservative and catholic. Peasants and fishermen make up eighty per cent of Cul-béni. As for the rest, well, there are a few *rentiers* who are succeeding in dying of hunger, a few retired men like the naval captain who writes articles about the newest new-found lands and the businessmen. And they are all Poujadists.'

'Like Blondel,' said Leroy.

'Blondel! It's not because he's a businessman that he's a Poujadist, but because he's a cuckold. Add in a few civil servants. Good. Now everything that all these people own wouldn't make up more than a couple of fortunes. One is Jaouen's. Grandfather Jaouen sold papers in St. Malo at the age of twelve. The son and the grandsons set themselves up with the oysters and the war. Oysters are not much now.

162

Finished. At least round here. But there you are, Jaouen had some pretty modern installations. Destroyed in 1944, it left him with a marvellous pile of war damage. He bought everything up as fast as he could, in '46. Then, no one had any faith in it. And yet see where we are! Jaouen's fortune is a new one. Now, the second one belongs to the lady of the château. She's a widow. Perhaps that tempts you! But, be careful, she's already eaten up three husbands! Her wealth goes back to the shipbuilders of the time when your ancestors went to pray to Notre-Dame-de-Grâce at Honfleur before going off to the New World. It's been constantly nibbled away, but it's still in existence. In land, mostly. Half the village is hers. You must have seen her, a fat woman in white, heavily made up with a big mug. The sixth of June was her very own Liberation! And that's Verville-sur-Mer.'

A little car drew up in front of a 'No Parking' sign. In a highly coloured transatlantic dress. Valerie appeared, carelessly displaying her fine legs. Arnaud, the *patron,* whistled through his teeth. Bébé got up as Valerie took off her sun glasses, but Abel signed her to stay. The Canadian girl half closed her eyes, examining Bérangère, as if she wanted to paint a picture of her. Loudly, she ordered a glass of milk and pulled a face when the *patron's* son brought the glass.

'What's this in the milk?' she asked.

'In the milk? What, in the milk?'

'That!'

'Oh, that's the skin.'

'Skin?'

'The skin of the milk.'

'At home, we don't have skin on the milk.'

Then Arnaud's son went over to the Florida pintable, with its pin-ups and its numbers in the tens of thousands. Women and money! Well, that's what America is! One by one, the little balls knocked against the clicking studs. Following the steel balls with the eyes in this abstract game of fortune and girls was Lucien's principal occupation.

No one at Abel's table spoke any longer. The Canadian girl had frozen them all. She removed the offending skin with a spoon. Her eyes never left Bérangère. She even held a piece of croissant stationary at the level of her breast, frozen by her own frigidity. Bérangère smiled, and turned to Abel:

'She's ever so nice, you know.'

It was impossible to know if she was joking.

Leaving Florida with a yawn, Lucien went over to the juke-box. *Mustapha! La salsa del pommodore.* Tomato sauce! And we're off!

'Hello, boy!'

A lively fellow, with a naked torso running waistless into legs which were too short, stopped on the spur of the moment in front of the terrace.

'The fun of it!' yelled Ray, jubilant.

The hilarious G.I. whom he had met at the Gates of War, was dragging behind him the girl who had been with him at Arromanches. Without excusing himself, he sat down between Abel and Valerie, leaving his girl to find herself a seat. He ordered a calvados in a beer glass and began to give shattering details of Charlotte's way of making love, while Charlotte, who knew no English, was repairing her make-up with automatic lip movements.

'Almost as good as Mamie!' said Ray, openly winking to Abel. 'And, with her, you don't have to rush it!'

'Mamie!' the word burst like a grenade. So this G.I. had known Mamie! In a moment the flower-bedecked terrace of the Père Magloire was far away, with Bébé and Valerie, M. le Maire with the silvered temples, and all those people in their Sunday best who were taking the air! Mamie, Mamie!

Valerie pricked up her ears. Abel asked her:

'Do you understand Ray?'

'He's not a well-brought up fellow.'

'However, pay attention to what this badly-brought up fellow is saying. It's interesting, this about Mamie and her fun and games.'

164

Abel turned to Ray, who, with eyes glinting, swallowed his calvados, then he called for another 'on the rocks, this time'. And he urged him on with a smack on the shoulder:

'Go on, man, go on.'

Caen in 1944 was a fantastic city. Sodom and Gomorrah after the fires of God. But God's fire had been partly ineffective because it was precisely through prostitution that life returned. Soon, the overburdened authorities abandoned the idea of repression and were simply satisfied to park the women, insolent under the open protection of the Allies. Their pimps appeared in spite of the risks, driven on by the desire not to let their meal-tickets go gratis to the victors. It's so easy to be patriotic when you're a tart. At night, the worms slid between the gaps in the walls, avoiding the patrols. Sometimes, there was a groaning and wailing behind the walls. There were streets where one walked on the heaps of glinting debris which reflected the moon's blue light, a vast gem of misery. The bridges of the Orne were destroyed, the quays broken down, the water poisoned with the pollution of diesel oil. On the walls, the German posters still ordered evacuation and cursed the Jews. Everywhere, worms crept out of the shade. And amongst them was Mamie, the incomparable Mamie, the stupendous American slattern, Venus among the ruins.

As soon as he had discovered this unbelievable fact, Jacques had wishes to show it to Abel. Abel had gone there through curiosity, for fear of the sarcasm of Simeon, through the desire that his mates would give him a bit of peace, through the difficulty of expressing disapproval, of being contrary, or merely different, by the childish fear of being cut off from the group, from the band, from the tribe, from the Chauds.

The spectacle of Mamie in her shop was unforgettable. Certainly, if the chaste Valerie could understand that from Ray's picaresques pronouncements, she would at last come near to the real Jacques. For a few seconds, Abel nearly

165

grasped a brilliant image: Valerie and himself were in a trap. Their quest was in vain. There was no longer any Jacques, even if there had ever been one. Valerie had her own Jacques and Abel had one too. Everyone who knew Jacques had his own version. But there probably never had been a *real* Jacques. Jacques was dead at twenty. At twenty, one is only the sum of a number of facets.

A long time after his demobilisation, in Quebec, while reading Bradford Huie's book, *The Revolt of Mamie Stover*, Abel had learned the the Mamie of Caen was no exception! Even for the name! So there had been another Mamie. You might think that wherever there were marines, Rangers, paratroops, gunners, or footsloggers, there would proliferate these enormous milch cows! In 1939, Mamie Stover was twenty-three, a big girl, a peroxide blonde. She had been disfigured by a scar which came from settling a few accounts, and could no longer stay in Hollywood. She took refuge in Honolulu. At this time, prostitutes were gathered together in a reserved quarter, had no right to mix in good society, nor even to acquire anything. They were whores unto death! Mamie wanted to make a few bucks. Since she had one talent, she used it. Now Pearl Harbour suddenly gave Stover her chance! With the war, the marines came in. Watched over by those white gentlemen, the Sea Police and their batons, these professional thugs swarmed out of the liberty boats and slid straight to the bars of their dreams, the Manhattan, the Los Angeles, the Soleil, the Hacienda. In the face of this irrepressible force, the administration appealed to Mamie and her companions and put aside the law on the public administration of prostitution. Supply and demand, the only rule which brooks no exception, came into play. Mamie went under contract as a singer. According to her biographer, she stayed there from December 1941 to July 1945. Mamie of Honolulu finished the war as a landowner, pensioned off as an officer's widow and decorated for services to the U.S. Fleet.

166

Valerie considered with distaste these males who drank like old sweats and insolently recounted their unhygienic stories! She had not heard the last of them.

Mamie's whorehouse stood high up in the town. Near the château. In what remained of Vaugueux, were Rangers and negroes who had gathered together, with haversacks on their backs. There were prostitutes with knife scars, escaped prisoners standing like bulls behind the counter. Naturally, the men fought amongst themselves to assert their superiority: fliers against Rangers, marines against the infantry. The Canadians used to pile indiscriminately into the fray.

'From time to time, a house would come tumbling down on someone who might be lying in his skin in a flea-ridden bed, while the tart was washing herself. Once, a patrol of the Sea Police, to protect their marines, was beaten up well and truly by a patrol of Military Police! You know how they went to work!'

'No,' said Valerie, her mouth dry, fascinated.

Abel broke in, puffed out his chest, lifted up his arm as though he was carrying in his fist a heavy police truncheon and beat it down methodically. He mimed the bludgeoned soldier, collapsed like a cork-screw.

'Exactly,' Ray agreed. 'I have some pals at Cherbourg and it was worse there. The police gave up running things. There was one district where they ended by shutting it off with barbed wire! Only, like it's always done Stateside, as soon as there was a scandal, an administration officer would listen to the complaints and pull out his cheque book. The others would glare at it, and they'd have a tear in their eyes. The officer named a sum. The others would bristle up in indignation. "Is that all? For an uncle we loved? It puts us in an impossible situation for disposing of the estate and then there's all the bottles your drunken layabouts have consumed! Your men are real stinking pigs, if that doesn't flatter you." The inspecting officer would push up the ante. "Good. But you

167

can't pay for a life with money! And the anguish of the orphan, eh?" The officer would make an exact estimate of the anguish of an orphan. "My dear sir! We've forgotten Aunt Sidonie. How she loved her Arnest!" Then the officer began to lose interest. "Take it or leave it. Otherwise, you'd better go to law. After the war."—"Oh, but one minute, one minute, let's speak. This is very hard. America is a great country. A very great country. Bigger than ever. And generous. Generous America. She wouldn't do that to us! Stars and stripes for ever! Fine. We must bow to you. And the formalities? Ah, good, we sign on the counterfoil. That's all? They'll win the war. Ah, it's written in French, too. Give me my glasses, Françoise . . . *I renounce all future claims* . . . And you're hard. O yes, you'll win the war. We can cash it at the bank? Just with our identity cards? Whenever we like? And who's paying for the funeral? The Army . . . Perfect, perfect. So long . . ." Isn't it funny?'

It was Caen, still the lunar city. Abel and Jacques went drinking in some dive where you slid in under a couple of curtains which stank of cat's pee. Abel, Jacques and Siméon —whom they called Sim in a bad humour—swallowed a few calvas. Abel's mouth felt rotten. But he felt the biting scorn of that swine Siméon who had infatuated Jacques. They left after listening to a few swing records by Django Reinhardt. *Georgia . . . Georgia . . .* Abel never forgot the overpowering beat of the guitar. *Georgia, Georgia . . .* From time to time, he bumped against a wall and swore. This was the first time he had been drunk. 'Well, you're stinking drunk, my lad.' *Georgia . . . Georgia . . .* They came out on to a sloping street, between the castle and St Pierre and came upon a couple of soldiers. These fellows were rasping out a guttural English. A civilian was arguing. A plump little Frenchwoman was saying, indignantly: 'Swine who don't want to pay . . . They both had their go at me and then they tried to skip out after-

168

wards . . . Well, but, look, what shall I do, then?' The civilian argued, gesturing. The girl yelled more loudly. One of the soldiers beat her round the face with his hand. She toppled over. Her legs beat the air. The civilian was still arguing. The taller of the soldiers dropped his fist on the head of the civilian who fell slowly. This was too much. The crusading Canadians put themselves up against the unidentifiable ally, who found himself looking at Abel, a man as big as he himself. The civilian groaned as though at his last gasp. The woman wept. Sim went down on all fours behind the toughie whose nationality was unknown and a straight right from Abel sent the attacker rolling over his back. The sound of whistles cut the air. The Chauds skipped off to the alleys. Abel staggered. The last image he had as he turned round, was of the electric torches of the MP.s fiercely pulling away the woman who was stretching her arms to Heaven, in front of the unconscious civilian, motionless beneath the moon.

Mamie Boyer was a young American living in France. She had been married in '39 at the age of twenty to a French flier who was shot down over Dunkirk. His photo never left her. She wept for him for a year. And then, without a transition, this still young and available Franco-American lady turned into the perfect prostitute, sleeping more and more often with more and more men, raising a scandal in Mantes, Mantes-la-Jolie, Mantes, with its factories. She specialised in giving her services to the occupying troops. With the landings, Mamie understood that she was running some risks. So she took up with the Yanks. That is how, at the end of July, the gang saw this five foot six blonde arrive on bicycle, superb in her summer get-up, her short skirt displaying statuesque thighs, freewheeling into the centre of the town to the cheers of the G.I.'s. A week later, Mamie's Place was in operation!

Of course, Ray had slept with Mamie. And Jacques, and

Abel; but Abel recalled above all the stunning, star-studded patterns of love. The details had vanished. Except Mamie herself. But her, he could have drawn, big-hipped, with a triumphant bosom! He made love to a tornado, a tornado called Mamie! Mamie had a square face, a coarse chin, large pale blue open eyes, a cow's eyes, shadowed with false black eyelashes, a square mouth outlined with lips which were too thick. Her neck was like a column. Her heavy deep chestnut hair fell to the small of her back. This magnificent animal smiled at Abel. He had mumbled: *'Bonjour, Madame!'* She had laughed, a throaty laugh, cooing in a low register. Mamie opened her peignoir with a flashing sweep of living pearl. Her breasts maintained the laws of American eroticism; beneath shoulders which were too wide, they hung high, pointed, firm, a huge soft barrier. They sagged only very little, firm in their swelling roundness. One might wonder that such a mass could still be kept in such condition after so much wear and tear. Unlike most adolescents, Abel did not have an obsession with breasts. Until now, they had repelled him. These, however, huge, crowned with delectable tips of warm amber, dried his mouth!

'Pretty boy! Gorgeous! Come along, now.'

Under the breastworks, the enticing path lead downwards through an ample blonde valley, which the cold tones of the peignoir made hot, hot, and led to the centre of her sex, as splendidly bedecked as the hair of her head. Her knees were round, smooth, superb. Mamie had incomparable knees . . .

'Come along,' she said impatiently, in a hoarse voice.

He rolled on to her, underneath the picture of the French flier. The flesh was cool, odorous, unending. It seized him, enveloped him, invaded him, cradled him, carried him away, drowned him, gasping all the time in the shock of love. Then he found himself again in the blue night, trying to regain his breath, stumbling through rubble which glinted like stars from the broken glass, the open eyes of the patterns of love.

The damaged Maison des Quatrans, a jewel among the

ruins, was looking at him. Jacques waited for him. He laughed cynically. 'We're going to drink a hearty toast to Mamie's health,' said Jacques. 'The greatest whore in the New World or the Old.'

No, Jacques was not mistaken. In one stroke he had regained his compromised prestige. And he had carried on by seducing a married woman. He never ceased to sing his praises of her complexion and the love she bore him. A baker's wife. The fact that he brought back all sorts of bread, fresh, crackly, odorous, croissants and brioches which they all still loved, so closely was their childhood to them. He had become the admirable Jacques once more.

Ray had had his fill of alcohol and called for Coca-Cola. Abel remembered a remark of Mamie Stover who had made it in the book about Mamie of Honolulu. 'Do you really think I need more than three minutes to polish off these little marines?' Indeed, nothing longer was necessary to spread out the carpets of love. He sent a look of gratitude to Bérangère. But, where had she gone? Ah, there she was near the newspaper seller, still with the mayor. He smiled at her page-like figure. Ray, exhilarated, was fondling Charlotte's thigh. His memories were much more precise than the Canadian's.

'We used to call it the pump! The building was narrow and there was always a queue. There was a Stars and Stripes flying over it. It had swing doors like a good Western saloon. And four compartments. It worked from midday to nine at night. It was like a Ford! In the first, you waited, like in the dentist's, but not for so long. And you coughed up there! You went into the second to strip and you gave your duds to a fat woman from the country round here. She sent you into the third room. Since Mamie had taken over the third with her imposing presence, all you could do was to land on the divan. That's where she waited for you! On her back, without any fuss! Boy, you really got airborne! As soon as it was

171

finished, the fat attendant took you to the fourth room, the washroom, and gave you back your clothes while the next one went from the first to the second to the third! Four-stroke cycle, like an internal combustion engine! Induction! Compression! Ignition! Exhaust!'

'This man is lying,' Valerie cut in, her voice steely. 'At least, Jacques . . . you're not going to tell me that Jacques . . .'

'Jacques?' What did she think then? Abel took a long pause. He was looking for the right words.

'Valerie . . . you see . . . war . . . the war, for women, well, as it was seen by the women . . . well, the war lay in between Mrs. Miniver and Mamie. That's right, Mrs. Miniver, the good lady in the rose garden. The one in the picture! The one who gives her sons to save her country and waits for them. And, at the other end, Mamie! What would you want them to do for the Mrs. Minivers, these little fellows who're going to their deaths with their guts opened up and their faces gnawed by the crabs? Of course, the boys had to take their consolation, otherwise they would have gone for the people in the liberated districts! And that sometimes happened! You can't send sex by wire. So you just have to stock up on the spot. Food arrived in containers, hermetically sealed and pasteurised. The good hygienic citizens of the New World preferred to die of hunger rather than touch the dishes pre-pared by these snail eaters, frog eaters, tripe eaters, these Western Chinks, these appalling guts with their mixed-up stuffings. So we brought in Coca-Cola, and vitamin biscuits and chopped ham! But when it comes to the girls, the Yank is not so fussy! With the preventative and penicillin,—well, get in there, lad! The moral of this story is that it's healthier to sleep with a piece that all the Wehrmacht has gone through than it is to sit down to a bit of horsemeat.'

Valerie stayed silent in the face of this unexpected bitterness.

'She was called Mamie,' he went on. 'Mamie! Do you grasp the point, Valerie? You, a sexologist? No? The ones who were not christened "Mamie" were given the name by the soldiers. They were all "Mamies". All of them! Mamie! for ever!'

He gave a deep breath and concluded, spurred on by the questioning expression on the face of the Diana from Quebec.

'I didn't understand 'till much later, very much later! For them, it meant "mama".'

She took the word like a blow and it knocked the stuffing out of her.

He got up, muttered between his teeth a brusque 'Now, you know,' and dropped his two hundred-odd pounds crushingly back on to the chair.

'These revelations have done for me,' he said. He passed his hand over his face as though he were washing himself.

'Will you lunch with us, Valerie?' he asked.

CHAPTER VIII

ABEL BATHED in the Norman richness, the union of the sea and the meadow, of work and idleness, a thick substantiality compounded of rich milk, camembert, sauces, sun-tan lotions, seaweed, the botanical flotsam which went to fatten up the land, a creamy state in between liquid and solid. The truck drivers from Nantes, Caen, Rouen and le Havre came in, bringing with them the spacious air of the highway, taking back with them the spacious air of the sea. Abel began to understand the housewives, the early risers at sea and in the fields, the building workers, the police and the railwaymen, without counting the hotel servants, the glistening cooks and the tired but smiling servant girls.

In the evenings, television taught him a great deal about this France which he knew so little. One night, a dancer in black tights came out of the little picture while the music of his war sounded forth.

The dancer was begging, holding out his hands to the well-to-do, the notables, to the generals and to the princes. The Ritual Fire Dance accompanied his gestures, as if it had been specially written for this contrived, despairing interpretation of man naked before the Gods. The man fell to the ground, raised his knees, body bent, head on the ground; then spun and bent down, rolling himself up against the cold, the snow, then stood once more, tapped with his heel, a *Zapatiado* of despair.

'Well, now, he really is supple!' said one driver.

For Abel this beggar represented the soldier, the eternal soldier, from Thermopylae to Korea! The soldier ran from bullets, grenades, rockets, dodged the sergeant and fatigues, took shelter under a bridge, clung to the earth, washed his feet, prayed to heaven, slept with one eye open, and re-ran the appalling race of the flaming German. He was begging for life.

The music announced that his time was nearly up. While Abel Leclerc stumbled around in the difficult search for himself, he ate oysters with the little Circe freed from the sanatoria, and trusted it would all pass away—and quick!

'She' was there.

'Look,' said Bérangère.

At the foot of a golden-thatched haystack, four nuns in summer habit were picnicking. The bus to Caen was passing St Bény—*'Cul Béni-sur-Mer'*.

'There's a Canadian cemetery,' she said. 'You can see it on the hill.'

All he saw at the fork of the roads were the gently rolling hillsides, the ripening corn and a few black conifers standing out harshly against the sky.

'We'll go, Bébé.'

'Not me. I'm allergic to cemeteries.'

Caen, on his return, had taken him by surprise. Vaugueux itself, shut in between the high cliffs of the reconstructed building, had become strange to him. The broken-down old block had shrunk. The same reasons of squalor which, little by little, had always brought together the very poor and the night-loving criminal into districts which were formerly aristocratic, were now concentrating in this historic, but wretched, backwater. Here were the exemplars of modern misery, the North African railwaymen, street cleaners and building workers. The quarter had taken on a resemblance to the Barbary Coast because of the 'Nordafs' who bunked up six to a room, without water or light, in the eastern filth which everywhere was so virtuously denounced. There were little cafés where records whined out music of a piercing nostalgia. It swarmed like Arabia in the places which not so long before had been the fashionable part of the town.

From Vaugueux, one day when he had gone out alone, he had investigated for a long time the enigmatic Maison des Quatrans, set like a jewel at the frontier of the new town. He was trying to find once more the precise location of Mamie's dive. It was raining hard and the warm drops washed on his face. He saw in his mind's eye the splendid showpiece of a house as he had done that night when he had come out of the magnificent Mamie's shanty, but there was no trace of the hutments now. A few men breaking stones were whistling as they took shelter under a tarpaulin. The town glistened. Sick and tired, he went and flopped down outside one of those modern bars which smell of Formica, at the back of the church of St Pierre. 'Perroquet' followed 'perroquet'. From

175

there he wandered about in the flurries of rain which made the macadam gleam, starting at the *Avenue du 6 Juin*. The insurance companies, the hotels, the banks, spread down to the neat banks of the Orne where the raindrops splashed noisily. Everything under the streaming trees was neat, immemorable; undoubtedly, peace takes everything to be permissible.

On that day, Abel got himself conscientiously drunk and, the next morning, he found himself in a grubby bedroom in the *rue des Chanoines*. An insipid blonde, Marie-Thé, gave him his coffee and croissants in bed and called him 'darling'.

When Bébé and her Canadian were not in the *Père Magloire* at *apéritif* time, the regulars were astonished. He used to throw out some pretty heavy kidding, typically Quebec. She would reply to him with the worst puns she could find, chosen purely because they were so bad; or she would explain to him 'the Countess's Album' from *Canard Enchainé*. When the Canadian laughed, the whole café rocked!

At the Père Magloire, formerly The Liberation Café, the customers came and went, greeted each other, drank at the bar, played cards, sought the tilt on the Florida table like fortune itself. They talked about the high seas and crime. They talked about apples and the farmlands. A constant stream came from their lips. 'So many words, messieurs.'

'Would you think, *mère Bertrand*? Old Jaouen's shot his dog!'

'Swine, he's the one who ought to be put away.'

'He was a nice little dog. Intelligent. But he'd go for the chickens. There was a bit of cocker in him and a bit of terrier.'

'That Jaouen's quite useless on this earth.'

'A layabout. He's got cloven feet right up to the knee. Give us another one, Marie-France. Your muscadet's not too bad.'

They spoke politics. They spoke about the calves. They

176

spoke about the wind, and the frequent rain and the summer. Abel was no longer *apart*. He gossiped with the postman whose moustache was stained with calvados. He made the acquaintance of little Yvonne. Every night she escaped from the grocer's shop. Julien's pals scrambled like tom-cats after this skinny little bit of skirt. The next day, Little Yvonne, fresh and well-washed, would chastely lower her eyes as she diddled the customers with short weight to pay for her stockings. One night, near the canal, she had brazenly offered him her tiny lemons and her little green peach.

'When you've had enough of Bébé,' she said, stung by his laughter. 'A slut that every man round here's gone through!'

Late one afternoon on a day which had continually hesitated between sun and rain, a man in black serge with a black cap came in, his peasant face marked with a pepper and salt moustache.

'Here comes the undertaker,' said Bébé in a low voice.

After having knocked back a glass of muscadet, the man began to hum a tune:

> Etoile des neiges
> Mon coeur amoureux

Bérangère burst out laughing. The man stopped, offended. The juke-box blared out a dance tune in a mad and rapid rhythm which infected all of them, like the racing movements which stir the paws of a sleeping cat.

' *"Embalmer's stomp!"* I really must write that number! I'll ask my namesake Felix Leclerc to do the music. Words and music by Leclerc and Leclerc! He has also been employed in a funeral parlour, you know. Yes, Felix Leclerc. It's true. I worked in one for three months, once . . .'

Nothing existed outside the mad whirl of the dance. He continued:

'I love watching you, Bébé . . . I watch you because I fear

177

you might fly away. Bérangère might slip off the terrace, with her pretty skirt ballooning out, so that in a flash you can see her underclothes in a foam of white nylon, and chiffon, flying, flying away in the wind. And then you'll fly off, with your skinny golden legs beating gently like an egg-beater amongst the snow! And I stay here all alone like a dog who's lost his master.'

He filled his Dunhill. Jennifer and Jacques returned.

'The past!' he sighed. 'I fear the past. However, I cling to it. It's fierce! It's the only thing no one can take away from us. God himself even! It's finished too late! He can kill me. But He cannot prevent me from having existed! From having been here. With Jacques. And the gang!'

'He can send forgetfulness.'

'I don't want to let myself slide into forgetfulness. I don't know what I shall do when I get back to Canada.'

Bérangère's lips quavered slightly.

'I don't know what I shall do, but probably there won't be any more radio commercials. Something's broken inside me. I don't know what's the matter with me today, my heart's sick.'

A truck driver from a soft drinks firm came rolling in like a sailor. He looked at the undertaker and began to guffaw joyfully.

'Well, then, you bird of misfortune, has someone pecked your nose?'

The driver got caught up in the frenzied dance and grabbed Annette by her apron.

'People live well here,' said Abel. 'They laugh. They live in the present. You see, at the radio station in Quebec, I've got some pals. Every day something new happens. Take the Dionne quins. You know them? But of course you do. The quintuplets. Remember? When they went into a convent? And one escaped into the Montreal night and her sister Emily found her again. After epilepsy and pneumonia. What a picnic! But it was news. The present. And it all passes

178

away. It stops one from thinking. Now there are some memories which come back. Now that I've discovered them, would you want to drop them? No, Bébé, my beautiful Bébé. I'm beginning to see the end. My misfortune is that I'm scared of life. I'm wandering, aren't I?'

'I like you like this.'

'The Chinese say that death's no more than an absence. In that case, Jacques is absent.'

'Jacques, Jacques! You're always talking about Jacques!'

She pronounced 'Jacques' in the French manner, with a light 'a'.

'Annette, un "perroquet". Not too much *menthe* . . . Ah, now, I fear an end which turns all our acts into nothing . . .'

She remonstrated with her finger, like a schoolmistress.

'Abel, you're thinking!'

'That's true. It's all beginning again. But what have I done to the good God to think like this?'

She placed her face in the V of her long hands, a slender feline face with slant eyes.

'He's called Gustave. The undertaker, I mean. Gustave, have a glass of wine with me!'

Gustave ceremoniously uncovered his white and grey hair, short and bristly like a dog's, plastered down in front.

'I saw you, Bébé. I've got to go to your place.'

Abel sat up quickly.

'People don't die often enough, in Verville,' she explained. 'So the undertaker has to take a second trade. Gustave is a carpenter. For three months now the aunts have been waiting for him to deal with a door which had warped. He always drinks small glasses of white wine. He's very often surly. It was he who disposed of my grandmother. A long time ago. He's always in the dumps. And always dresses in home-spun suits. There are the arms of the town, on his cap. He makes a habit of creeping into darkened mourning rooms, rooms with only one streak of sunlight which they haven't been able to block out. Rooms in which you can hear weeping, heavy

179

breathing and muttered prayers. After two or three coughs to attract attention, he will say: "Would you care to see him for the last time? I'm going to screw down the lid." You say you wouldn't. But it's stronger than you are. You go. That is Gustave, the carpenter.'

Who was right, Bébé who no longer wanted to dream of anything, who wanted to live only in the present; or Abel, trapped helplessly in the past?

'I tell you, I've done the same job! Yes, they didn't keep my job for me at the radio station in the rue St. Ignace, in 1945. There were others who hadn't had the notion of joining up. I turned up at old father Polyte's place in the *rue St Joachim*. I told myself that death was the thing I knew most about. In Canada, we don't keep the dead in the house. It's not hygienic. And then, well, they're dead, they're dead . . . we are not Latins, you see. Not at all. We used to wash them, brush them, paint them, comb them, varnish them, polish them up, and make them shine! Then we'd put them in a salon. Like a hairdressing salon. The families never came back. "He looked fine like that . . ." It's comforting. Wholesome. You pay by cheque. Now for the next one! At first it sickened me. The clients creaked. Later, I used to put a bottle of Coca-Cola right beside the dead body. In the basements, there was a cold room in which the customer was placed after he had been brought out of the ice box. In order to give him his toilet, he must not be too hard. Amongst the equipment there were some large planks of polished timber for the ceremonies. Every so often, the cold room was empty and between the cremations, we used to get really fed up. I made up a table tennis table with the planks and some trestles. One day, the head embalmer caught us at it. I have the ball in my hands.'

He finished his perroquet.

'You were speaking of your grandmother. I adored my Aunt Mamie, Aunt Jolicoeur. She was the one who brought me up. She was the being I loved most in the world. The

180

undertaker carried her off, like yours. But I keep her alive among my memories. I can still see her, you know, I see my aunt . . .'

From the naked crown of his head to his solid chin, he was coloured a variety of reds as a result of the differing effects of the sun on a skin which did not tan well and peeled. There were some spots the colour of ripe corn, a few suggestions of baked red mullet, and some light strawberry pinks. His eye-lashes were turned an albino blonde.

'I used to call my Aunt Jolicoeur "Mamie". There were plums at the bottom of the garden. Little bags of golden juice. "Mamie, a golden plum, please." Ah, Mamie was good . . . They were Reine-Claudes, you see . . .'

He stopped dead and his sunny expression was abruptly leaden. Dazed, he repeated:

'Mamie!'

The secret archers had just let fly their arrows.

'Oh, Bébé, that's appalling!'

She took his hand.

'Abel! Abel! dearest . . .'

'I used to call her Mamie. Like the big whore at Caen! My God! Mamie . . . for the soldiers—"little marines in three minutes". And all that really means is "mama"! I knew it. I explained it to Valerie. But . . . I never made the connection with my own Mamie . . .'

Tenderly, she caressed the arm which bristled with hairs.

'I'm sure that the tide is coming in,' he murmured.

The undertaker emptied his glass, and, standing up very straight, he put it down and went out between them.

*   *   *

One night, at the Embruns, they were half asleep, she huddled up in his arms. It was raining fiercely against the little house, in gusts of wind from the sea.

'Have you and Valerie never made love?' she asked.

181

'Bébé, what do you think? With Jacques's fiancée?'

'That's right, with "Jâques's" fiancée. The admirable "Jâques", who behaves just like his pals and gets the wives of French prisoners pregnant!'

'Bébé!'

'What do you mean, "Bébé!"?'

'Why do you say that?'

'Why do you take it all so seriously?'

'But . . .'

'Because it doesn't surprise you! Abel, you must look the thing in the face. Your "Jâques" was a man just like the rest. A man, and that's all there is to it.'

Between the gusts of the storm, the phantom bell was sending spasmodic distress signals.

'Did you ever hear Jacques talk of a baker's wife?'

She had reverted to the French pronunciation of Jacques.

'Yes. He told me he had a friend who was a baker. In Caen. He often brought back croissants, brioches and raisin rolls. Why?'

Outside, the waves from the mounting sea crashed down tempestuously. She did not say one word more. She went to sleep a long time before he did.

Abel recognised Sunday from the pealing bells. Valerie had no patience with him.

'Abel, today's the twenty-ninth of June. Wednesday. When are we going inland?'

Abel did not want to go inland. He had still a lot of time. More than a month. The flies were stinging and a violent quarrel had broken out between Lucien and his father. It was on the matter of la Luzerne. Once again Valerie considered with scorn the little world of the *Père Magloire*.

'To say it is for that reason that Jacques . . .'

'Valerie,' he said deliberately, 'many of Jacques's friends, who weren't twenty years old, died in the same spot, in the same circumstances as la Luzerne. To be specific, with their faces gnawed by the crabs.'

That day, he had drunk only beer.

'On the Rives, in front of Jaouen's oyster beds, there is a bridge. This bridge had not moved since 1944. A Sherman broke down the river bank and foundered with its crew. Its body now serves as the base for the bridge which the engineers made. It is by way of this bridge that la Luzerne came to prowl round that night near the property of old Jaouen. The Bridge of the Dunes. A pretty name. "I'll meet you at the bridge of the Dunes, darling." '

Very carefully he scraped out his pipe. More Canadian than ever in his studied slowness, he began again:

'Valerie, you will have to go back to Quebec without worrying about me. Now, let's see, the departure from le Havre is . . .'

'Ten minutes to midnight on the twelfth of August.'

'Wonderful Valerie, as exact as a watch! Yes, go back to Quebec. There is still time. Valerie, listen to me carefully. You have built up for yourself a certain character for Jacques. Oh, I'm well aware that the story of Mamie shocked you. If you carry on like this, you're going to kill him a second time. Look. I've said what I was going to say. We'll go inland whenever you like.'

'You make me afraid. I thought when you said "No!" it was definite. Tomorrow, Abel, tomorrow! Tomorrow morning, Abel. I'll come and pick you up. I'm counting on you, Abel.'

She was happy. She was radiant. To think that she was going to find her 'Jâques' again!

He snorted. She went on:

'Are you staying in this café? It's not very . . .'

'Suitable? Shall we meet at the Bridge of the Dunes? No? Well, then, wait for me with the car at the calvary, near the canal. That's suitable, isn't it? Calvary?'

*　　　　*　　　　*

His anguish broke out again in the promenades which were shadowed by the lime-trees which lay along the two sides of the main road. Here too, it was inevitably called the *Avenue du 6 Juin*. I am surrounded by the war. It is in me, and in my town. A patrol broke down the doors with rifle butts. I have become your country, Bébé, your country, with its good people and its little swine, its neat and laughing housewives, my good friend Marie Harel who invented Camembert, the Norman farmer's wife, in sabots, with hard-working arms, the fecund female, pink and brown, with butter-milk breasts, whose sisters all make the same sigh, at love or at the washtub.

But not one word was spoken. He drank, and tried again.

'Bébé, I think . . .'

'Yes?'

'I dote on your country, as I do on you.'

'Why, you're making me a proposal!'

'It lives as it can, just as it is. From day to day. A country which is living is wonderful, Bébé.'

'Take care! Don't idealise too much, my fine fellow. Calvados and war damage! Neglected religion and busy holidays. The frigidaire and the television. The rest of the world can go hang! Do you remember the wedding party of the Lemaresquier girl? Round here, you mistrust everyone else. You talk to send them to sleep. You mistrust the ones who see a little farther. The priest, the teacher, your own mother. You mistrust the wind and the rain. God. And women. The mayor. And men. You are born mistrusting. But you yourself, you don't know how to mistrust.'

'Bébé, you're not spoilt. You're tied to nothing. You give everything. You're a bubble. You're a saint . . .'

She gave an embarrassed laugh.

He recalled in his mind's eye the happy months which now were ending. The wedding and the aunt who died, the little boy and his mussels, the cursing Barentin grandfather, the undertaker, Jaouen, the overpainted sign of the *Café*

184

Libération, the cocks on the dungheaps and the shrimping net against the monument to the dead. He gave a gesture with his arm as though he were sweeping everything off the table.

'We must go for shrimps,' he said.

'Oh, yes, tomorrow.'

'Right. Tomorrow. Ah, no! Not tomorrow, Bébé.'

Tomorrow was the rendezvous in the Valley of Death. What had been the Valley of Death in '44! An unworldly silence was going to encompass Jehosphat. In the corn, some of the dead waited for farmers to discover them, others were swallowed up by the sands like that poor little bastard in front of the bunker. Others rushed into the seaweed at the danger zone; and crabs, shrimps, lobsters came to get their quarry. That's what I feared at the time of the Landings, in the Valley of Death! My legs are still trembling! That's right, fear, my fine fellows! Fear of being doused in the sea, like the lads at Dieppe, with those little bastard shrimps eating out your guts! Those nauseating Nazi shrimps . . .

Part Three : Mad Meg

Ton geste cependant restera ignoré—comme tant d'autres—puisque tu n'es pas lá pour faire taire ceux qui forgent une histoire à leur profit. . . .Tu t'es donné! Je te salue—dans l'oubli.

Major Michel Gauvin
June 1944

Your gestures, nevertheless, will remain unknown—like so many others—since you are not here to silence those who write history for their own profit. You have given yourself! I salute you—in forgetfulness.

CHAPTER I

THE APPLE trees, with their twisted, mutilated branches, stretched upwards from the rich grass. The sap ran out. Jacques was sleeping with his face in the hay. They had collapsed with fatigue some time before. Abel consulted his watch. Three hours had gone by. They had come from the other town, the one which was nearer the coast, through the little valley, by the fortified farm and sleeping bridge and the stagnant little stream. The war was rumbling on to the south and they were no longer in sight of the sea. Their clothes stuck to their skin like wet cardboard. Fatigue burned into the soles of their feet, into their stiffened calves and the backs of their thighs. In some misery, he tried to bring back the life into his legs, but each boot weighed twenty kilos. Jacques had taken his off. He was going to suffer when he put them back on!

There was no news of Petitjean and it seemed that the bulk of the regiment had by-passed Bény-sur-Mer. With the sea behind them, Bény was 'ahead and to the left'. Abel had never been strong in direction-finding. For more than two days they had wandered, and he had conceived a gregarious desire to find his pals again, to find the N.C.O.s and the right to complain unceasingly against the brasshats, to find his happy irresponsibility. Abel bent down, picked up a grass stem and tickled the sleeper's nostrils. Jacques waved away the grass with a mechanical gesture. Suddenly, Abel threw himself to the ground. Three hundred yards away, in the

188

village, a cloud of violet smoke rose up, accompanied by a heavy crash. Jacques did not awaken! That would be a funny way to die: the soldier sleeping: death comes; and for all eternity he does not know if he is dead or if he is sleeping!

'Hey, Jacques, act like Greater Germany and awaken!'

He imitated the whistle of a prairie train and shouted in Jacques's ears.

'All change!'

Jacques got up in one bound, rubbed his eyes, passed his hand under his bearded chin, and yawned interminably. How cool it was, in this orchard under its blue shade! A cock was crowing. Abel went up to the ruined farm. Now, where was this damned bird? Ah! In the ruins of a barn, a brash white chicken was flaring out its feathers. He chased it off with flailing arms. The bird darted away, indignant, calling vainly to the farmer's wife. Abel picked up an egg which was still warm, together with another one which was cold. He went back to Jacques who was trying to put on his boots and uttering little groans.

'Here's breakfast,' said Abel.

Jacques took the egg. An untidy soldier picked up an egg. The soldier was rumpled, in his wool and iron. The egg was smooth and fragile. The soldier looked at the egg, with an imprint of the hay on his cheek.

'How do you open this thing?' said Jacques, laughingly.

Abel blew.

'Is it hard?'

'No, it's fresh.'

'Then why is it warm?'

'Because it's just come out of the chicken's arse.'

'That's disgusting!'

Abel took his knife and delicately cut the shell at each end, then he sucked. The violet pillars still rose into the air, smoke from inferior candles which had just gone out.

'Do you remember Stoneham?' asked Jacques. 'The notice, "Eggs laid while you wait."'

189

'Just what had happened today!' But the eggs sharpened their hunger. Abel and Jacques gathered up their kit, put on their helmets, left the coolness of the shade and went into the village with dilated nostrils.

It smelled of frying bacon. The living room of a single-storey house opened into a small yard in which hydrangeas had been planted, with rose bushes borne down with flowers. The table was set with bread, a soup bowl, an opened bottle and four dishes. Abel pushed the door, worked the metal handle in vain, tried to force the door and raised the window. A clock marked the time. It had a big bull's eye in its centre. The pendulum swung majestically to and fro and worked a mechanical picture. A boy was climbing an apple tree and the irate farmer was holding out a stick behind a hedge. When the thief was at the foot of the tree, you could no longer see the proprietor. But when he was at the top, the farmer in his blue Norman blouse and cotton cap, came out from behind the hedge brandishing his club.

Jacques shinned up through the window and put his legs through. He was in his socks. He had knotted the laces of his shoes together and held them in his hand.

The serving ladle was in the soup tureen, but the soup itself was cold. An oil lamp, studded with pearly highlights and flanked by two rolls of fly-paper, was swinging gently. Between photographs of a man with moustaches and an old lady in a waisted jacket, there stood a calendar from the Post Office showing St Thérèse de Lisieux. All Frenchmen are cousins. They have the same narrow whitewashed rooms, the same water pots, the same flowered crockery, the same oil-cloth on the tables, even the same jars for sugar, pâtés, rice and salt on the chimney breast.

The two soldiers, for an instant intimidated, looked into the cupboards and found a small ham with some salt butter. Outside, an angry cock called out through its trumpet of flesh. They ate, sitting on the edge of the chairs, with the overpowering sound of the clock.

Suddenly, a key moved in the lock. They jumped up, knocking over their chairs. In the parallelogram of light was outlined the figure of a large woman in black.

'Jesu Marie! Soldiers!'

It was the millennial encounter between the peasant and the soldier. But these soldiers were from the age of the bad conscience and the woman looked tough!

'Good day, madame. We saw the open window . . .'

'But you speak French like us!'

'We're from Quebec. Régiment de la Chaudière.'

'Quebec. Quebec. That's not Caudebec, is it? No. Heavens above, you're eating cold food! That will curdle in the stomach. Terrible!'

So this is how they're waging war—with kids! Dear God! we'd have to tell the kids about the Boches who've been dug in at the school and in the presbytery for four days now, fifteen or so support troops who reached forty years or more of age.

'I'll make you some coffee, at any rate. No one's going to say I let you go without something hot.'

She ground the coffee, lit the fire and had the water boiling in the twinkling of an eye. Jacques hid his boots under the chair. And they drank. They said: 'It's good, madame, although it was unspeakable, this concoction of barley and malt! And when they left, she put some red and white roses in their arms. That is why the two lost Canadians as they went away, wished each other a wife of this kind, the Evangelist's 'strong woman'. They laughed, Jacques's face hollowed with dimples and they did not dare to throw away the 'flowers of friendship'; so they slid them into the camouflage nets and marched proudly, as if Normandy were to be liberated by divisions of men crowned with roses!

A shirt-sleeved man came out of a porch, the pillars of which were surmounted by a cross of corn, the primeval sun cross of the last harvest. The peasant was leading a huge brown horse.

'Whoa there, Jewel, whoa, whoa! Jewel, whoa.'

Over the front of the farm, two flags were flying, the blue verging on mauve while the red was nearer scarlet, hastily sewn together. The countryman hardly noticed the soldiers. He'd seen many of them since the Hundred Years' War. The two Canadians arrived in front of the town hall, which also was bedecked with flags. In the centre of the square, the monument to the dead showed an infantryman, the tail of his coat drawn heroically up over his puttees, fixing his bayonet, whilst behind him, a fine lady with a bare breast sounded a bugle and pointed theatrically to the tobacconist's shop. A one-legged man in a military tunic came out of the café with the carrot-red sign and beckoned to them to go in. The bistro bore the sign: *Café des Sports*.

Inside, the *patron* was crushing flies with a fly-swat. The one-legged man offered them a drink. This veteran was wearing the blue of the French soldiers of the 1914 war, the blue of the wash-houses, the *poilu* blue.

'Be careful, there are still some Boches around the buildings. They're sharpshooters, after officers.'

The old man told the story of a neighbouring town which had been taken and retaken several times the day before, with the French flags appearing and disappearing by turns. Then, pensively, he considered Jacques's feet.

'In '14 I went into Charleroi like that. Julien, haven't you got some shoes for the soldier?'

Julien and the old man went away and reappeared. They had dusty hunter's boots, worn-out football boots, shoes, peasants' footwear, summer sandals, all more or less worn out and they heaped them up on the tiled floor where Jacques was sitting.

'Ah,' said Abel to Jacques in a melodramatic voice, 'I've found you out. I was watching you. I came to spy on you.'

He ended by taking a fancy to a pair of espadrilles which

were anything but uniform, lifted up his body with extreme care and raised his legs. Gently he placed the soles of his feet on to the earth as though it was a hot-plate and stood on them with anxiety. Then he smiled, happy.

'Hallo, lads,' said Julien, handsomely established behind the bar which carried his signature in copper plate writing.

Two civilians came in abruptly. The thinner of the two, an edgy man, with a slim black moustache, and an olive complexion, was wearing a shirt in thick blue flannel without a collar, and washed-out brown trousers. Into his belt he had slipped two revolvers, one large and one small. His companion swaggered in, a big negro with the colour of a dark plum.

'Are they English?' the newcomer asked, indicating Abel and Jacques with his thumb.

Julien, the landlord, scowled. This was a fine way to reply to his greeting!

'Canadians,' said Jacques. 'French Canadians. Régiment de la Chaudière.'

The thin moustached man's forehead creased in a network of innumerable wrinkles.

'Wait. Wait! They've gone by, the Chaudières. We met them yesterday, didn't we, Banania?'

Banania was knocking back cider.

'Pass by, yastaday, the Showays. Not here.'

He pointed to the south and laughed with a flash of teeth. He really did resemble the famous laughing poster.

'Bény-sur-Mer?' asked Abel.

'That's right, Cul Bény-sur-Mer, because there's no sea there. That's what we call it.'

The olive-skinned man had the bantering tone of one who is not to be had. Brusquely, he clicked his heels and introduced himself:

'Commandant Maxime. Fifi. Where's the H.Q.?'

'The H.Q.?' said Julien.

'The headquarters of the Resistance!'

193

'Well-l-l!' said Julien, quite undecided. 'I expect it's opposite, at the town hall, with the ration cards.'

With the brisk walk of a staff officer, Maxime went to the door and signalled with his arm. Nothing! Then he bawled out. He must really be a soldier! From the corner of the street, there slowly emerged one, two, three, four, five, six men. They advanced in fits and starts, singly, and crossed the little square as if it were being swept by a withering fire. They came puffing into the café.

'A fine team!' said Julien, between his teeth.

Two of them were wearing rough tunics of a blue-grey without badges and trousers of the same colour. Like Maxime, the fattest of them had strapped on a belt from which hung a bayonet which bounced against his plump thighs. He looked like a cheerful butcher. The other, in the same indeterminate uniform, was thinner even than Maxime. He swam inside his tunic. He wore no hat and his shaven head disclosed the surprising bumps of a skull rich in geographical accidents.

'You know these birds?' the one-legged man asked in a low voice.

Julien indicated that he did not, the corners of his mouth drawn very low.

There were eight of them. One, very well shaved, very young in appearance, with very white hair was munching wheatstalks. Two others were wearing brassards fastened with enormous nursery pins on which were roughly inscribed the letters: F.F.I.

'Group William the Conqueror,' the commandant announced. 'We've chopped off the enemy's rear. Show them your pocket, Banania.'

Banania showed his teeth and drew out of his pocket six belt buckles which he threw on to a marble table. They carried the inscription: *Gott mit uns.*

'Hell! Just like the other time,' said the veteran. 'They've not changed at all with Hitler!'

194

Abel and Jacques looked at the buckles, then at the partisans, their chief Maxime and this Banania who, his eyes sparkling with amusement, slowly ran his hand like a knife across his throat.

The last of them was in workman's blue. About forty, with a blond moustache and a low forehead. He had the fine happy laugh of one who doesn't give a damn. The two men in the dull blue military coat—but from which army?—set up a portable transmitter.

'E.R.17,' Maxime explained. 'From the arms depot at Vaucelles. Infantry model of 1940.'

The big butcher put on the headset.

'William the Conqueror calling,' he said in the mechanical operator's voice. 'William the Conqueror calling. Hallo, Sardine. Do you read? Do you read? Over. Over.'

The big man operated the change-over switch. He listened. Everyone listened.

'Well, then, Dix-de-Der?' snapped the commandant, impatiently rubbing his moustache with his finger.

The operator took off his helmet, made Maxime repeat his words and shook his head.

'Sardine's not listening out,' the commandant grumbled. 'What a shambles, this Liberation is!'

He turned to Julien.

'Any collabos in the village?'

The landlord shrugged his shoulders.

'You'd better tell, because we'll find out.'

'What's this F.F.I. mean?' asked Abel of the jovial little rotund man.

'French Forces of the Interior.'

'Franch fosses of th' Inteer,' Banania repeated.

'Where you from?' asked Jacques.

'Guadeloupe.'

The word in his mouth took on the timbre of a velvet flower.

Maxime cut in.

'We don't have to take your word for it, *patron*. No collabos? Extraordinary. We're going to check for ourselves.'

'Oh, indeed! Pardon me, your lordship! Just a minute,' snapped the landlord, turning instantly a beetroot red.

He beat the fly-swat down on the counter with all his might.

'If you adopt that tone of voice, F.F.I. or my balls, I'll chuck you out of here! Since you want to get some action, go and see the mayor! Shall I ask for your papers? No one here knows you.'

Maxime weighed up this resistance to the Resistance, hesitated and went out, taking with him the two men who wore the brassards.

The sky was overcast. The artillery fire did not let up. The warning sirens sounded, intermingled and cut through each other, quite indecipherably.

'We're going to strike in a thousand places,' said the big butcher who was called Dix-de-Der, to the quiet young man with the white hair.

Under the severed lime trees, the commandant Maxime was in palaver with the mayor, a stout, lively little man who spoke with his hands. Dix-de-Der left the cards for a minute and, saying 'Don't mess up the pack,' he returned to the E.R.17, worked it without result, took off the headset to scratch his scalp, and went back to the game. Opposite, the F.F.I. commandant and the tubby little man went into the town hall. Suddenly, there came a familiar whistling. Abel and Jacques flung themselves on to the ground. The others looked at them, stupefied. The air cracked drily as slate and plaster spattered to the ground. The shell had exploded between the lime trees, at the foot of the monument to the dead. The smoke cleared slowly. Nothing was left of the arm of the dame who played the bugle but the shoulder.

Banania stood up and, with white eyes, asked:

'Doesn't anyone know where the beach is?'

196

'Sod you and your beach,' snapped Dix-de-Der. 'The swine! I had a full house, jacks and kings.'

But the man with the moustache in the workman's blue remained flat on his belly on the steps, his head lying low. Commandant Maxime went out of the town hall at a tremendous speed. The mayor followed him, taking off his hat and mopping his brow. Behind them a kid, whose eyes were popping out, was carrying a ham between his arms, like a baby. Maxime started back in front of his comrade stretched there on the ground. The mayor leaned over, prodded the body, turned it over and stood up again, wiping his knees. The commandant said, in a voice strangled by emotion:

'Adieu, le Grêlé! You have died for France. I entrust him to you, *Monsieur le Maire.*'

The mayor, taken aback for a moment by the tone, signed to the boy who went into the Café des Sports, put the ham behind the counter, went into the yard and returned pushing a wheelbarrow. The tubby partisan and the young man with white hair put the body on to the barrow, tenderly, and went with him towards the graveyard. The mayor went into the café, sat down and took out a piece of paper.

'That's understood, then, commandant,' he said, solemn in his turn, 'The heroism of the children of Normandy will be honoured in the appropriate manner in Cuverville. But we must do everything according to the book. You will take quarters in the Café des Sports until some new instructions from your H.Q. . . .'

Julien, the *patron,* gave an eloquent grimace.

'Everything's red tape,' said Maxime.

He repeated: 'Red tape, red tape, red tape.' The doctor-mayor shot a lively glance at him, then began to write.

Once more, the walls shook. Abel fell on his rifle, a reflex from close-combat training. The patron vanished behind his counter. The room stank of powder! That was a close one! The mayor was transfixed with indignation, his fountain pen raised. A smoke cloud, blue in the shade and red in the light, disappeared irregularly.

'Dammit, that was dangerous,' said Jacques.

Abel and Jacques burst out laughing. They fancied this gag. One of the veterans who had got out of Dieppe had told them about it. His wife had written to him: 'I'm worried, darling. Isn't it dangerous?' This time, it was so much more dangerous because the gun was fired by the partisan with the harelip. He stood stupidly still, looking at his smoking pistol and he swore fearsomely in Spanish! The mirror in the café was decorated now with a round black hole, from which spread out the imprint of a medallion star. Julien came out from behind his counter, with astonished eyes and his mouth like an O. He creased his eyebrows, glowered at the commandant who was beating on the table with his fist, at the Spanish thug and his smoking pistol, at the two Canadians who had roared with laughter; then he turned and saw his broken mirror.

'Well, dammit all!'

'Bloody swine,' Maxime blustered.

The miscreant gave a gesture of incomprehension. One could guess what had happened. He had been a volunteer in the Spanish War! He was not acquainted with this gun and he had been caught out when he was stripping it. But, anyway, this was nothing to get steamed up about. After all, there was a war on!

'You'll have to add the cost of the mirror to the requisition order,' said Maxime. 'The incident is closed. The essential thing is to have everything in order.'

Dix-de-Der at the radio set, unflappable, started operating again. It seemed that no time at all had elapsed since the entry of the commando into the Café des Sports, for the actions of the happy butcher and his R/T procedure, so stereotyped and incessantly repeated—'over to you, over'—were identical with the earlier session.

'Drop Sardine,' said the commandant.

198

The mayor had finished drawing up the order. He held it out to Maxime, who read it, read it again, signed it and gave it back to the mayor. The mayor, as he went off, stopped in front of the Canadians.

'Good luck, lads.'

He was wearing a thin red ribbon on the clerical grey of his jacket. He shook Jacques's hand, then Abel's. The pressure of the hand of the mayor-doctor was insistent; but, he left at once. In the little square, he skirted the shell hole, gazed at the bronze soldier and his mutilated muse and disappeared into the flag-bedecked town hall.

A woman in a green apron was venturing out under the lime trees. A dog barked furiously. A child came in to ask for some matches. Julien served slices of ham with the blade of the knife. The William the Conqueror Group and its commandant munched away. No one thought of death any longer.

'At Cricqueville-les-Caen,' Maxime explained with his mouth full, for he had a wolfish appetite, 'there is an internment camp. We were all there for acts of resistance, insulting officers, with their bicycle pumps (we call their dirks "Bicycle pumps"), listening to the English radio and distributing leaflets. Everything, you see.'

Abel and Jacques, their eyes opened wide, were impressed. Were these really the fighters of the shadows, the desperadoes, the men with the Molotov cocktails, the partisans?'

'On the fifth and the sixth, Cricqueville was bombarded. We didn't even have to cut through the barbed wire.'

'But what about the German belt buckles?'

'You're always saying "The Germans"! We call them the Shloos, Fritzes, Mouldies, Green Beans. And always the Boches. The Boches! Well, you're Canadians. These Shloos were sleeping in a prefabricated hut. Banania just took his shoes off. He didn't even make a squeak. We shoved 'em under a dungheap.'

'We going to the beach?' asked Banania.

'A pain in the neck, that lad is,' was Dix-de-Der's opinion.

Abel gathered his kit together. He'd had enough of the *Café des Sports*. Jacques followed suit, with his shoes round his neck and his espadrilles on his feet. But Maxime got up. 'Wait!' He got his things together. 'We'll come with you.' It was peremptory. Behind the two baby soldiers in their floral helmets, went three *francs-tireurs*. The clumsy Spaniard, Dix-de-Der and the man from Guadeloupe took the place of the extraordinary prisoners of the day before. It started to rain with huge warm drops which melted into the dust.

At Bény-sur-Mer, an officer from a support company directed them to *Les Fermes à Loiseau*. They advanced from covert to covert. They slipped into a farm. Some hundreds of chickens were cackling, a horse was pounding its hoof in the stable and the machine was standing outside, a gas-producing tractor. But there was no other trace of inhabitants. Jacques threw himself down at once on a pile of straw and fell immediately asleep. Maxime consulted a map. Abel was becoming more and more ill at ease. The General Intelligence had not ceased sending him messages in cipher. It did not know what was going on, it could not interpret but it sent him little sparks of anguish. And Jacques was asleep! There was no question of closing his eyes, although they were sore with lack of sleep. The Spaniard was snoring. The infantry battle was crackling on outside. Abel got up. The Guadeloupean also. Abel went right round the barn, cluttered up with agricultural machines, harrows, mowers, a host of disused equipment. Banania followed him. He was uncertain, anxious. Abel returned to Jacques. Maxime had not lifted his nose from the map. 'Above all, do not sleep; or awaken Jacques. Sleep in turns.' Abel found himself nodding off. He dampened his eyes with saliva, beneath his chin and behind his ears. He must not sleep. Sleep. Sleep. He shook himself. The Chauds were all close by. He would sleep later. Don't sleep. Don't sleep. He would hold out. Everything was

200

becoming vague and blue, a deep blue, a fabric on which sunflowers slowly danced.

Abel awakened with a jump.

The screams of a stuck pig came from the barn. He stood up, kicked Jacques in the shin and leapt to his carbine.

With what he saw before him, Abel was going to burst out laughing, but the laugh choked in his throat. Banania, sitting with all his weight on the swarthy partisan, was stuffing goose's feathers into the man's mouth. The Spaniard's cries were becoming fainter and fainter. His body gave a few violent convulsions which were mastered by the powerful thighs of the hilarious negro.

'Commandant Maxime!' yelled Abel.

The commandant was shivering over his map. The cheerful Dix-de-Der had vanished.

'That's enough of that.' Abel told Banania. 'Let him go. Hear me? Let him go or I fire!'

Half choked, the Spaniard was flailing violently with his legs. The feathers flew about.

Abel pressed the trigger.

He had fired into the rafters. The din was terrifying. The Guadeloupean turned round. The whites of his eyes glistened in the dusky plum-coloured skin. He stood up. He kept his legs bent, elastic. The feathers fell innocently back on to the ground. Banania brought out of his pocket a blue streak and, at once, he jumped. The buckles . . . ! The belt buckles . . . ! The Germans under the midden! A new blast hit the air. Then there was nothing more than the scarified caterwauling of the chickens.

Banania had fallen with his face to the ground, his hand before him, open on the razor which had fallen from his grasp. He gave a few more convulsive starts and then lay still. The last feather fell in capricious flakes.

Abel went up to the body, his knees trembling. He picked up the razor, folded it up with a chill shiver that travelled down his spine, from joint to joint. He tried to turn Banania over. He weighed a ton, like a dead animal. Jacques, only half awake, helped him. They put the negro on his back. At a range of ten yards, the bullet had smashed his chest open. The purple blood boiled up. His eyes were still open in fury. The Spaniard with the hare-lip was panting. He lifted himself up on his forearm, coughed, coughed some feathers and spat them out from his hare-lip. Abel tried to close the eyes of the man from Guadeloupe. It was impossible. They were like rubber. They stayed open in their uncomprehending anger. Abel threw a sack over the face.

Maxime pulled some Gauloises out of his pocket, and offered them to the stupefied Canadians. From his haversack he pulled out a huge pack of safety matches. All the matches had been cut in two. All that was left was the tip and a tiny piece of wood.

'Less heavy that way,' explained Maxime.

'Who are you?' asked Abel. 'You and your friends?'

Maxime looked away.

'Banania? He was interned at Cricqueville-les-Caen. In the regional asylum. The razor, you see. The Spaniard's also dangerous. He killed his mother.'

He winked sadly.

'Put yourself in my place. "Commandant Maxime, of the F.F.I. Resistance Group of the Cricqueville Mental Hospital." Well, it's true. I formed the William the Conqueror Group. With a bloke from Verville, who had been interned on the orders of the mayor, a dirty collabo, who'll lose nothing by waiting. Maxime Friquet! Controller of Taxes. Lieutenant in the reserve. They put me with the male nurses and the student doctor. Then I'd had enough of listening to the shouts. Shouts! Well, I don't know what I'm going to do now...'

He relit his cigarette, burning his fingers because of the short matches, held it out to Abel who lit his own and then Jacques's. They were the first Gauloises they had smoked. They coughed.

202

'Now, my group is split up. We must keep things regimental!'

He yelled.

'Fall in!'

No one answered—and for good cause!

He went up to the negro lying stretched out under the canvas. The Spaniard continued covering the body with feathers. The Controller of Taxes and Lieutenant of Reserve Maxime Friquet, gave a violent kick at the body of Banania.

Walking backwards, Abel and Jacques went out of the barn . . . They slipped out under the porch and broke out into a sunken road. Some short bursts of fire crackled out and the bullets whistled into the wet wood. But this was better, much better, than the bizarre doings of the comrades of William the Conqueror!

CHAPTER II

THROUGH THE OPEN window, Abel followed with his eye a group of dancing swifts. The Poor Sister was entertaining the Canadian. A white speck on her eye gave her a look in which the credulousness in their blueness was contradicted by a series of blinks, like the winks of a pensive owl. The Poor Sister was taking advantage of the absence of her sister to tell the Canadian all the bad things one had to know about the Rich One, a woman who, proud of her two happy marriages, reproached her even for the salt in her soup. 'I would go into a home,' said Berthe (Or perhaps it was Marthe? No, it must be Barthe . . . or Merthe), 'except that it would make her too happy.' In this way they went continually over and over their half-century of old hostilities. They were the best of friends.

Bébé had promised to be back by eight. They were going to dine at the café belonging to the ex-colonial. On the Continent, time was not as important as in Quebec and the carefree Bébé was by no means precise. One wondered how this creature of charm and fantasy could submit to the exigencies of teaching. It was true that she did not teach much . . .

'Be distrustful,' said the Poor Sister. 'Be on your guard! She's sixty and she's still looking for a man!'

Abel was looking at the photograph of a thin man with a big Charlie Chaplin moustache, posing full face, with a stupid expression. The picture was in a heavy brass frame. This was the Rich Sister's first husband, founder of the fortune of the house. This fellow, so solemn and official, resembled the Controller of Taxes of Cricqueville-les-Caen, the famous Commandant Maxime.

'This gentleman was Berthe's first husband . . .'

Ah, Berthe! So this was Marthe speaking. He was always wrong about them.

'He was a fine man, our Monsieur Victor. He was called Victor. He was as straight as a die.'

Abel vaguely heard: 'Tor. Or. Otor. Totor.'

'An authoritarian,' Marthe went on. 'Well, one has to be. But he was a man, for all that. Sergeant-major during the war. Well, this fine man who was well set up, comfortably off, had everything, and his parents owning a house, that's to say a second house and, well, my sister turned him into an imbecile! She's a man-eater!'

He returned to the picture. The resemblance to Maxime was now distant. For Maxime, the story of the reconstituted commando William the Conqueror had lasted six months. Maxime had the uniform of a battalion commander. And then the group was destroyed. Only Maxime survived, but they took him back to the asylum. He was still there. When

Leroy had told this to the Canadian, a few days earlier, Abel had given a bitter laugh. Another witness to his past! And in that state! Clowning and putrefaction! Shakespeare for ever!

The bubbles from the fountain followed each other in a mechanical succession. Emptiness, fullness, the past, the present. No Bébé. The sentinels had re-awakened. Orders were whispered down the line. The odd little bell which no one operated gave a few feeble rings.

'My own husband was a travelling salesman. Yes, when I was about thirty, I married—at last. He travelled in hosiery. But those tarts who keep the boutiques are all really fly customers. Monsieur Alphonse was a weak one, in spite of his two hundred odd pounds! I've seen some of them. And they come in every shape and size!'

Attention, attention. Take care! Let nothing go by. Everything may be a sign. No one must sleep. Even a silly old gossiping woman may let a word fall.

'One day, I found him, sitting in front of a café at the side of St Pierre! He was parading round with some little tart. My blood boiled. I threw them out on to the road, glasses, plates, saucers and all; and the girl fell on her backside, kicking, kicking away so that you could see all she'd got!'

'Does it often happen that Bérangère is so late?'

Marthe lowered her eyes.

'Bérangère's very free, Monsieur Abel. Her mother died when she was only fifteen. Then there were the men! She's lively and airy, a real gadabout! Just like her mother, our youngest sister, poor Laurence. Ah, there were not many good examples in this house. And the little girl's grandmother let her do anything.'

The telephone jangled. Bébé's voice was very near, as though she were talking from the next room. Everything she said was spoken in an unusual tone of voice. He must not worry. Nothing was wrong. She had been detained. She told him about it. It was not serious. She was coming. She loved him. So long, darling, be with you soon.

The engine of a trawler chugged away outside. The anxiety which the telephone call should have dissipated, had not been appeased. A quarter to the hour sounded on the clock, then the hour itself. Where the hell did these damned Westminster chimes come from, with their reminder of black-out and stout! Ten o'clock! At last, footsteps sounded on the staircase. Abel stood up. Everywhere, the networks were busy, recollecting the memories, the images, the words heard on the telephone, exactly as they had functioned in the same country, once before, from the instant when Maxime and his Group William the Conqueror came on the scene.

She opened the door, too violently, and said:

'Have you hidden my aunt under the bed or inside it?'

This was indeed her manner and her style of joke, but her voice did not ring true. He moved the pear-shaped switch which had amused him on the first night. The cold flood of light from the ceiling lamp fell on Bébé, in front of him, her hands opened in an awkward gesture of offering.

'What's up, Bébé?'

'Nothing. What should there be? Just because I'm a bit late!'

Indeed her voice did not seem natural. She was gurgling out the vowels, stumbling over the consonants and she tried to cover up the whole effect with an excessive smile. The young woman gave a sweeping gesture with her right arm, as though she was throwing to the wind this contemptible story of lateness.

He took her by the shoulders.

'You're sick,' he said, tenderly.

'Don't be so stupid. I'm fine. Don't be so stupid.'

She gave a drunken laugh, danced in a futile attempt at a lightness of movement and it was he who stopped her falling on to the white elephant. General Intelligence wired the message: *Careful. Delve into the past. Try to recall similar situations. Urgent. High priority.*

Gently, without letting go her shoulders, he said:

'Bébé, I have antennae, you know...'

'Butterflies have got antennae, not gorillas...'

She made an effort, but his gentleness carried weight, her attempts at being comic faltered. Her face seemed as though it was being reflected in a distorting mirror. The difference which he often noticed between her cameo-like profile and her less perfect full-face, was now turning to caricature. Her chin had hardened, her colour had changed, and was spotted with mauve blemishes. It was impossible to hold her eyes.

'At any rate, you're not normal.'

'Oh, dear, it's you who are not normal. You're beginning to get on my nerves. If you're talking about morals, that's on the other side.'

'The other side?'

'Yes; this lad doesn't understand anything.'

Once more she made a gesture, too exaggerated but calculated, not at all feminine when she was usually the very essence of femininity. Ah, so she meant: 'On the other side of the sea. On the other side of the Atlantic, in Canada.'

He let go her shoulders. A rocking movement, forward and backward, took possession of the young woman's body. Her neck seemed to be too long, her shoulders too sloping, her pelvis too heavy and she had put all her weight on legs which were spread apart, with thickened calf muscles and flat feet.

'What's the time?' he asked, talking of nothing in particular to hide his discomfort.

'Six, perhaps.'

The clock with the stream of time on it showed ten past ten. Like V-for-Victory. And Bérangère had the clock right in front of her. The idea of calling a doctor flashed across his

207

mind. *Take control of yourself. Keep calm. Watch and wait. Wait and see. Do nothing.*

There was a noise in the shadow behind the bed. Excusing herself too volubly, Marthe entered.

'I've brought you a *tisane,* my dears.'

'Come and sit in the chair and tell me what sort of after-noon you've had.'

'Oh, an afternoon, just like all the rest.'

Her expression was bitter, sour, of evil intent. Where now was the princess of the seashore? *Watch,* ordered the General Intelligence. Her head too erect, her profile scornful, pretty but oddly rigid, Bébé was walking like a model who was showing a collection, but a model who was just failing in all her gestures. She tripped over the carpet and dropped rather than sat on the chair.

'Tell you what? If I have to tell you the story of my life, I'll be here until tomorrow morning, Canada! Now you're looking at me like that. It's true, you're looking at me, it's annoying. You're fussing round me. Be damned to it! I've come a bit late. Well, that's because I couldn't do anything else. You're not going to make a scene.'

She gave the same laugh, oddly forceful in its vulgarity.

'This would be funny if you were my husband. But if I did have one, I'd have to chuck him out.'

The laugh went on, in the same artificial manner. Some of the old modulations returned to her voice, but the general texture of the words was woven from a succession of related places which had nothing in common with the sparkling personality of the Messalina of this extraordinary bedroom. The Westminster chimes sounded, recalling ginger ale, the tide on the Thames and Whitechapel under bombardment.

'What's the time?'

'Six, or seven. I'm not hungry.'

'Bérangère, we should have dined at the *Diable de Mer.* It's a quarter past ten.'

'Don't be stupid.'

208

'Look. Look at the clock. It's just struck the quarter. Quarter past ten.'

'Ten, in the morning?'

'Bérangère, it's dark and your doves are asleep.'

He did not dare call her Bébé any more. Incredulous, she considered the room, the clock, the cage, and the Canadian, then shrugged her shoulders. General Intelligence was working furiously, but they did not come up with anything helpful, just vague memories, anecdotes about mental illness, recollections of reading or the cinema, in particular *Snake Pit*. He took up again where they had been before this talk about time, shocked by the accusation which Bérangère had just made.

'Bébé, I've never had any idea of asking you to account for your actions.'

She passed her hand over her forehead, then rubbed her cheeks and her eyes with her fingers.

'I've been to Graye.'

She had now set her heart on giving him this account for which he had not asked.

'I met Adrienne, a friend from my childhood who also has a daughter at the *aérium*. We saw the doctor together. Then I had a *perroquet* to drink to you. The doctor was with a pal. He wouldn't let us go.'

One hour earlier a doctor had been with her. And he had noticed nothing odd. So? Abel remembered what she had said to him, both heart-rending and tender, about the world of the dead and the superimposed towns. Who was this young woman who had stolen Bérangère's countenance, now a little puffy, and whose head now was held too high, now was slowly rocking too and fro? No, the same woman could not show two faces so very different!

She stood up. He thought idly back to the *perroquet*. Suddenly . . . But yes! The loss of any sense of time, this confused diction. These unco-ordinated movements.

'Bérangère.'

'Now what's Bérangère done?'

'She's drunk too much.'

'Don't be so stupid.'

'She's drunk too much.'

'Oh!'

'She's drunk too much with the quack and her childhood friend. Now Bérangère's drunk. You're tight, my love.'

He looked at her, somewhat sickened.

'You're not going to get high and mighty because I've had a glass too much! You're not in a good position to do that, Canadian.'

This was also Bérangère, this pretty stumbling girl about whom people in the street had been able to say: 'Now what's she been up to?' The quack from the *aérium* must have brought her. There had been the sound of a car, just before the young woman's devastating entry. At the time, Abel had not given it much attention. Now curiosity took possession of him, not malicious, but sad, sharp and fraternal. The young woman's eyes were dilated and her gestures still lacked precision. She began to speak, her legs apart for better balance. Like a bumpkin at the ball accused of drunkenness, she was going to demonstrate her balance on her feet; she raised one knee in the air, put her left elbow on her raised right leg, and made a face at him as she tried not to fall down!

'Me drunk? Don't be so stupid. Look at this line on the floor.'

It was just as he had foreseen. With concentration and a fixed eye, placing one foot before the other, she followed the line, her arms out for balance. She wavered. She stood up once more, putting her heels together and brought her hand to her temple in a grotesque military salute. It contained some clear symbolical sense for her, but not for him. She sat on the bed, suddenly collapsed, her skirt tucked up above her golden knees.

'The doctor's nice. He's in love with my daughter. She's beautiful, my Christine. That's true, you've seen her. The

210

doctor came here. A fine lad. He looked after me. He meant well, you know. But me? Well, now ... ! '

She had this terrible little laugh. *She was speaking from the depths of herself. This was like looking under an overturned stone. The woodlice! Remember. Make an effort. Drunkenness frees the interior forces. They come to the surface. They show themselves uncontrolled. They take possession. Drunks invent nothing. Repeat: drunks invent nothing. They do nothing but spit out what is inside them. It's the same with you when you're in that state.*

Bérangère kept up the smile of those who think themselves alone in their comprehension, in the superb naïveté of drunks, of lovers and children.

'You see, the beautiful Roman? She's giving her little tit to the beggar! She's a girl just like me, but she's got a lot more than me! Yes, she certainly has more than me! You can't deny it.'

She pulled out from behind the nylon her little clear white breast. Abel looked, divided between tenderness, desire and disgust.

'The pattern on those drapes is bloody! Don't you find the pattern's moving? One day you told me something about patterns ... Can't remember any more. When I was a little girl, I made patterns, too.'

'You won't need to this evening.'

'It was orange, blue, green, red and it turned round like butterflies. You're right, you big ape, I don't need it tonight. It must be that I'm getting young again.'

A trace of humour returned to him, as to her, but he could not hide his sadness. These wandering words tarnished the wonderful memory of the patterns they had discovered together on the dunes.

She threw off her ballerina slippers into the other end of the room and stood up, her hair about her shoulders. She

211

looked like the Marguerite of his childhood home, a long way away, far into time and space in the Royaume. She looked like Mad Meg, but a Meg now very young, desirable, sadly too desirable!

Her voice changed.

'I had a child who died. He would have been ten now. I had him when I was twenty. As I left college. He was a boy. That's why I don't like cemeteries. He was called Christian. And that's why my little girl's name is Christine.'

Tears flowed into her green eyes.

He began to revolt against this degredation. In spite of the violence of his desire, he did not know if he would ever again touch this lovely young woman with the bare breasts, whom drunkenness had made dirty.

'Obviously, you're going to make fun of me. Because I fear for the little girl! I hate cemeteries. What are you going to do? You're not going away, are you? Abel, what have I done to you?'

She stood up again, but she could keep erect only with great difficulty. He hit her twice, quietly, as one slaps a drunken girl one wishes to awaken. Like Grandpierre, poor old Grandpierre, who used to forget to breathe! If he is still in this world, he must still be taking knocks and saying 'Thank you.' She opened her mouth into an O, like models in the glossy magazines.

He must get out, leave the coast, find a hiding place somewhere. But where? Arromanches? And find his antiseptic Canadian Diana once more. Hell must be something like this, with no place to hide. Bébé was weeping warm tears.

'That's not a good thing to do, Monsieur Leclerc. I'm a lady, Monsieur, Monsieur Leclerc.'

The Poor Aunt, who had come soundlessly back, was carrying a tray on which two bowls were steaming. How long had she been there? Before or after the slaps?

'I'm a lady, Monsieur Leclerc. And I've known Canadians before. And there's not one of them would behave like that

212

towards a lady! Well, it's the way of the world, I suppose . . .'

The way of the world, indeed, of a world opened up anew, unforeseen, suffocating, an abyss. As her tears fell on to her naked breast, she seemed covered by a thin, glistening film of moisture. So this was shame. He desired her like this, more and more strongly, with all his male strength, ready to tear her, open and penetrate her, storm and pillage her, then to gasp and die!

Marthe was mindlessly twisting fingers deformed by arthritis.

'You have this, Bébé, it'll be good for what's the matter with you. Ah, my husband! There were lots of times, it wasn't very nice, when he would come back to me . . . Don't you go away! She is so fragile and she loves you so! Don't you see that the poor little thing's not well?'

Bérangère slumped down, weeping. Another Bérangère had come into existence, an impossible Bérangère, probably the one whom 'little Yvonne', Lucien and some others had spoken of with such venom. What was worse, he had obscurely known about it from the very first day.

He took her into his arms, raised her up and stretched her out on the bed, moist, defenceless, trembling. He took away her hands which were clinging to him like seaweed.

'She's so hot. It's emotion! It always stirs up when she sees Christine. The father was a swine. Oh, men!'

Bérangère twisted and turned on the bed, her hair loose. He put his hand on her shoulders.

'What's the time?' he asked.

'Don't know. Must be late. Look at the clock.'

'Don't you remember that I've asked you the time a number of times.'

'Why?'

She lifted herself up and stared at the clock.

'Twenty to eleven! As late as that! Oh, my poor darling, I've made you wait so long!'

He breathed deeply. She was coming round.

'Abel, listen to me, it would be better. I must explain. I'm not a woman, Abel. No, I'm not a woman. I'm a boy. I've always lived like a boy. Oh, what a headache I've got.'

She was not lying, she looked ghastly.

'My mother, Laurence, died too early. Without telling me why she was alone and why I had no father. It is from that, that all my stupid actions grew, much later. And I've done a lot of them. But I've never been a bitch, never! As Marthe!'

Marthe was approbation itself! A certificate of good living and habits. But the blemish on her eye and the unction of her gestures pleaded ill for her protégé. The Westminster chimes sounded.

'I've told the truth,' said Bérangère, once more stupid. 'Every time I tell the truth, a bell rings.'

The word stuck. *Truth!* Bébé's odder statements pointed to Jacques. 'Heroes who made the wives of French prisoners pregnant.' Before he had even considered the matter, he questioned her.

'Stories about Vaugueux. I'll explain to you. Not tonight, I've a headache. And also, I'm sick of your Jacques. I'm sick of it, sick of it.'

'You're sick of me as well.'

'I'm sick of it, sick, sick. Sick of it, sick of it!'

In the repetition, the words lost all meaning, grew into a thickness of absurdity, a wave of lava which engulfed everything.

'Sick, do you see? Sick of it all! Sick, sick, sick . . .'

'Drink up, Bébé,' said Marthe. 'Monsieur Abel is going to let you get some sleep, dear.'

'See you tomorrow,' he said, as he went.

As he was going, she called feebly to him, then sank down without awaiting his reply, drowned in her hair. Abel went down the stairs, left the Embruns, walking blindly, blindly forward. The iodine smell of the Channel had become the very odour of despair.

214

CLOSE TO the dark calvary, the sea was frothing, milky. Bérangère must be sleeping, between the turtle doves and the white elephant. Now, in the morning, Abel did not see any part of last night's scene from the same angle. A tender pity invaded him. Three blasts on a car horn made him jump. Valerie! She had come early! She inspected him and he felt ill at ease. However, he had slipped on a white sweater and light blue slacks.

'I think it better if you drive, Abel.'

A stale scent of toilet water filled the little car. He creased his nose, opened the quarter-light and engaged gear. From time to time, Valerie glanced at this silent driver from the corner of her eye. At the crossroads of Bény-sur-Mer, he was tempted to shoot off towards the dark woodlands of the cemetery. No, he would go alone! They went through Caen, slowly down in front of the University with its lawns, its abstract statue and the students chatting in front of the château. As he went past, he saluted the Maison des Quatrans, the remains of Vaugueux, St Pierre and went down to the Orne by the *Avenue du 6 Juin,* on a day which was brilliantly scented with the smells of the beginning of the world. At the bridge over the canalised river, he braked violently and threw Valerie against the windscreen. But the avenue was empty.

215

Caen, powdered over with white dust, presented a dismal picture to the truck drivers. Wires sagged sadly down from the topsy-turvy telegraph poles. At the side of a blown-out Tiger tank, a kid's bike was standing, its front wheel buckled. With a fearsome din, a bulldozer was driving a passage through the debris, sending papers flying. The two Abbeys, the *Abbaye des Hommes* and the *Abbaye des Femmes,* spoke to each other above the shambles. It was Sunday. An old lady in black came out of a broken-down cottage, holding her missal closely against her dried-up bosom. With great care she locked her front door, although there was a hole in the wall you could drive a horse through! The Canadians called to her. The bells rang out, bells amongst the ruins. Bells of Caen, your ringing metal tears the spirit! ... The old woman had a brave smile. The trucks roared past. Caen stank of death. And even so, the bells rang out their full peals. They stopped. In a roofless church from which you could look at a hoped-for heaven, a thin priest with a sour face was saying mass. The Canadians were singing in accents as rustic as flour sacks.

> O Canadiens, rallions-nous,
> Auprès du vieux drapeau,
> Symbole d'espérance
> Ensemble, crions à genoux
> Vive la France.

In the nave, civilians were weeping warm tears for their free, ruined town.

He turned the steering wheel violently this time to avoid a genuine vehicle, and the past vanished. The road climbed. Abel accelerated. It was good to bowl along this interminable road which once they had taken such a time to cover, mostly on foot. Jacques had found more comfortable boots after he had been decisively bawled out by Sergeant Benjamin. They had been greeted coolly. A story like that could end in a court martial! We'll keep an eye on you, my lads! Higher up the chain of command, Petitjean had also been well and truly reprimanded. He did not appear until forty-eight hours later, with a wounded arm. He was a fine sight, was Petitjean, encased in a green and grey layer of mud and pebbles, with dust stuck to his eyebrows and a varicoloured beard. He was so dirty, you would not have thought he came from this war, but from the previous one!

Soon, Abel and Valerie came back to the river. A railway ran along parallel to the road. He felt once again the contrast which had struck him so forcibly between the murderous wide open fields to the north of Caen, and these tiny plots, scooped out of living light amongst the hedgerows where the infantryman could look after himself. Abel slowed down and stopped in front of a whitewashed fence. A brown and white cow mooed close to a dead willow.

I believe that this is the valley. Close by, there's a village...

'These are the co-ordinates,' Lieutenant Petitjean would have added, in his high-pitched voice. Petitjean, Jacques and the past entrapped Abel, at the intersection of space and time.

The strain of the search had hardened his expression, giving him an antique nobility, the rough beauty of primitive masks or the busts of Saïs, of ancient Crete or the Etruscans, or the great ages of ancient China. The rain, sun, sea and wind had finally succeeded in bronzing his recalcitrant skin, which was peeling off in pink streaks, uncovering tiny precious veins in the material from which this manly head had been hewn.

With the windows down, and the roof open, they went slowly along. An open car overtook them like the wind and the passengers made angry gestures. The wildly growing oats had spread over the milestones. The road followed the capricious route of the cool river which slipped along from wash-houses to mills and rubbish tips, reversing in its mirror the willows, like full-bottomed wigs, on its banks. This countryside in all its caprices was like Bérangère. Like Bérangère when . . .

The beating of his heart quickened.

He suddenly read a half-effaced name on a signpost, engraved in letters and figures which went back to the time of horse travel.

ANGERVILLE

2 Km 7 hm

The valley widened. Soon the village appeared. Abel stopped on the shoulder of the road, got out, on to the verge which had been disfigured by greasy papers. This, then was the village called Angerville. At a first, and overpowering, impression, it seemed to him too tiny. But the bombardments which had defoliated the countryside had also changed its configuration. What's more, the flooding altered the major contrasts between the earth and the sky. And then this smart tourist route, outlined in green on the map, was not their road. The old military road had slid across the open plain, through this vast shallow depression which today was stretched out under the high tide of the ripe corn. His heart beat too hard. He didn't like it. He didn't like the silence of the intelligence services.

Abel had been relying on the belltower. Yes. This could be it, this unusual structure, a belfry made up from two superimposed pieces, the lower one squat, ancient, heavy, in contrast to the other which was airy, fragile, delicate in its octagonal spire. The slope downwards of the roofs of the choir, the apse and the porch was typical as well, as if the church had gone up without pride, a cousin to the barns the nearer it reached down to the peasants. In his memory, however, the belfry had been more slender, blue, and the roofs were brown. Now, the roofs of Angerville were all blue. The descent of the roofing timbers like a staircase no longer

218

seemed to him to be the same. The rhythm was less acute, less evident. 'You're thinking, you're thinking,' Bérangère would have said. Little trollop! Why did she have to uncover her poor little life as a woman with too much freedom who no longer believed in anything? *Don't think of this young woman any more. She's played her part. Now she's vanishing away.* Well, things were coming back to him. More than he had ever thought possible. Thus, as far as the difference in the angle of the roofs was concerned, he had to account for the fact that he was now looking at the village from a higher position. At the level of the corn, would it not be different? Two tractors of a brilliant red came out of the village. A girl on a bicycle appeared. She gave them a quiet sign of greeting. She was as pink as the apple blossom underneath her kerchief which flew way, way out in the wind.

Abel exerted all his strength, collected together his re-collections, called up in himself every memory and all his will.

Shaking like a big ship at anchor, suddenly he felt his body relax. The tension fell away.

He was incapable of moving any farther into space-time.

It was collapse. His will was broken. He was thrown there like a heap of seaweed which is cast up by the last wave. He was at his equinox. Certainty had fled from him for good, just when he thought he had it in the palm of his hand. He would go no farther. Angerville was, *perhaps,* the village which he had seen rise up from the dead waters of Josaphat.

Forgetfulness now flooded back into every part of him, insinuating itself, infiltrating itself. A voice mocked at him, croaking like the crows on the railway line: 'What's the good? What's the good?' or repeating 'Sick of it, sick of it!' How had he been able to believe that he would again find in these smiling valleys of life, of birds, of carts, of fishermen, and pretty girls on bikes, how could he find here his Valley of Death?

The Valley of Death was no longer!

In spite of everything, this was good news. Death was dead. Until a new order of things. Until a newer war.

What was to be done?

The dice had stopped rolling, but their numbers were illegible. And Valerie, behind him, was imperative, cutting off all retreat.

There are few moments when a man decides, beyond recall.

He turned round.

He smiled, at peace.

He looked Valerie in the face.

'This is it.'

There was a very long pause, broken by the scream of a motor-scooter.

He was firm, easy, free and purposeful.

He added:

'Jacques never got to that church.'

Jacques died in front of the gates of the kingdom. The kingdom started on the other side of the town. He had set himself down on the Normandy coastline where the apple-trees soaked their roots in the waves and he had possession of the damp world of the high grass. She murmured: 'Jâques, Jâques, my little Jâques.' And the little word 'little' fell badly from her lips. She had lived almost long enough since the death of Jacques to have been his mother. Henceforth, she would be the mother of a boy who was fixed in the past, immobilised in his adolescence. She understood, then, with a visceral revulsion what Abel had said about Mamie of Caen, that woman expressed a natural maternity for the soldier, whatever his age. This was the thaw.

The fellows on the tractors attacked the corn. She sat on the bank with her head in her hands. Precaution was useless. The whole of Normandy came flooding in, in waves, beneath the young sun: the emerald green of the evenings in the

220

steep-banked roads, bordered with the black acid fruit of blackberries. Where Jacques had cut his face, the damp green of the woods which were like the velvet coat of a gigantic game warden, and Jacques had slept among the trees. It was an immense undulating tapestry, in a green like the celebrated *verdures* of Bayeux and Angers, where each thread was a tree, the discreet apple-trees, the chestnuts in the blue shade, the taciturn beeches, the airy green of the acacias, silvered with the Italian poplars, erect as the distaff of a fair-haired queen, the tinny green-grey of the willows near to the slow rivers where the fishermen dozed in their punts, the glass-green of the rivers in their mossy culverts with the sharp sparkling waters in which trout pass like memory itself. Jacques had been an endless sleeper in the shadow of the chestnuts, the soldier tramping over the mossy bridge. Jacques had seen the trout leaping. But Jacques had never gathered the red apples of the discreet apple-trees. He had been stopped when the apples were green. He had never been as far as the village.

All discretion gone, she sobbed.

'Jâques, Jâques, my little Jâques. Jâques, oh Jâques. My big Jâques, little Jâques!'

She was mumbling with mouth to the ground.

'My God, send me Your grace! Have pity on me. Send me grace from the seat of Grace, as our fathers asked when they left for Canada. Dear God . . . Do not let me weep in front of this man. Abel has always spoken of the Valley of Death, of Josaphat, and then he gives me this lovely garden! Have pity on me, God!'

Abel remained useless, stricken as a butcher who had killed badly.

All the sunlit greenery of the abodes of Pan entered with force into Valerie, subjugating her, pummelling her, possessing her; the green of water, green of opal, oyster green,

Rouen blue, the green of that beetle which, between the woman's face, scarcely two inches from the ground, and Abel's huge feet, went on with its beetle's life, organically, irresistibly, eternally a beetle. Tears brought out all the lightness, the freshness, the mists, the fogs, the fine rains, the transparent skies, and the pale milky greens of the Norman dawns. She was chewing a blade of grass, dampened by the last shower. She spat it out raised herself on one arm. Abel went to her. She nearly shouted and he recoiled.

I must finish off this woman. Just as it should have been finished with . . .

He turned pale with horror. Yes! Yes! Abel ought to have been finished off. This was the first time that he had dared to tell himself it. No one had had the courage for it . . .

A small wall ran round the cornfield. They went to it and sat down. Her lower lip, usually so thin, sometimes scornful, sometimes cruel, was swollen with grief, human at last.

'Is he in the cemetery?' she murmured.

He shook his head.

Come now, we must have done with this now, and shout the truth about the death of Jacques, since he had not been master of himself sufficiently to invent a decent death, acceptable, comforting for the survivors! He must pour it all out, now that Valerie is beginning to ask questions again. A feeling of hatred rose up in him against this almost ageing woman, with her reddened eyes, her pretty blue frock with white polka dots, and a wave at the hem. A hatred against Eve, the evil companion, the usurper, she who, long, long ago, took the place of the wonderful Lilith.

'I've told a lot of lies, Valerie. But I could not do anything else. First, when we got here with the party, I was ashamed of this Normandy which had changed so much. I was like Tom Thumb when he threw out crumbs of bread and the birds ate them up. Previously, in Quebec, I did not recount it. Not all of it. Here, what I had to tell you was becoming too horrible. Do you understand?'

'No!'

'Ah! Well, you've got this obsession about finding a grave. A grave which does not exist.'

She crumpled up a damp handkerchief, her head lowered, her neck bare.

'Why did you not explain it to me earlier?'

'I must have changed my skin, like a snake. I even think that it happened to me last night, but that's another story. Look, Valerie, between the bend in the river and the bell-tower, the village was circled with water. The railway was cut in ten places, impassable. An armoured train was hanging from a broken bridge. The road we're now on, I don't know whether it even existed. The engineers had unrolled another road, which passed across the village, and which came to *terra firma* again two miles farther on. Altogether about three and a half miles long. Jacques saw the church, but he never went into the village. Jacques died. Jacques died along this road, which provisioned the armies in the Falaise pocket.'

Christ, other people's deaths really give a man a thirst!

'You've heard of the Patton Road, haven't you? This was like it.'

She did not understand anything. He had to explain everything to her, step by step.

'It was Patton who launched the slogan: "A pint of gas is worth a pint of blood." We nick-named him Old Blood and Guts. Well, after Caen, a pint of petrol really was worth a pint of blood. Do you understand? Every vehicle which broke down was immediately thrown on to the soft shoulder, in the places on the road where it narrowed to a single track. Here, the road was only single track. I must tell you about it again. After our adventure on the landings, we have been put back together and . . .'

A lark passed over very high.

'. . . and Jacques became a driver.'

With her eyes wide open, she looked at the plain, and the moist corn, shining under the sun, which a light breeze was

223

sweeping in a brown wave, the cottage gardens, the orchards, the river banks and the smiling village, the village which was never reached by the truck driven by Jacques Lafleur.

CHAPTER IV

A JOLT threw them against each other and their guns clashed together. The wagons of the armoured train stood out clearly on the railway. The first and the last trucks had remained on the permanent way while the trucks in the centre were hanging down like an enormous bicycle chain.

'Let me drive,' said Jacques. 'You won't get thrown about so much.'

With Jacques, you always got this damned annoying petty boasting.

Four in the afternoon! The sun was burning on the road. One thing they thought amusing was to place a burning hot helmet on the hand of a dozing neighbour. God! he'd jump! What a laugh! The column was stretched out through the dust. Now and again it would be passed by convoys coming in the opposite direction. Then there were catcalls, yells, animal shouts, cusses, followed by a general collapse of those who had stood up in order to yell more loudly as the movement of the clutch threw them violently onto their seats. Since the road was not very wide, it was necessary to slow up at each meeting. Then the heat mingled with dust. At first, they pointed out to each other the sunken carcasses of animals, but at the first human corpses, they said nothing more.

224

From the heights of Caen, you could see, like luminous bubbles in the blue, the silver balloons, which marked out the Mulberry harbour. After, nothing! The marine convoy was away in the misty distance. A never-ending bend in the road drew the right-hand row up on to the bank and the soldiers collapsed swearing on the left-hand row. In the long sweep of the country ahead, Abel recognised the dull leaden sheen of the hostile waters.

'There it is,' he told Jacques, who had not done the run.

From here on the traffic would be on single track. Noisy jeeps, squat Dodge trucks, the laughable Ducks which sometimes allowed themselves a comical detour in the water, tanks, tankers, crane-trucks, bulldozers, transports, all went forward unceasingly.

With a grinding of brakes, the camouflaged trucks stopped. A column was coming towards them. You could see it beyond the village. It vanished into the broken-down cottages, then the first elements re-appeared on this side. Men jumped out on to the ground. Siméon was munching a steak-and-kidney pudding with his rotten teeth. A disgusting fellow!

'I could have sworn I'd already been through there,' said Jacques.

Abel made a non-committal gesture. The artificial lake took on the irregular shape of an ivy leaf out of which arose apple-trees, hedges, pylons and the savaged village. The sun glistened on the windows.

'Hey, lads! Here are the Boches!'

Three, five, eight Dodges ground on to the solid earth, shaking their loads of prisoners who were as grey as their uniforms. Siméon, who had enlisted for the duration for reasons which it was better not to explain, shouted:

'Hallo, Greater Germany, going on your travels?'

Benjamin spoke harshly: 'Shut your trap, Sim.'

Siméon was on the point of continuing; and this would not have been the first time that he had defied the red-headed sergeant. But it was not the moment for sarcasm. He contented himself with grumbling:

'They're only Boches, for Chrissake!'

Germans and Allies, vanquished and victors, all had the same earth-covered appearance. The G.I.s who guarded the Boches, with their round helmets and their kids' smiles, threw out some slangy jokes which the French-Canadians did not understand. Somewhat put out, they went back to chewing their gum.

'Hey, Piccadilly Circus this way?' asked Siméon.

The policeman worked his arm like a dummy. They all laughed, but too loudly. The road bent under their weight. Some truncated willows appeared, with their trunks engulfed in the waters. Out of a muddy crater two legs protruded, and the onlookers were continually amazed that they did not move.

The countryside exhaled an odour straight out of the Old Testament, of confused stories from the Red Sea and the Dead Sea, stories of the heavy waters and the lake of Tiberias. But what fishers of men would come here to cast their nets? Abel looked at Jacques and noticed that scornful expression on his face born of a false indifference. The face of fear. Their foreheads trickled with sweat; sweat from the heat, sweat from the tension, sweat from sea-sickness, as violent as they had experienced on the boat before the landings. This was indeed the Valley of Death. Because the Valley of Death was not that sandy stretch of lousy beaches. Death, like itself, needs the primeval swamp, cloying, like the womb. A kestrel dived on to a Tiger tank marked with the white and black cross.

'He's going for the rations,' said the indefatigable Sim.

What was the good of trying to put on a brave face? They contented themselves with wishing with all their might to be alive half-an-hour later, to have passed that stinking needle-shaped bell-tower, which came no nearer. The engine raced. And the hideous contraction returned to the pit of the stomach because the tracks were slipping. The truck slid round. It went backwards. The truck hesitated and trembled, without moving. The men went quiet. The driver's mate jumped down into the slime which splashed up as he landed. There was a good foot of it. He chucked some sacks under the caterpillars. He swore. He got back. He hung on to the running board, and signalled to the driver. First time! It slid to the right, to the left, teetered, vibrated and set off. Well! This was a free warning to the trucks behind! They all turned their necks to get a look at the vehicle immediately behind them, a tanker standing high on its wheels like a dancer.

Abel smacked his neck, crushing under his hand one of those little black insects which cling to the battledress cloth. They were cattle flies, but they preferred men.

The village was still six hundred yards away. The road was only a stony causeway across the flooded plain, supported by logs, bags of unspeakable earth, heaps of faggots, and planks laid across the deeper parts. Abel looked at it. It was better to have your attention fixed on something. He waited. The soldier is someone who is always waiting. They went on to a section of prefabricated bridge. Abel was thrown sharply forward. Time shells and percussion shells fell together. From the 155, at least! They burst in quick explosions, lifting great geysers of coffee-coloured water. The men stepped heavily on to the running board, putting their weight on to the caterpillars, slipping down, falling flat, going under. The heat of the motors rivalled the heat of the sun. Across the road, between the caterpillars and the chassis, they could see the live trout of the air playing, the fighter planes which sped into joy, into cleanness, and clean white linen.

'I'm inclined to think it rather dangerous,' said Vadboncoeur heavily.

The joke was worn out. They have even forgotten its origin. The shelling lasted for some hours. Actually for four and a half minutes. They breathed, and looked, not wishing to believe too much in the miraculous silence. A crow cawed.

They were bringing back a driver with a bleeding shoulder wound.

Petitjean gave the orders in his pansy voice. Jacques was to replace the driver and he was not happy about it. 'Fine, then we can rely on Sophie.' Sophie was the name of the truck. He re-adjusted his equipment and floundered through the mud. Abel picked out the village with the old church as through binoculars. On the right, there was a corner of a meadow and the cows were poisoning themselves by grazing on seeding grasses with flowers of a nauseating yellow. With swollen udders, they were lowing pitifully. There were apple-trees at thirty yards, at the side of a bank of earth. The men got back. The motors coughed and started. All of them. A miracle.

The village showed them a black gap which they had not noticed before, an open jaw to swallow them, a huge barn which the engineers had gutted to win a couple of hundred yards. The sappers had not bothered to knock down the walls and the roof, so the road passed underneath its roof timbers. They breathed awhile. They started to laugh.

And, all at once, it started again! This time, it was serious. The vehicles got bogged down, slipping in the treacherous waters. At the back, a high blue flame rose higher even than the tall poplars. The explosions lingered in their guts. Abel waited, with his nose to the ground, his world reduced to this cluster of dandelions whose flowers were sticky with sump oil. Swinish Germans! Scum! Shells burst round him. Men coughed, spat, choked and were blinded. Then it became calm, in a riot of spattering fireworks. The greenish mist mingled with the smoke which a ragged sun was unable to disperse. A group of sappers, laden with tools, came out of the village. As well as the tanker-lorry which was roaring into flame, a transport had been struck. In front of them, lying on its side, half engulfed in the mud, it was showing its cater-pillars. 'Sophie!' Abel slipped, ran, waded and bustled Petit-jean out of the way.

228

'Jacques! Jacques!'

Where it was lying, *Sophie,* or the shell which had hit it, had ripped up part of the road. For some yards, the pre-fabricated road was slanting crazily and he had to take hold of the sharp edges of the grill from which lumps of muddy concrete were falling. Abel went relentlessly onwards, on all fours. A mechanic lent him a hand.

'What about Lafleur? The driver?' he asked, haggard.

But there was Benjamin, the N.C.O., with eyes that were too blue and a red moustache.

'Leclerc, go back to your truck!'

Abel was looking stupidly at *Sophie,* which was even more deeply embedded in the mud at the back. The sapper officer came running up. Petitjean, behind them, was panting. He also clambered up like a crab on to the metal trellis.

The sapper officer was an English-Canadian, a precise and cold giant. For a week now, he had seen nothing *like* this shambles. He seemed to consider the matter as a simple matter of military traffic control.

'Jacques, Jacques, Jacques!'

The first vehicle was already revving up, shooting out a stream of burning gas. Abel, clinging to the mudguard saw Jacques at last. His trunk was coming out of the mud. He was ashen. Abel felt that he was on the point of disappearing. Behind him, someone was explaining in a sepulchral voice: 'The other one's underneath. You can't see him any more.' But where were Jacques's legs? There was just no room there for legs! Jacques's eyelids were closing. He looked so old, so pale, so tortured! Petitjean called out!

'Leclerc, get back to your truck. That's an order!'

Jacques yelled out.

'They've done for me! Kill me! Kill me! Kill me! Kill me, you cowards! Abel, kill me! Abel, Abel, Abel!'

Abel clambered forward, and put a foot on a stone. It held. He wished to slip behind Jacques. No good! The stone turned over and his boots plunged into the mud up to his knees. The screams of the wounded man were terrible.

'Stop!' the doctor shouted.

Two medics shouted. Everyone yelled at once. The convoy officer was bellowing at Petitjean. The quack, holding on with one hand, was attending to the wounded man with the other, hanging over him like a monkey. The Medical Corps badges on his new uniform shone. From beneath Jacques, red mud rose up.

'We must press on at once,' said the convoy officer.

'*At once,*' the sapper officer affirmed.

'You can't go on with a wounded man under you.'

'Cut away the reeds,' said Petitjean.

'No,' said the big phlegmatic man with the red face. He signalled.

'What are you doing?' asked Petitjean.

'Bulldozer.'

'Swine!'

Petitjean's fist smashed the sapper lieutenant full in the face. He reeled back some yards, put his hand to his belt and, somewhat regretfully, pulled out his revolver and slipped the safety catch. Petitjean looked at his grazed knuckles. His face had a childlike expression of distress. You could have thought he was going to cry. The sapper officer, who had not put his revolver away, spoke in a very slow French.

'You're out of your mind, lieutenant,' he said.

The convoy officer, who knew Petitjean, and was also from the Chauds, dropped his arms. The doctor stopped feeling under the water, spoke to the medics and vomitted. Jacques groaned.

Then, the bulldozer appeared in front of them, out of the darkness of the barn.

The doctor stripped an arm and gave an injection, held up by his aides. He got back, jumped down on to the road, breathing deeply, and exchanging an eloquent glance with the sapper officer, he looked at the others. The men watched the officers, who stared at each other.

230

'How long would it take to pull it out?' asked Petitjean in a strained voice.

'Three hours.'

The clatter of the bulldozer was becoming deafening. The engineer officer whistled. The bulldozer stopped, twenty yards away. Jacques had almost lost consciousness from the effect of the jab. He murmured:

'Abel . . .'

'Is it bad?'

'Better now.'

'We'll get you out.'

'Three minutes,' said the engineer officer, his face set, the lower lip protruding.

Dumbfounded, Petitjean looked at the chief of the convoy. A motorcyclist slipped between the stationary wagons. Petitjean slowly dropped his hands. The quack had already gone off. Benjamin repeated, without conviction: 'Get back to your truck. Go forward. Help no one. Leclerc! Leclerc! I'm talking to you.' A flare burst overhead and came slowly down. Jacques had closed his eyes. He was sleeping. A mad desire to get it over took hold of all of them. He's done for, done for! We can't let the rest get slaughtered! The flare was a signal to the Boches' gunners. They're going to start up again! Off! Get cracking! He's dead, for God's sake!

Abel jumped on to the road and waved.

'Take him away,' said Petitjean.

The contact of hands brought Abel out of his stupor. He shook off the men's grip, screaming in rage.

'Jacques! Jacques! Swine! Swine! Swine!'

Four husky privates pulled him away from the front of the wagon where he had clambered. They didn't exert all their force. Abel pushed, shook himself free, ran down on to Benjamin in a rush of fury. The N.C.O. knocked him down with the butt of his revolver. Abel lost balance and fell into the mud. They picked him up. 'Don't be a fool, man!' Sergeant Benjamin sadly studied his gun.

231

The sapper officer climbed on to the bulldozer. The roar of the motor became unbearable. Another flare burst over the apple-trees. The bulldozer ground its way forward, shoved, disengaged and crunched forward again. The wagon resisted firmly, then shivered, rose slowly up, stood on end, huge, like the circus elephants who wave their forelegs to the big top. The members of the convoy, armed with crowbars, pushed feverishly, helping the bulldozer. There were twenty of them to shove Private Jacques Lafleur to his death.

With an incredible slowness, the wagon over-balanced and was swallowed up.

The marshy waters boiled with huge yellow bubbles which broke the surface of the loathsome water.

Going in reverse, the bulldozer went back to the village. The engines snorted with happiness and followed it, nose to nose, as if they were shoving each other impatiently forward.

Stretched out on the floor of the truck, his head full of lightning strokes, Abel lay on his back. Above him he saw the stormy sky seem to wobble. The jolting movement bruised his back. Abel realised that he was alive and, in spite of the horror, was happy to be alive. To be shaken like this, he was going to let go, he was going to fall into the sky, into the spot where the flash of an early fused shell was visible, while the bombardment began again, farther off, uncertain, irregular, ranging on the mutilated willows beside the river.

'SHE MADE love with the light on.' It was an insult to say that of a woman in virtuous Quebec! Bébé made love *only* with the light on! And Valerie? This idiotic idea crossed his mind, settled in it, turned obstinately like the red tractors in the plain. I am talking about Jacques's death and I come up against a woman who wants to make love with the light on. Bébé, the light on, but not too brightly. And Valerie? And Valerie? In a farm, a man with a heavy Mongoloid head was playing a harmonica. The others were drunk with a nostalgia for the countryside. They pined for their prairies. Night thickened in the parallelogram door of the open barn. A peasant with a head like a pig, nicknamed Cinderella, was beating time on a saucepan. A horseshoe was swinging, hanging from a beam beside a string of onions. These were the Chauds, at rest. The Chauds, after Falaise. I never knew that these were my family. Now, I'm an orphan. An orphan since '45. An odour of sweetness rose from the swarming elderberries.

Abel sighed, amid the full triumphal summer.

'I was only nineteen, Valerie! When I see boys of nineteen today, I no longer understand anything. We play at war with kids. Even if they weigh two hundred pounds! A week later, I woke up in a field hospital. A good sign, there were nursing sisters there. One, a brunette, said to me: "Falaise has been taken." I didn't give a damn for Falaise. When they asked me

233

how Jacques Lafleur died, I had to make an effort. I did not remember about it. Everything had melted away. Like a handful of sand. I saw nothing any more, nothing but the plain, the road, the clattering trucks, the belfry with its two slopes and Sergeant Benjamin, cussing sadly. But all that meant nothing to me! I was sick of it all! Sick of it!'

He thought of Bébé, of her: 'Sick of it, sick of it.'—like an incantation. Poor little sister ...

'Shocked,' said Valerie, seriously.

She certainly would never change! People don't change.

'That's what I was told. As I came out of hospital, I went on a long soak. They took me back there completely drunk. I was cured. Valerie, I'm thirty-six. I'm a brute. Oh, yes, you've thought so a hundred times. Well, now, I often awaken in the dead of night, covered with sweat! Once more I see the wagon standing up like an animal. There was Sophie, the name painted on top in white, in a flowery scroll. I can see Sophie again, I can feel the chassis. I hear Jacques. The shout: "I'm coming." And I can't move. I'm the one who's being sucked under. I move my legs. I'm floundering. I cannot go on. I'm being swamped by *today!'*

He raised his head. His expression, from being inward-looking, now turned outwards. And his focus sharpened.

'The report left the sombre story of Jacques right in the shade. Driver Lafleur? Oh, he was already dead. Or it's like . . . Anyhow, as far as we're concerned, we'd seen nothing. Nothing at all! Just as though there hadn't ever been a Sophie on the side of the road, or a tough sapper lieutenant, or his diabolical bulldozer or the German artillery to set the game going! I came across Petitjean later, in the Rhineland, because he had been posted. We had a cigarette together without saying ten serious words. We couldn't. And that's all there was to it.'

Slowly, they went to the car.

'On my way back to the regiment, I passed by here. The water had gone down and the immense dried crust of earth

234

was cracking. Many vehicles which had come to grief were being cleared away. There was no trace of Sophie.'

A mirror was fixed inside the sun visor. She turned it to her and wondered who this woman was with the face of stone.

'Did you see *Mrs. Miniver*?'

'The English film with the woman among the roses, and her children who went off to war ... ?'

'That's right. Well, women look at war like Mrs. Miniver. Good red blood when one is wounded, a bullet clean between the eyes when you have the bad luck to die. Well, it's our fault. We have lied about it since the stone ages. We never told them: "Your son died with six feet of gut sticking out of his belly and he screamed like a stuck pig." Never! So they build for themselves the peaceful image of the soldier's death. It allowed the older of them to carry on presiding over their societies and left the younger ones with the hope of taking their place.'

'Let's go, please, Abel.'

He drove slowly. It had done him good. It kept the beast in him quiet. He just had to talk now, merely to fill in time.

'There were some formations where they gave strict orders of secrecy. But everything is always known. Patton was the prototype, Old Bloody! He always kept his smart revolvers at his belt, revolvers with pearl handles, encrusted with jewels, fabulous, just like they were in the time of Buffalo Bill. Even in Buckingham Palace, he did not take them off. A clown! Or an actor, rather! Patton, the man who thought he was Patton. I saw him once. At a couple of yards range. Scornful. Men, for him, were dummies. He said one day that our names would be written in history on the monuments for the dead. He was a cynic who forgot that the names of ordinary soldiers are only inscribed on monuments in their own villages.'

The town of the living appeared in the centre of its crown of orchards, displaying its shady tree-lined square, the bronze column surmounted by a weathercock, and the church shooting its spire with two slopes up to its sky. Valerie listened, sorting through her memories. She did not know how to interpret or understand. She had travelled right through this story in which she had played an important role, without understanding it.

'General Patton, himself, wrote his name in History,' Abel went on. 'I saw him in a photo at the Gates of War, at Arromanches. But not Jacques! General Patton is dead, he broke his neck in a car accident in Germany, in December '45, at the age of sixty. A broken neck. I often wonder how, for he didn't have one. There was his star-studded jacket and then, straightaway, his helmet! This is what he used to say, brave old General Blood and Guts! I used to recite to the lads to give them a laugh. "Soldiers, all Americans like the turmoil of battle. You're here for three reasons. First, to defend your hearths and those whom you love." Who's he kidding, between Caen and Falaise! "Second, for self-respect, because you would not want to be anywhere else and real men like a fight." That brought out a general laugh from the real men who liked a fight! Patton, General Patton. In August 1943, he met a fellow who'd had a nervous breakdown and knocked him down, saying he was a coward!'

'Let's get out. I'd rather be sitting at a table outside some café.'

There was an inn ahead of them, with brown half-timbering, straw-coloured rough-cast, pointed roofs, tables with red and white check cloths, everything washed, waxed, painted and completely Norman. It was called the *Reine Mathilde.*

'Why do you speak to me about Patton, Abel?'

'Because Patton is war! He used to train his men to endure the extremes of heat, with nothing to eat or drink, in the Desert Centre at Indio! March or bust. What a fine German general he would have made. Patton equals Rommel, Rommel equals Patton, same number of letters, same structure to the name. The only difference between the two was

236

that the Barbarian was more civilised than the civilised! I can still see the swine ...'

Hatred had not diminished in sixteen years.

'... engaged in his fraternity of arms, as they say. Round face. Wide, short neck, hard little eyes. Silver hair, close-cropped. Smelling of the bathroom. Little teeth like grains of rice. Four stars on his helmet. All that no longer stops him sleeping.'

Abel thought a moment. 'Just wait a minute, darling, and I'll tell you about the Liberation of France.'

'There was a pipe like the large intestine, which was rolled out from the coasts of England on a huge floating drum. Petrol went from the trucks straight to the front line troops. Bulldozers gutted villages to gain a hundred yards. Valerie, Jacques's appalling death was war, true war. Guerre, Krieg, Guerra, call it what you will.'

Mad Meg, sword in her hand, passed by. He drank from his milk, and made a face.

'It's pretty bad.'

He asked the waitress if there had not been an engineer's road across the village during the war. But the girl was not a local.

Valerie was regaining her composure. This was evident from the way in which she ate, agreeing to find acceptable the *omelette aux champignons* and the *caneton à l'orange*. Well, a good job well done. But she remained pitiful in her statuesque beauty. He was sick of being with her.

'It would have been better if I had been left behind,' he said.

He read in the woman's blue eyes a calm 'Yes.'

He shook himself. No! That was really too unjust. To hell with pity!

'I still sometimes see the German. He comes out of the bunker. Listen to me, Valerie. He is running. He is flaming. The flames reach up a yard above his head. The flame is blue at the bottom and white at the top. You don't understand.

237

The Boche continues to run. Poor old Boche! You wouldn't
have thought it possible to run so far. And he falls down into
a heap of carbon, with a smell of roasting. How do you like
your meat, eh? Well done or rare?'

She lit a filter-tip cigarette, with the deliberate gesture of
one who is desperately trying to keep control.

'I ask your pardon, Abel. I've been thinking some frightful
things and you guessed them.'

'Thirty yards and charcoal at the end!'

She put her hand on Abel's hairy paw. Valerie's hand was
dry, but the gesture was significant.

'But you're the one who's right, Valerie! Oh yes! I ought
to have been gobbled up by the shrimps, on the sixth of June.
What good am I? You've said it. I drink perroquets. I sleep
with Bérangère and I know that she's been with others, many
others, and she'll see a lot more of them after me. So what? I
am nothing. I do nothing. I don't like myself. I don't believe
in anything. I no longer believe in God, and I'm too much of
a coward!'

His voice became harsh, heavy, emphatic, with fanatical
inflections, now brutally revealed in this apparently apathetic
man.

'If there is no God, there are only two solutions. One must
continue respecting man as if he were God. Or blow out one's
brains. I've done neither one thing nor the other. Ah, yes,
you're right, Valerie. I should have stayed behind.'

'I never said that!'

'You thought it.'

'I did.'

'When? When we went to Arromanches? In front of that
boat? You remember . . . boat *We Three*?'

'Yes, I thought: "Why is it he who is here?" '

'I knew it! Have you often thought this?'

'Yes.'

'In Quebec?'

'Yes.'

'Before we decided to come on this trip?'

'Yes.'

'On that day of the wasps?'

'Yes. I thought distinctly: "Why is it this one who's come back?" I hated you! Abel! you have always been good. It's unusual for a woman to have been as unjust to a man as I have been to you. But what poisoned everything was that you were the one to announce his death. Abel, I don't know how I'm going to live with this new knowledge. It's something quite different. I am overwhelmed. You just can't believe that war is like that. That's how it is, then. This . . . this vileness...When...when the world is so beautiful!'

She made a gesture with two hands, as if she were caressing and holding to her the smart tables, the lime-trees, the war memorial, the village of Angerville, the church in the middle of the churchyard and was presenting it all to heaven. Her hands fell.

'The bill, mademoiselle,' he said.

'Yes, monsieur,' said the waitress. And she lifted up her little snub nose as if she were answering quite another question. 'And what you asked me earlier. About the floods . . .'

He stopped. His broad, bent shoulders awaited the axe blow.

'The guv'nor asked the chef's wife. She was the first to come back in '44, with the priest. It's true, there was a military road. In the floods. You ought to ask the teacher who's also the mayor's secretary.'

He pressed a crumpled bill into the girl's hand. There! It's finished! Settled up and paid. On all counts. They would never know anything more.

ABEL ORDERED a glass of milk. The record player gave out another version of *Mustapha.* The jingle now, through the fluttering addition of an Arab flute, took on a penetrating quality, a sense of dignity, the melancholy of the exile. At one extremely old-fashioned house, the *Hotel d'Armorique,* the sad little Araby of the Vaugueux chanted its song in the midst of the robust Norman indifference. At a neighbouring table, were some young men, masons and painters, all from the building job, who were soaking up cider, speaking very loud. One dark young man in particular, who was tight.

'So she said: "Nothing doing tonight." I wouldn't get my bit. I said: "Come on out, the weather's fine. There'll be a moon." '

The laughter was delightfully salacious.

'Wait! wait!' The girl went home all the same! I didn't know how it would turn out! The boy was right opposite. I went in it. The bitch! In the meantime, the old woman had come up.'

'And then?'

'Nothing. Just a hell of a row!'

Abel asked: 'Are they talking *patois*?'

Bérangère laughed. 'Only the old ones speak *patois* nowadays.'

'Your pal's late. Does she know where to find us?'

'She's always lived round here. She's called Fleur. You'll see, it'll be all right.'

He wanted to question her about Fleur, but he held back. It was always better not to question Bérangère. One always learned a lot more from her spontaneity. Too much, sometimes. However, this girl who was now beside him was *his* Bérangère, amused, roguish. A girl with whom one would prefer to live much longer than for a few chance weeks on a foreign shore, a green fairy of the waves, a princess of the sea, the Norman Tanagra, broken and mended afresh. The difference between the girl he had met the other night and his companion of today had become inconceivable. When was she herself? Which was the true one? *Stupid question. She's both of them. With women, the principle of a separate identity does not apply.*

'Pour some *cassis* in my milk.'

Yahia, a red-blond Berber with frizzy hair, and blue wrinkled eyes, repeated: '*Cassis?*' Incredulous; then he picked up the bottle and poured it out.

'Like that?'

'More.'

Disgusted, Yahia considered the mixture. Bérangère burst into laughter.

At the bar, stone masons were showing each other photographs. One of them fell to the floor. Abel picked it up. It showed two cupids in a Renaissance style. The sculptor had been freely inspired by the attenuated elegance of Jean Goujon, and his work was contemporary and old-fashioned at the same time, quite out of fashion.

'The château's of the same period as the one at Anet,' explained the young man in the overalls. 'They've asked me to replace some of the pieces which disappeared during the war.'

He spoke naturally about the 'last' war. For him, it must seem far away! Bérangère leaned her cheek against Abel's arm. Well, the sculptor was certainly young. Twenty?

241

Twenty-one? He was sporting a small brown beard, under his lower lip, like those worn by the Francs Tireurs of 1870. Bébé smiled at these two lovers who were standing arm in arm.

'You're happy,' said Abel.

'Happy?' said the stone mason, in surprise. 'Yes. At least, I would be happy if it weren't for my military service just round the corner. It's me for the hills!'

Attention, attention, attention! Nothing is irrelevant. No detail must remain uncovered. Precise explanations can come from anywhere. Alert to all services. To all units. General Alert. Look particularly at these two cupids arm in arm . . . winged cupids arm in arm. Winged cupids . . .

There were, indeed, two winged cupids, of a deliberate crudity of technique, of the same *genre* as the sculpture of Bourges, Rheims or Strasbourg. But these were perfectly formed. They had nothing of the character of the big-bottomed cupids of the Regency or baroque periods. These were a pair of adolescents, a boy and a girl, beautiful in their slenderness. The two figures, side by side, had interlinked their arms and each held the fist of the other hand solidly against their thighs. They leaned together with arms, shoulders and wings forming one corner-piece of stone. Set at right angles, each to the other, their wings formed an indestructible block.

Bérangère gave the picture back to the sculptor.

'May we see the stone?' asked Abel.

'Certainly. I'm finishing a replica of it for the Château. It's still on the plinth. A light limestone. A wonderful grain! Is this your line?'

'No.'

'You need only ask for "The Song of Roland" ,' said his friend. 'He's Roland. And he sings all the time. So we've nicknamed him "Song of Roland." Or else Barbiche. Or Bibiche.'

'I envy you,' said Abel. 'Above all, because you can invent

242

two figures, who are holding each other by the arm, knotted together like rope, yet they will hold something very heavy up above them.'

He resumed his self-depreciating tone: bitter, slightly theatrical.

'As for me, I sell the wind. I sell words.'

'Well, mademoiselle,' said Roland, alias Bibiche, 'if he sells words, he doesn't do too badly at it. Monsieur, you've just explained to me what I've been doing. I did not know before. I mean it, you know!'

It started up again, as with the fisherman, as with the little boy. An unnatural, honeyed halation surrounded the customers of this odd little bistro tucked away in the old warm streets. The little square window panes gleamed brightly. Marie-Thé, the tart, would perhaps come in and say: 'Well, good evening, here you are then, Canada!' Or it might be Mamie: 'Beautiful boy, come on!' A beautiful boy, who'd take three minutes to deal with, like the little marines.

'I didn't invent the idea,' said Roland. 'I just happened upon it on a scrap of drawing paper, in Rouen Museum. A piece of sanguine. It wasn't terribly clear, but I saw it in these two cupids. Like spots of ink ...'

If she had been there, Valerie would have said: 'Rorschach test!'

But the symbol of the two figures with linked arms did not escape him. And this was the symbol which afflicted the Canadian, harrowing him like the death of Jacques. It falls ill with men to glimpse the ideal.

'Your friend's taking her time.'

'Fleur promised me. She's a good little bourgeoise; not scatterbrained like me. I've lost the address of her new flat.'

'Listen, Bébé,' said Abel, rousing himself. 'You've been the smartest of girls. You must tell me the rest. The rest about Jacques.'

She answered him. 'Because you want to go back?'

'I can't stay here for ever.'

Why couldn't he stay here for ever with Bérangère and the liberated population of Normandy, such as they are, the confused song of the Arabs, the sculptors and the boastful masons? Why did he not think of settling himself in this land where the lovers linked arms? General Intelligence sent instantaneous signals. *'Nothing doing! Impossible. We will answer for nothing. Remember the bad sister. She would want to be one of the two angels; without doubt. But she cannot. Unstable. Incurable. Incurable. Bérangère equals Maya. Beware of illusions. Your life is elsewhere. I say again.*

'My life is elsewhere, Bérangère.'

She pursed her lips. The way in which she had posed the question showed that she did not really believe in it.

'One had ties, you understand, Bébé. One is tied. One has one's roots in a country. You can't please yourself. You're unhappy, but you're at home. You're not in exile. Here, I'd become an exile. A vagabond. You're tied. You say you're free. But you're tied. D'you understand?'

'I understand. But not me. That must be what is wrong with me. Not being tied enough.'

He leaned over and stared at the table. His shining bronzed skull glistened. He muttered some stumbling words.

'I don't think that you're a one-man woman.'

'That's true,' she murmured. 'Every man wants a one-man woman.'

Two Arabs got up, and stared at the street through the bottle-glass windows. At one side, the loud-mouth went on with his tale.

'Well, the other night, that was it! There was a w.c. but there wasn't any water. She noticed at the last minute. So she had to go to the fountain! And then, this popsie said to me: "What's your job?" As true as I'm standing here! And me, I said: "I'm a plumber."'

A Rabelaisian laugh swept the company. The cider jugs were refilled. Bébé made a move.

'We can't stay here for ever. I'll just leave word with Yahia in case Fleur turns up.'

They said goodbye to the two masons. The young man with the beard smiled at Bérangère and Bérangère returned it. She smiled at men. She was like that. She was a free woman. The stone figures of the loving angels who together held up a load marked the frontier of a forbidden land. However, Abel was never to forget the image which had been carved by the friendly twenty-year-old mason who could make a thousand of them; this image of two cupids who linked arms to support something heavier than they.

Abel had a physical love for Caen, so close was it to his own Quebec. It did not worry him to have to seek out Fleur. What was there anyway to expect from in anything that concerned Jacques? Bérangère had no doubt yielded to feminine romanticism in imagining that Jacques had left a child on the Continent! A cheap novelettish kind of story.

An old lady in a violet headscarf was sitting on a cane chair, lying in wait for wandering tourists who stopped in front of the mansard windows.

'You're still in France,' she said.

'I should hope so,' answered Abel.

'Yes, but it's no joke to be hanging on. It's no longer the same world. Well, there you are, Bébé. You're not saying anything, Miss Silence!'

'How old are you, maman Malvina?'

'Getting on for eighty-seven. Don't worry, I like my Vaugueux well enough. I like it better than those rabbit hutches, the government puts up! I've never left it, even in '44. I was waiting for death in my bed and she didn't want me. I reckon I'll be alive for the next war!'

'Have you seen Fleur while you've been sitting here?'

'She was looking very nice in a new dress. Early in the afternoon. She went into the town. You'd have said she was a

245

princess. Today, all women look like princesses. That's what puts them on their backs!'

They went off.

'So you know this witch?'

'Malvina is a witch. But she's nice.'

'What did she do when she was younger?'

'She was the madame of a house. It was the only industry of the district.'

Bérangère as a little girl and her friend Fleur had jumped on to the knee of this Norman Celestina. Each new characteristic which was revealed to him etched in her disturbing fragile figure.

They passed by some beautiful houses of the seventeenth and eighteenth centuries, now condemned to death. Some unspeakable courtyards were revealed. Skinny dogs wandered about, foraging in the dustbins. Now and again, the new road cut like a knife through butter into the old houses. From Kouba's place, the rival of Yahia, right up to the *Hôtel du bras d'Or,* emerged a whining music and there Abel could see once more the same window-card which had amused him so much previously. 'Rooms by the month, Rooms by the night.' No doubt, Mamie had found the right spot right away!

'Will you tell me the story of Jacques and Fleur?'

'Now, look, I'm not certain. It's just an idea I've had. Will you trust me as much as Valerie?'

'In some ways, more. You've got all the nerve of the devil!'

'How d'you mean?'

'With Valerie, you always receive the notion that Valerie has of herself. But with you, you come right out with a thing. You don't beat round the bush.'

He waited for her, jostled by the passers-by. One woman, bursting with pink health, said, without batting an eyelid:

'The fool, he damn near busted my bed. You should have seen it, what with me and my hundred and sixty pounds.'

246

A picture story in a stained glass window told of a boar hunt. A spicy smell rose up from the butcher's shop. Bérangère came out at once. Nothing there. Farther on in the *rue Montoire,* she went into a bagwash. Then into a highly coloured fish shop, which featured a huge mosaic showing crayfish, giant lobsters, tunny, blue mackerel, crabs and sea-spiders. The real fish were sardines, herring, skate and shell fish from which a strong odour arose. It had not always been there. Abel tore himself away from a contemplation of the wares of the shop which superbly displayed the flesh tints of young womenhood.

'Have you made your peace with the shrimps?'

There she was his exquisite Bérangère!

Retracing these old steps reduced Abel to a state of shock. He walked round the medieval town, returning to the present with relief as they came up against the invisible transformation which marked the limit of the old part of the town. Bérangère went into a house, came out of it again and shook her head. At the end of the *rue Haute* they received, in all its brightness, the full view of the new town. A huge urban expanse opened up, in the mists of the evening. The Abbaye aux Femmes stood up haughtily. The bells of St Pierre began to chime.

'I'm going too far! I know where she is! Fleur is a bitch! She would have saved me a heap of trouble if only she'd come to Yahia's.'

They went back a few steps and she entered a courtyard. Two puny acacias with yellowing leaves were growing in the front of an ancient yellow house, where the wrought-iron work was red with rust. It began to rain, a small fine rain as sad as past time. Bérangère reappeared in a halo of copper light which burst out of the end of the dark corridor. Her smile, a smile of pure joy, contrasted with everything that Abel, for the last few days, had learned of Bérangère's life. She signed to him. He followed her, climbed up the staircase and came upon an apartment with high ceilings, only the

247

interruption of the frieze showing that it had been partitioned.

'Well, so you're the Canadian.'

Fleur was a handsome forty-year-old, a fine blonde with a touch of Titian in her hair, a big woman but supple with it, a slim waist with plump, rounded shoulders, shining with health, the same type as Mamie, but quite different from the 'sophisticate' of American glossy magazines.

'She's a beauty, isn't she, my Belle Boulangère?' said Bébé.

Belle Boulangère! Jacques had talked enough about her. It was only at Caen that Abel, through a chance remark by Vadboncoeur, learned that Jacques had bought the famous pipe, the Dunhill, the sister pipe of the one Jennifer had given him. Yes, he'd bought it! And Jacques had let it be known it came from the favours of Jennifer! Abel hadn't taken that at all kindly. He had taken against Jacques who was making a buddy of that swine, Siméon. As far as the baker's wife was concerned, there were those in the company who believed Jacques and those who didn't. Abel was among the unbelievers.

'Forgive me,' said Fleur. 'I agreed to meet you at Yahia's. At the last moment, I don't know what took hold of me. So, you're Jacques's best friend. Let me ...'

She pronounced 'Jacques' in the French manner, with the light 'a'. She went to look for cider in the refrigerator. A chill mist was deposited on the bottle. She held it out to him. He uncorked it, holding the stopper in his hand. The cider shot sparkling out, with its odour of apples.

'Bérangère's told you about me. Well, that's neither here nor there. Where does it get us? My name's Florine, Fleur Leclerc.'

He almost yelled.

'You too, eh? Bébé, you might have told me. My name's Leclerc too, madame. Oh, no, it's not possible! It would have struck him. And I should have remembered it!'

'Just a moment, now. Leclerc's my maiden name. Did you know that, Bébé?'

'No.'

'My married name is Dujardin. Was. When I knew Jacques, *my* Jacques, I was married. He would not have known my maiden name.'

The dance of uncertainties began again.

'I was married in January 1940. I was just twenty. My husband was in the 39th Rouen Regiment of Infantry. He was taken prisoner in May. That was the time I knew Bérangère best. She was no longer a little girl. How old were you in '44?'

'Fourteen. A round number fourteen in '44.'

'She was a darling. She still is! She ran about everywhere. But a little devil! Oh, yes, you were a little devil.'

'She still is,' said Abel, won over by the tender complicity of these two wounded women.

'I'll tell you all about it. Don't be frightened. Oh, yes, all you Canadians! . . .'

She also used the plural.

'My husband was a prisoner until May '45. I kept the shop going and it wasn't easy. Obviously, I never went short of bread.'

Bread! The bread of war. The bread of the Liberation. The bread of the sixth of June, which went so dry. The bread of the deserted bakery! Lucette, with her bra strap which kept falling down!

'In France we've made a bit of a fetish about the prisoners. There were two million of them and they weighed heavily, particularly on the women.'

'That's true,' said Bébé. 'Everyone called you the Belle Boulangère and they held you up as an example to the trollops who went off the rails.'

'I stayed in Caen during the Liberation. An animal life which lasted for a month. The Canadians came. We saw the first on the morning of the ninth of July. They came down from Carpiquet. For us, they were water, sun and life. Were you there?'

'Yes,' said Abel.

General Intelligence had warned, but he was too deeply immersed in the storm of memory.

'Do you know what you were for us?'

The blown roses, the roses in the helmets, the roses of Arromanches, the war which was going to burst out farther on, like a wounded beast; women, the laughter of women, the dirty kids, the handshakes of the solemn men. In the cellar, Lucette, her children and desire like a whip. The little girls who jumped on to the trucks to kiss them, some who sought the cheek and others who sought the mouth...'

'It was clear you were all happy,' he said flatly.

'Yes, well, you were gods!'

Her blue eyes sparkled.

'I don't know how it happened. I forgot that I was married, that I loved my husband, that he was in Pomerania. There was no post any more. Nothing. The houses were crumbling about us and I was twenty-four. He left a month later.'

Abel calculated quickly. Everything she said coincided with the dates and with the statements made by Jacques, about his superb...

'I found myself alone once more. Played for a fool! One day, the postman brought me a letter: *Kriegsgefangenenpost*. It was from my husband. Dated the first of June. He wanted to sell the Bakery. He asked me to send him some Flavigny *anis*. The *anis* woke me up! I was pregnant! I loathed your Canadian! Just a kid, too! That's why I didn't want to come this evening. It brought everything back and it felt bad. Anyway, it's over and done with. I put the shop in the hands of a manager and went to have the child at Port-en-Bessin. I left my little girl with a nurse. In 1945, in May, my husband came back.'

She spoke in a murmur, so low that Abel could not be sure of having properly understood her.

250

'I slept with my husband. It gave him such pleasure! Me too, you can be sure. But, in the night I confessed. He got up. He got his working apron which he'd not worn for five years; he had to tighten up his trousers with his belt. He was more handsome, thinner, with hard eyes and white teeth. I loved him to distraction, but this was not the same man. I had just made love with quite another man! I would have far preferred it if he had beaten me! He went down. An hour later, I tiptoed out of the bedroom. There were noises in the bakehouse. He had stripped to the waist and was kneading the dough. He was making bread. He made it well. It had to be really good, that bread did!'

Abel choked. The smell of the bread! The deserted bakery and the pack of famished German prisoners!

'The divorce wasn't long delayed. No one had any pity for the wives of the prisoners. He kept the bakery. Sometimes now, I see him. He greets me. It's worse than if he never noticed me. He's never remarried. Women's life is really stupid when war gets mixed up in it.'

The door opened with a gust of wind and a tall girl came in breathlessly.

'You're not at school, Gisèle?' said Fleur. 'It's all right, isn't it, at the *lycée*?'

'Finished. Not too soon, either!'

'She goes into the sixth form next year.'

It was Gisèle, daughter of the Belle Boulangère, who was no longer a baker but was still beautiful, and of a Canadian named Jacques who never came back. She was beautiful, she was tall. Her eyes were of the same blue as her mother's; yet in shape and especially in the slightly Asiatic fashion of their tilt and in her smile, she recalled Jacques. But as far as Jacques's eyes were concerned, Abel had to confess that he was unable to be certain about the hint. Blue, yes. Dark blue. Very dark? And her mouth? Her mother also had a slightly pouting mouth. Her dimples, then? Ah, yes, dimples in her cheeks, in her chin. That's the lot. Alas!—

251

'M'man, I'm going to the *Pile au Face*. Raymonde's waiting for me. She's coming with us to Port-en-Bessin. When are we leaving?'

'Monday.'

'Bye, bye. Love, m'man.'

The clatter of her heels could be heard going down the stairs, through the corridor and into the courtyard.

Abel had kept in his wallet a photograph which showed Jacques, a few friends and he himself, right in the ruins of Caen. The picture was not bad, but it was small. He held it out to Fleur. She put on glasses and studied patiently the faded photograph. A wasp banged against the window. It was beginning all over again! The Belle Boulangère took off her glasses, gave the picture to Bérangère and remained thoughtful.

'Who's this very thin lad at the right?' she said at last.

'It's me,' said Abel.

'Well,' said Bébé, 'so it is. It's you.'

The wasp was buzzing madly round in its snare.

The Belle Boulangère rose, walked a few steps, showing her slender waist and her inviting hips.

'What became of him? That one? In the photo?'

The question was its own answer. Fleur had not recognised Jacques. A woman who was merely doubtful would not have had this melancholy lack of concern, this sad smile, just like Gisèle's. The girl certainly resembled her mother. The father had passed away without leaving any traces.

'Jacques died in August,' said Abel. 'He was driving a truck.'

'How tall was her? Smaller than you?'

'Smaller?'

'Come and stand beside me.'

He hesitated.

'Go along,' said Bébé. 'She won't eat you.'

Fleur was standing beside him as beautiful as a ripe peach. She smelt wonderful. She took him by the shoulders.

252

'How much smaller? Like that? or like that?'

He no longer knew. It seemed to him that she was in his arms for a long time. He reddened. Uncertain, he looked at Bébé and Bébé had a troubled smile.

'Like this, I should think,' he said, lowering himself.

She shook her head and dropped her hands.

The wasp buzzed away. Wasps are the true colour of mourning, striped honey and black velvet.

CHAPTER VII

BIKINIS WERE drying on the bunkers. The band was out again for the fourteenth of July. Le Dernier was thundering against the electors who had voted for de Gaulle and regretting the time of the F.T.P. One day he surprised himself by saying: 'I can do just what I like when I get my holidays with pay!' And then he took courage. He had to see his pals in Nantes and St Nazaire, in the shipyards of the Loire-Atlantique! When he spoke about his friends in Loire-Atlantique, Vauthier's eyes went misty.

In the changeable splendours of the summer, half sunny, half rainy and with the flood of holidaymakers, the little world of the inn lost its individual character. It became annoying, mechanical, especially when Lucien, displaying his disgust with himself, put *Mustapha* on to the record-player. The nagging question: 'Are you certain that it happened at Angerville?' no longer disturbed him as it had done before, like a bell in a lost station. No, rather he wondered now what motivation had driven him when he had engaged himself to the pursuit, and he became angry with himself when he could not find a clear answer.

The papers carried their usual ration of catastrophes, scandals and events sufficiently bizarre to give a well-varied diet. Berlin. China. The Congo. *Skytroops leave Stanleyville. 'How my sister was raped!'—Girl's story.* Lumumba. Mau Mau. Nuclear tests. The French and the thorn in their flesh, Algeria. De Gaulle in Normandy. De Gaulle at Cherbourg. At the Arsenal. De Gaulle at Bayeux. *If you want to be happy, live in between Caen and Bayeux.* But there was also the carelessness, the 'I don't give a damn' spirit. *Russians launch man into space.* Brigitte Bardot is wearing a wig and Annette Vadim has got a divorce. *Record start to holidays— 25% Up on 1959—Rivière Gives up the Tour de France.* Crime doesn't pay and lovers are famous. In Algiers, naked bathers are machine-gunned by the *fellahin*. Torture is spoken of openly. Eichmann. Six million dead. And then the rest of it. War, like an iceberg, only displays part of itself. The huge bordello of Cherbourg, a non-man's-land of vice! Mamie's dive! The Nazis. The Nazis who massacred the Canadian prisoners, amongst them my pal Tit-Rouge. On the eighth of June 1944, in the Château d'Andrieu, prisoners from the Royal Winnipeg Rifles were murdered. There were nineteen of them. Seven others, included six from the Queen's Own Rifles. The Canadians intended to bring the criminals to justice. But of 21,000 SS there on the seventh of June, there were no more than 60 by the time of the Falaise battle.

Falaise! Falaise! On the seventeenth of August, the Canadians occupied the shambles of the town. Convoys ground the corpses into the earth. There was a thick fog. Everywhere there were green, yellow and blue flames, a black smoke, rotting horses whose bones, of a soapy yellow colour, stuck out of their burst skin. Everywhere, there were intoxicated flies. 'That's where I got my depression. That swine Patton! Old Blood and Guts!' By fits and starts, this

254

holiday among his Continental cousins brought with it highlights which shone red and then vanished. 'But certainly, it's because I've identified myself with that lad in Sicily that I hate Patton so much. This was war at its putrid worst, seen at last in all its nakedness . . . My fear, my fear in the belly since the first minute of the landing—on the charming little beach which was so very dangerous! A fear so much more difficult to bear because I did not lose my head and I had to guide Jacques about.' The prisoners who stuck so close, the madmen with the Commandant Maxime, Mad Meg, the black Guadeloupean with the razor. Margot, war and madness. Mad Meg.

Galloping towards the left in the sulphurous light of the Apocalypse, was the helmeted witch with a pointed nose, with hair streaming, with the glinting round bird's eyes. Her neck was thin and corded, her bosom dry and flat beneath the cuirasse and she was carrying the great sword into the smoking countries, perhaps in anger, perhaps in indignation, perhaps through the revolt of the peasant who has seen too much. She was still carrying her housewife's basket on her left arm. This was *Dulle Griet*. Marguérite, Margot la Folle, Mad Meg, war and madness in a single Fury. Crowding round the archers in the cauldrons, the carriers of oriflammes painted in fading rays of light, there were dwarfs brandishing a mass of arms, lewd monkeys raising pikes, the death masks, the reverberating countryside, the human puppets with bird's heads, the marauding mercenaries, and the hangmen, the ghoulish midwives whose crooked fingers did their work of castration. And dancing on high at the top of the greasy pole were all the frog-like demons of the feast of St Jean, all the incarnate furies of midsummer, the longest day of the year, the anti-Noël. Christmas is in the heart of the night, but is the festival of Light. The feast of St Jean is, in the heart of the day, the secret festival of Darkness.

255

Where was this terrifying image which had struck him so forcibly as a child? In Quebec? On the banks of the Chaudière? No, in the Royaume of Saguenay. His uncle had brought the picture back with him from France, Uncle Elie Jolicoeur whose fate it was to be assassinated by a maple tree! His uncle, as a soldier, had cut the reproduction out of a special number of *Illustration*. The name of the painter is Brueghel, Brueghel from Hell. His subject is entitled *Margot l'Enragée, Dulle Griet* in Dutch, this huge harrowed and harrowing carcase which is sowing death. The allegory, had pleased the Canadian who was always ready to think in pictures and speak in proverbs. At the house of the Jolicoeurs, they called it Marguérite. Mamie Jolicoeur did not like this madwoman. No one wondered any longer what she was doing there, brandishing her sword eternally, in the flickering light of the torches. It was just one of uncle's fancies, that's all. Uncle was always odd. Especially since the war in Europe. But it was not very pretty to hang up in the dining room! Margot had fascinated Abel. He only understood today the significance of it, and it threw on to the tide a biblical halo which increased him to the size of the Prophets.

'Oradour,' growled Vauthier.

Abel had, in his mind's eye, the officers of the administration paying out compensation for the dead, Jacques in agony under the truck, in the turmoil of dodged responsibilities, without the charity of a *coup de grâce*.

'I'd like to ask you a question, Monsieur Vauthier. During the Occupation, I imagine you saw quite a few things?'

'Yes, indeed.'

'Good. Then, if it were to do it over again?'

'I beg your pardon?'

'If we had to do it all over again? I mean . . .'

Abel spoke with difficulty, annoyed at his own timidity.

'Friends who were denounced, tortured, deported and shot.'

'Certainly.'

'With no hesitation?'

'None.'

'Even if it leads to that?'

Abel indicated the newspapers. They had been full of catastrophe for some days.

'Well, yes,' said Vauthier.

'Even Algeria?'

'Yes.'

'And de Gaulle in power?'

'Even then.'

'And the militants who do a bunk or who vote for the General?'

'Well, we have to see. You mustn't generalise, if I may coin a phrase. But all the same, yes. Yes, yes. Everything. I'd start it all over again.'

Under Abel's burning regard, Le Dernier, suddenly intimidated, slid his wounded hand with the stumps for fingers underneath the table.

Blondel, the garage proprietor, would always have been jovial, were it not for the worries caused him by his flighty wife who continually urged him to spray himself with cologne. He sat himself down in front of Fontaine, the lawyer. Time passed and yet did not seem to pass. Marie-France laughed from out of the centre of her spreading fat. 'What a laugh, messieurs, what a laugh!' Jaouen used to come to show himself off at about seven. One night, happy to find a new listener, he explained his profession, putting into the explanation the fine passion of men who speak about their jobs!

'About 1920, there was an epidemic. The "horse's hoof", which you could catch with a trawl, monsieur, yes, a trawl, disappeared. We started to improve the flat oysters of Brittany. Mine came from Cancale. We replant them in the beds like vegetables. I'm not joking. The government have put us under the Ministry of Agriculture, and my oyster-washers are agricultural workers! Then there were the restrictions of 1940. With its other victims, the war killed off the oysters, monsieur. They were the most innocent!'

One morning in the last days of July, the police took Lucien away. Some fishermen had seen him at the side of the Pont de la Dune on the night of the crime. Calumny spoke, and jealousy! Certainly he couldn't say where he had been that night. And then, he did not care much for Ratier! Ratier used to say that one ought to cut off the hair of the girls who went with the paras. That couldn't be forgiven. But to go as far as this . . . !

Lucien came back on the third evening and the police turned up next day as though nothing had happened. The laughter did not break out openly until later when they heard Lucien's alibi. He had been with the girl friend of a senior officer of police, the girl who was called 'the gendarmeress', because she was so sweet! Lucien, the rogue, had conducted himself like a gentleman!

It came about that Bérangère and Valerie went out together one day. They went for a whole day, to lunch in Honfleur, leaving Abel at the Père Magloire. He questioned Valerie on her return, but she did not tell him anything. And Bébé laughed like a cooing turtle-dove. It was not until later, in the bedroom with the clock which displayed the bubbles of time, that she agreed to let drop some light on their conversation.

'I told her the story of Fleur,' she said. 'You would never have told her yourself, would you?'

258

He felt choked. It was a treachery towards Jacques. Bérangère was smoking, naked, stretched out on the bed, and her gaze followed the smoke which vanished into the hangings with the green and red palm leaves.

'You need a woman like that.'

'Ah, no, no, no, that would be a joke.'

Bébé turned over on to her belly. The sinking of the bed curved her hips. She was golden at the back and across her shoulders, on her thighs and her legs, while her buttocks were white, and dimpled. Across her back, the scar could be discerned as a razor-thin mark. She turned her malicious expression to him. 'Her cameo profile!' It was better to think that she was taking a rise out of him. He caressed her and she purred. He wanted to say: 'I love you, Bébé, you're an idiot'; but the words never came.

'Jacques is a ghost between you and Valerie,' she went on seriously. 'You think you're looking things in the face. You don't look at everything in the face, you know.'

'What about you?'

'Me? Oh, I cheat. That's easier. Listen, your Jacques came to a terrible end. But he was just one soldier among many. Pay attention. You must kill this ghost.'

'That's why you told Valerie . . . the story of the Belle Boulangère?'

'Yes.'

'But we're not sure about it. Fleur didn't recognise him. Not at all. It's crazy!'

'Child or no child, Fleur or no Fleur, there was a baker's wife, wasn't there?'

'Yes.'

'And others?'

'Yes.'

'That's what Valerie must know. Your Jacques is a vampire. He's eaten up half of your life.'

She pressed herself passionately against him.

'I've accustomed myself to the idea of your going, Abel.

259

But I'd like you to leave a free man. Freed from yourself. Between us, my lad, don't you think you owe that to yourself?'

'Do you think the statue of the Cupids with the linked arms meant nothing to me?' she went on. 'I wept for it one whole night! I'm fully aware that that is really living. But I've come to know it too late. It would last three months, you big ape. I've already told you so. I'm a teacher, but that's just by the way. I'm the shipping agent. I'm here to receive the Canadians who've not been able to go home, the little sister with the big heart. I'm paid by God's Tourist Office to help lost soldiers find their lives again.'

She was joking, of course, joking.

'I take them by the hand. I give them a turn round the country and then send them back to Canada. I'm a secret agent. So secret that I do not know whom I'm an agent for!'

She gave a cracked laugh which echoed long; then she lay on him, burning yet cool, like a stream disturbed by currents; and his heavy male palm lay on the scar as though he wanted to make it vanish.

Bérangère went to see her daughter at Graye. Let's hope it doesn't end as badly as last time! It was six o'clock on this fine August evening. The wind was getting up. Valerie and Abel were having a drink on the terrace of the Père Magloire. Once more Abel had ordered a cold milk. He pondered on its flavour with a studied incredulity. Valerie took off her glasses. Since Bébé had told her that she was better without them, she often took them off.

'I'm no longer myself,' she said. 'A little longer and I'll be sleeping under the trees.'

At the kerbside, under a 'No Parking' sign, a black Peugeot had pulled up. Two civilians got out with two uniformed policemen. Leroy, the mayor, was with them. He looked bored. They went straight to Jaouen.

260

'The examining magistrate has issued a warrant for your arrest,' said the older of the two civilians. 'Monsieur Jaouen, you are charged with the murder of Ratier.'

Jaouen leaned back, slowly, reddening, sitting on the chair with all his weight.

'The night of the crime, you told your wife that you were going to Cancale. You made a pretence of getting on the road, you left your car on the side of the Rives. You went on foot up to the house, passing over the Pont de la Dune. It was two in the morning. You saw a light in the annexe which serves as the forwarding office. There, on the couch where your workmen sometimes sleep, you came upon your wife, and Ratier. You had been warned by an anonymous letter.'

Jaouen stared at the inspector, a gleam in his eye.

'You were carrying an angle iron such as you use to fence in your oyster beds. The iron was about eighteen inches long and had been sharpened. You could use it either as a cudgel or a short sword!'

'The bitch!' breathed Lucien.

'Shut up,' said Arnaud senior.

Jaouen held his place, but Blondel and the lawyer, embarrassed, stood aside.

'Please show me the warrant.'

The police officer held it out to him. Jaouen put on his spectacles and read it. He pushed the paper back with the tips of his fingers.

'Your wife shouted. You struck Ratier twice, the first time with the angle-iron used as a bludgeon, and then you hit him a glancing blow at the base of the skull. The second time you cut through his thigh, using the iron as a sword. Monsieur Jaouen, the iron was found in the lock with traces of blood still on the shaft, although it had been carefully washed . . .'

Valerie seized Abel's hand.

'These people are frightful . . .'

'Finally, your wife made a statement. Oh, she could not avoid doing so, or she would have been an accomplice.

261

Understand? Your accomplice in the murder of her lover.'

Jaouen scratched his hair. The police were looking at Lucien out of the corner of their eyes. Clearly, the Arnaud boy was regaling himself by thinking about the wife of this bastard Jaouen, who made love well, and sweetly, and of the swine Ratier who, although taking her away from him, had not transported her into Paradise!

Jaouen swung his heavy body, and with his elbow forward, leaned his fist on his heavy thigh.

'I did it in self-defence,' he explained deliberately. 'This swine had picked up a bottle and would have laid me out. It's just too easy to go around cuckolding people and then knocking them off so that you can devour their money with the wife! I've got proof, you may be sure.'

Jaouen took a paper out of his portfolio. The police officer unfolded it, read it, folded it up again and gave it back, disconcerted.

'All the same, you must come with me, Monsieur Jaouen.

Jaouen emptied his glass. He rose. He said: 'Goodbye, gentlemen. See you later. I'm within my rights.'

At the door he said it again.

'Within my rights!'

The neighbours hurried along on the footpath, the roadway and the terrace, bustling Valerie and Abel, climbing on the chairs and tables, and little Yvonne clapped her hands, highly excited, whilst the car carried off to Caen the man who was within his rights.

Abel was speechless when he learned a little later the contents of the paper which had been shown to the policeman. After he had wounded Ratier, Jaouen made him sign a confession of adultery, on a sheet of Jaouen's own business letterhead, marked: 'Jaouen, Cultivation, Consumption and Despatch of Oysters, Verville-sur-Mer. The Oyster—refuge of the pearl—pearl of health!'

His wife had also signed it. Then, Jaouen had showed him the door. La Luzerne had dragged himself to the threshold.

262

He had not dared to call out. He had struggled to the road. Losing blood, he must have ended up by sliding into the ditch where he was swallowed up by the mud, exhausted, releasing his last bubbling breaths of life.

CHAPTER VIII

ON THIS AUGUST Saturday, mists were floating in the distance. About midday, they lifted and it was another still, fine day; but one of the last, because the *Samuel Champlain* was sailing the following Friday. The narrow road wound down into the plain which was cut up by fences and made copper-coloured by the cut corn. After the second crossroads, the car stopped in front of a place which was enclosed by a dark wood. There is always a breeze here, a high place by comparison with the generally flat countryside. Far off, there was a milky streak: the sea. Through the clanging at the entry, some young trees were waving. The lawns were as neat as in the New World. Valerie followed Abel into this pilgrimage which she had desired so much. At the end of the lawns, two wings of a building rose up, rough-hewn. Abel recognised them at once. They were pointed, with a rectangular base, ornamented with dark green foliage which was too heavy for

263

the breeze to move, almost petrified in air under glass. These were the Towers of Silence. It was a good cemetery, shaved, watered, hoed, but empty apart from this man and woman who walked timidly along the central paths. A stone table stood between the two towers on which had been engraved, in the English of Shakespeare

Their Name Liveth for Evermore.

'Their name!' The Patton business all over again!

'I've come home,' Abel thought distinctly. Dew sparkled on the clover. The wind stirred the leaves of trees which were still young so that Abel, the city-dweller, was unsure of himself in spite of his country childhood, ignorant of whether they were really maples.

After they had crossed the line which divided off the Towers of Silence, he found the cemetery straight ahead. Out to the far distance the graves were ranged, set in herringbone pattern. The dead slept in their oaken uniform, as tidy as the pink models at the Gates of War, in the same state of attention.

In the empty cemeteries, you could hear the birds. They nested in the tranquil hedges which bordered the field of rest. Birds will only put up with men who are in their graves. Distant motors, the heavy rhythm of tractors, the snarls of the scooters, the deep-throated beat of the trawlers united to form a feeble echo, reminiscent of the tape recording of the disembarkation.

In the rows separated by the wide paths it was possible to move without difficulty round the vertical headstones. Rectangular, slender, with a delicate concave at the top, the only curve which the architect had allowed. They were marked with a lightly engraved cross and a maple leaf leaning to the left, stylised and inscribed within a circle. It took a little time to realise that some carried an inscription in Hebrew with the Star of David. There were even a few Arab inscriptions. At the foot of the graves, rose trees were growing.

264

657546 Private

M. CADIEUX

Le Régiment de la Chaudière

le 22 juillet 1944

If the rank—that of a simple soldier—was in English, the name was indeed in French! In French, were also engraved the name of the regiment and the date. Private Cadieux died on the twenty-second of July, before Caen.

Before them unrolled the slow film of the English and French inscriptions, the first the most numerous, the second shared between the Régiments de la Chaudière and Maisonneuve.

YOU'RE NOT FORGOTTEN,

BOB DEAR

The quivering inscription burst in upon them, lightened by the unimaginably sad smile of the mother. Abel and Valerie could not see this faceless mother, or this gentle wife, but they were listening to her voice: 'You're not forgotten, Bob dear.' The familiarity was foreign to the haughty austerity of the place

WE'D GIVE ALL THE WORLD AND MORE TO SEE YOU COME

SMILING THROUGH THE DOOR

Each word made its point. They could see the soldier's smile, so frantically desired, a smile which must have been so notable when he lived, a smile full of dimples, like Jacques's, a soldier for whose return good people would give 'all the world and more.' He'd push open the door of their house. He would smile. But never again would Private Denis come pushing open with a smile, the door of the past.

The English phrases, with their everyday language, were more earthy than the French. Even here, the English-speaking Canadians were separated from the French-Canadians; but they had reversed their traditional positions,

265

for the English were usually considered to be more rigid, more conformist. Here they had let themselves go after death, rejecting cant and pride, while their French brothers were stiff in their attitudes; and the next headstone said in French:

HE DIED FOR HIS COUNTRY
MAY GOD SAVE HIM

The roses also followed in line, superb in their full blossom, purple, violet, tea, golden yellow, rose-pink, broken-white, dead-white, sulphur and saffron. Now and again, a flower dropped its petals with a sigh.

They walked as one knits, point by point, stitch by stitch, row upon row.

Valerie, a few yards back along the path, followed him as one does in a nightmare, when one cannot catch up with the guide. Standing quite upright, she spoke, and her voice fell, intimidated by the silence.

'I'm not feeling well. But I'm going on.'

'Do you want to go back?'

'I want to go to the end.'

She pointed to the distant wall of the cemetery. They'd be there for hours. She came closer to him, step after flagging step. She pointed out the field, with a wide movement, as if she were evoking a mass of suffering never before imagined. Several times she bent her breast.

He set off again. The light wind played with the fallen petals. Suddenly Abel stopped. She heard a groan from him like a wounded animal and standing behind his huge immobile form, she read:

Private
G. LECLERC
Le Régiment de Maisonneuve
le 3 juillet 1944
Age 21

Abel could not leave this stone which shouted his name.

266

Valerie touched him with her fingertips, with a hint of supernatural fear. A burst of joyful song arose from the starlings in the hedge.

'I never heard tell of this Leclerc,' he murmured.

Gently she pushed him on. He resisted. Jacques was beside him and looked at the grave. At last, he went off. They walked round the grave of G. Leclerc,—Georges, no doubt— to get to the fifth row. The checkboard now presented a different perspective. The first stone carried the inscription:

LET US NOT FORGET HE DIED
THAT OTHERS MIGHT LIVE IN PEACE
FREE FROM FEAR

'The official response to the famous question,' he said, 'Impersonal.'

He did not approve of 'good reasons'. Carthage had had good reasons. So had Darius who had visited the cemetery of the Persians. He stumbled, overtaken by the vertigo of time. No, he could not stay here. He could not be contented with this facile reaction. *Free from fear.* Yet he was touched in spite of himself.

Words! Words, words, words! or only the simple truth debased by the usury of language? In the white symphony of the headstones, the human element entered: *free from fear.* Again he thought of himself, of the Leclerc at his side, the Leclerc who died that others might live, free from fear. Perhaps! This G. Leclerc was twenty-one. 'They'd have had to put "19" for me.' G. Leclerc was the elder brother he had lacked. Georges . . .

'Come along, Abel.'

Jacques was walking with them. The book turned its pages of stone, beneath the Towers of Silence, guarded by invisible sentinels.

Age 22 age 21 age 19 age 25 age 27 age 18 age 19

Bees flew by, intoxicated with the roses.

267

Age 22 age 23 age 20 age 19 age 19

TO ONE WHO DIED BEFORE HE HAD A CHANCE TO LIVE

But none of them had had his chance to live!

The stones began to dance. She was showing up again and was now some paces behind him, in the previous row. Jacques was between them, his arms falling heavy, at his side, as they did when he was fed up.

'Valerie,' said Abel firmly, 'it would be more sensible if you went back to the car.'

'No, I must go on.'

Pigheaded! She was a real Canadian!

Headstones, maple leaves! The taste of childhood came back into his mouth, the sweet taste of the sugar of the Royaume, the maple sugars, dirty fawn, granular, resinated and cracking in the mill into the form of a leaf. He swallowed.

Age 20 age of Jacques age 19 age of Abel 19

age 26 age 24 age 20 age of Jacques

The graves made a mute harmony in the bass line. They approached the central cross and Valerie was dragging more and more behind.

Sergeant
Claude Benjamin
le Régiment de la Chaudière

Benjamin! Tough sergeant Benjamin! The one who'd met me after the fiasco of the lost commando! The one who'd been there when Jacques died. 'Go on! Go on! Help no one!' Was this fate really worth the trouble of being such a pig? *May the Lord God Have Mercy on his Soul* . . . Yes. I agree! And may He have pity on mine, at the same time, if I have one, that . . .

The heat was making thin columns of air shimmer above the lawns. *Like a solemn choir of peasants who come to sing from below the earth.* Peace lay more lightly about them each time the route of the paths lead them to the forested banks.

268

But peace itself crushed down, in the centre, under the sun.

The dead sang with unknown words, and, above them, the blue pines sustained their voices. Bells were heard and, in the humming of distant motors, the staccato of a tractor. HE GAVE HIS LIFE FOR WORLD FREEDOM. *Free from fear!* Words, words, words. 'Clowning and putrescence.' No, no. It's not possible. Not everything cries stinking fish! NO! NO! NO! Not everything is 'merely words'! Otherwise Abel, my brother, lie down on the earth and bury yourself in the soil and a stone will grow about you! *Free from fear!* There is something true there! If it isn't true, it must become true. You must make it true. You! You!

I?

Alone!

Like le Dernier.

Abel was haggard in the midst of this shimmering geometry. His ears were buzzing, his heart beat in time with the tractor. *'For World Freedom!'* Yes. Yes. Perhaps. 'Oui'. 'Ja'. What? Who said 'Ja,'? Where are the ones who are singing 'ja'? There is none. They are in another cemetery. One cannot, in any event, put the murdered with the murderers.

Flaubert. Masson. Robert. Age 27 age 24 age 20 age of Jacques 19 age of Abel 19 age of Abel 19 age of Abel . . .

Rows of graves and one, two, three, four, five yards and some dozens and hundreds more, to make a cemetery which joins the plain and the coast and stretches between them in a steppe of the dead.

He was alone. He looked over the checker pattern. She was on her knees, five rows behind him. Jacques was nowhere near her. Abel signed to her. She had her face in her hands and did not see him. He lowered his head. A green cricket with thighs like an acrobat was swinging on a plantain leaf. The din of a tractor followed him from the other side of the hedge, systole, diastole, systole, diastole. On the lawns the dandelions flourished, little fat suns. *Age 21, age 19, age 34.* Heavens, a grand-dad in the world of turbulent young dead! Listen, Abel, this one is your age now!

My name's Lauzier. I'm thirty-four. I was with the Chauds. I was killed on the fourth of July 1944. Don't ask me why. Say an Ave to heaven for me. For Private Lauzier, ALL YOU WHO PASS SAY AN AVE TO HEAVEN. An Ave, an Ave, give me an Ave, I beg you, quickly a little Ave do not ask me why if you knew how bad it is when you're dead if you knew how much time I've put into dying don't ask me why I've longer to stay dead than I was alive. An Ave an Ave it's not me who put that on my headstone. Give me a true Ave a little Ave. I've so long to stay dead. Give Private Lauzier a little Ave don't ask me why give me an Ave, a smile from the child I never had the glance from the young woman I would have married and who is now happy with another lad in Trois Rivières.

Abel reeled like a thunder-riven beech tree. The cemetery with its ranks of graves lined up on the left, went out of shape, rising up to the sky like a kite, wobbled, spun abruptly and fell back. Abel put his hand on his heart. He regained control, listened to himself and breathed. No more, this time. It was nothing. Everything circled round to the left, as it had done in Bérangère's bedroom, but it could be controlled. Abel put his hand on Lauzier's grave. The stone was warm. 'Sorry, old man, I weakened.' 'Oh, make yourself at home. There's a lot of pleasure in the touch of a pal's hand.'

Valerie was over there, a long way off, turning slowly. Yes, there she was, in her frock of polka-dot blue, going away, casting off the lines, slipping askew under the porch of one of the Towers of Silence, swallowed up by the shadow.

Slowly, the sickening spin slowed down.

There were still many rows. Except for the relatives of the dead who were buried round the central cross, no visitor could have the courage to press on too far. Like those kids at

270

school who are called Xavier, Yvain, or Ziegler, those distant ones are at the end of the alphabet of the dead.

A butterfly hovered. It was odd, something yellow and alive.

Thanks, Lauzier.

'Not at all, think nothing of it,' said Lauzier.

The world had taken on its reassuring immobility. His heart beat out a heavy rhythm, with an abnormal irregularity, but outside him. His heart was no longer in his body. Outside. An outboard heart!

He walked slowly.

A man in a starched blue blouse with three others burst out on top of one of the Towers of Silence. The man in the blouse was beating a little drum. He must have been beating it for some little time. In a fantastic itinerary, his three companions were going from grave to grave. They were unrolling a ribbon which they wound round the headstones. Abel went up to them by way of the central path. His temples were moist.

The smallest of them, a round little man of about forty, and as red as a tomato, was counting the stones already decorated. But it was not easy to wind a ribbon round a vertical stone. The ribbons fluttered down. The little man was cussing. One of the two larger ones was running, abruptly here and there, in a succession of broken movements which the arrangement of the rows imposed since, in order to catch the ribbon as it flew away, it was necessary to start off in the opposite direction, to do the same operation two or three times before finally bringing it back to the headstone!

Then the three men decided to knot the ribbons round the rose trees. Having found this solution, the plump man mopped his brow with a check handkerchief. He consulted a list which whipped in the wind. They turned their backs to Abel, then went to another row. They came nearer. They stopped at last in front of Abel. The clumsily-built man had a comical head on a very long neck, crowning shoulders

271

which were shaped like a bottle, ending up as an endless torso which crushed down on short legs.

'Hello, Abel! What a riot, what a riot! Abel! How are you, man?'

What the devil was Ray doing here, the G.I., Mamie's man, with the other two and this peasant in a blue blouse in a Canadian cemetery? It seemed that Ray had unearthed these two pilgrims at Bény-sur-Mer, on the terrace of a café where they were filling themselves up with courage and calvados. They were old Chauds. Bastarache and Lagite had sworn to decorate with the colours of Quebec the graves of the Chauds they had known. There were seventeen on their list. Ray had been carried away by the nobility of this enterprise. He would go with them. America would never let its allies down. They had already found twelve. They searched vigorously for the other five. They resumed their quest, exaggerating the zig-zag imposed by the graves with the zig-zag derived from the calvados.

Ray took a flask out of his hip-pocket, drank a long pull, wiped the mouth with the back of his hand, held it out to the second man who drank in his turn, threw it over the graves to the fat little man who took it like a rugby pass, drank and showed it to Abel. He hesitated. He refused. The man with the drum made a sign. With a superb pass, the fat little man sent the flask to the drummer who drained it at a gulp, demonstrating the excellence of the Norman training.

Ten minutes later, Bastarache and Lagite had decorated sixteen stones, but the seventeenth remained undiscoverable. They were cussing away—well, this was the dreaded end!— when Abel had the notion of consulting the register in one of the Towers of Silence. He reappeared and indicated the grave with his hand, the second in the first row. Carried away by their enthusiasm, the lads had overlooked it at the start. That's it, mission accomplished! They were drifting out towards the entrance when the fat little man—Bastarache was a butcher in a Quebec suburb—looked at the remaining

272

ribbon. They were not going to take any ribbon away! They were there in order to decorate, they would decorate, in spite of sun, wind and any obstacle! The idea of obstacles must have been as vague in their heads as in their diction. But the thought was firm! Lagite approved. This Bastarache ought to stand for Parliament! Ray did not understand French, but he gave his opinion, with confidence. Did the rest of them have no right to the ribbon, just because they weren't personally acquainted? In some ways, this idea of personal pals is petty. Shabby! They swept it away with a broad gesture. There was ribbon left, and they would use it to decorate the graves of all the regiment. Of course! Of the entire regiment. Long live the Chaudière and up the Chauds.

Finally, the ribbon was finished. But there were still some graves undecorated! Injustice returned. Abel considered this mad scene with a deep sadness which was not able to drown a sombre laugh. The pair of them were blind drunk! Beside them, Jacques was laughing his own deep laugh. Under the headstones, the Chauds could not get angry. They would even pay for a round! Undoubtedly Bastarache was a leader. Like many butchers, accustomed to chopping things up. There are butchers in every revolution. He chopped. He cut until there was no more ribbon. The only thing to do was to return to all the graves which had been done, snip off some little pieces of the blue ribbon with the fleur-de-lys design and then it would be enough. Bastarache threw out a command to the drummer and he, without leaving the slender shadow of the hedges, began to drum, somewhat faster now because of the calva.

Abel left them. Without him, the participants in the ritual carried on the job, quicker and quicker, more and more tottery, coming and going, leaning over, cutting, snipping, becoming discouraged before the growing number of the dead. They were drinking in huge gulps. The drummer was rolling about, larks flew out like the arching flight of a thrown stone, the wind snatched away the blue and golden butterflies

273

and made the ribbons spin madly, like insects and petals, while the three merrymakers collapsed at last on to the grass and the drummer rejoined them in the returning silence of the huge cemetery on which the sun beat down.

THE BEAUTIFUL day was sailing towards its death, at the storm-filled horizon where an armada of clouds were passing by. Valerie was happy to be leaving, but did not dare to say so, because of this thick solid mass which was Abel Leclerc. 'Valerie's bedroom's really a man's room, there are so many cigarette stubs about,' thought Abel. This was the first time he had been in it. He hurried to get out. He went to the door which opened and Simone appeared, bringing tea. She had a coquettish gleam in her eye, but when she saw Valerie on edge and Abel scowling, she put on the smile she reserved for 'stuffy' customers.

'I'll leave you to get ready, Valerie. My bags are already in the car.'

She hesitated, and with false gaiety, she said:

'So you really are going, Abel?'

Could it still be doubted? Once more he could see the lovers of Vaugueux, the Cupids linked by their arms. And Bérangère? Bérangère was the honey of love, but daily bread was necessary too. She had confessed what he had guessed, that night with the poor aunt. Boldly. Yes, there had been Adrien the doctor. And before him, the mayor, Leroy, la Luzerne and others. They were the 'uncles.' 'I live like a boy. I don't attach any importance to it.' He could see once more the damp, her gay flame and the staggering scar, the four-poster bed, the understanding Roman matrons and the clock with the stream.

275

Memory burned within him, a memory of this thin scar which had made him furious with desire. He wanted to shout until he burst! Through the window he looked at the peaceful beach. In front of the dead landing craft, children were being led gravely along on ponies by a dwarf dressed as a naval officer. There were also Bébé's words: 'I can't give you children. Marry Valerie, she'll give you some fine kids.' It was so ridiculous that he laughed. Valerie blurted out: 'God, but this man is crude!' However, it's true that Valerie would give fine children to the man who could put up with her. The beach called to him. He went to the door. He ventured a word:

'You've never had the idea of getting married, just to have children, have you, Valerie?'

'Certainly not!'

Diana had returned, the Amazon, the man-woman. She gestured and her hand was a sabre.

'Abel, listen to me. We shan't have this freedom again. Life on the boat . . . Above all, in Canada . . . We'll get caught up by work and our surroundings . . . Well, I want to thank you.'

'What?'

'Yes, truly. Abel, I said some terrible things to you. I've called you clumsy, a drunkard, a layabout! I've not been easy in mind since. I was wrong. You're a man. I did not even know what that meant.'

He remained at the door with his hand on the knob, uncertain.

'Now I've had the opportunity of talking to you, Abel. You know when I realised it?'

'No.'

'In the cemetery.'

'I see.'

'I went to the end. You carried on.'

He released the knob. She took his hand and pressed it with all her strength.

276

'There. Yes, you're a man, Abel.'

He opened the door quietly.

'And that's what separates us,' she murmured.

The whole half-timbered hotel was like the interior of a yacht. Half engulfed in the darkness of the stairs, with his bronzed bald head, he was like the departing sailor of the novels.

Abel reflected the sky and the weather. In the rock-pools were the shrimps. Nazi shrimps, Allied shrimps, unshed traits of childhood kept into manhood, there was nothing but shrimps! But, the previous night on the war memorial at Verville, a swastika had been painted in tar. There are still people willing to burn the Jews, gipsies, prisoners and the children in churches! You burn everything that's *different*. Eichmann! Six million dead! And after all, Eichmann did nothing but obey orders. How many bureaucratically innocent Eichmanns would have killed how many people, if Hitler had won? It was the plague, as Vauthier said, le Dernier. The brown plague. The Nazi plague. The madness of war. Madness. Mad Meg who still dominates her world of youth, in the realm of the maple trees. The William the Conqueror Group and its chief, Maxime! When did I ever understand that I was in business with fools! Before Jacques, certainly. Jacques never tried to find out. He only tried to please. I was distrustful, certainly, but I understood too late! I was worried in the *Café des Sports,* but I did not understand. Just as I did not understand until very late with Bébé! But when Maxime showed me his half-sized matches, that was the time to be aware!

We must not let this swastika pass! Ten thousand Eichmanns installed for a thousand years. Iron rule. Racialist frenzy. The death of all liberty. Even if the word 'liberty' is nothing but bait, it alone can carry hope to men. Fine. I agree. Nazi slavery?—Never! But these indifferent Normans? The smug Jaouen. 'Within his rights'? Lucien and his piggish father? Little Yvonne who was already turning into a pretty good tart? The deceptions, the frauds, the corruption, the denials of confidence. War damage! The rules of the game. I buy back. I sell again. I am seller. I am buyer. I live on death. Understand it well. I buy, you sell. I sell what you buy. You sell, I buy. We sell, we buy at a lousy price. Lousy! The prices are always lousy. Mercury is the God of pigs.

This is it, then, the liberty that cost Jacques his skin. Is it worth all these graves under the Towers of Silence?

Far out, the sea is going down. At Arromanches the colours are fading. We mustn't have the show burnt down. The Gates of War are closed. The plump holidaymakers are having a stroll before their aperitif, so different from everything that had bowled over this tough lad with the copper-coloured pate, who was going resolutely to his own finality, alone, quite alone in the face of this one question: 'And if it was all to do again, Vauthier?'

After Abel had gone, Valerie scoured the streets to find once more the figure of this unwilling killer. In the glory of the setting sun, the evidence of life and death moved towards the sea. There were some incomprehensible hesitations in her walk. 'I must do up my bags.' But she did not remember Simone. The accomplice, the docile servant. He must have got her on her back! Suddenly she scared herself with the vocabulary she had employed; thoughtfully, her eyes followed this man who became so important as he got farther away. Was Bérangère possibly right, when she suggested to her that she would marry Abel? Because she had told her so! These girls had a continental experience! No! The idea of a man in her bed made her flesh creep. There was, however, one point on which Bérangère was right. *I have taken refuge in Jacques to protect myself from other men.* How had she known that? Bérangère knew things, from within, without

278

having learnt them, while she, Valerie, had to learn everything from outside, paying all that time more than the fair price. She bridled at it. She hated Bérangère, as good dogs hate birds, because of the unfairness of wings.

Where it came down to the earth, the sky was a silvery blue, except for a menacing streak of deep blue beside the Chaos in the direction where they searched stupidly, on the first day, for Jacques's ghost. The mass of the pontoon cut into the wet sand. It was nearly as big as the church at Angerville. Like the church, it also was hollow. To be precise, it had been one unit of the harbour wall, marked with the number 449. The front plunged into a sea full of little crabs which the kids were catching. Sharp shouts came out of the gutted pontoon and the landing craft acted as a sounding box to give them an outstanding prolongation. Little boys and girls ran round. One of them gasped, out of breath: 'He won't get us. He won't get us.' Abel stood stupefied in front of this marvel: children playing in the ruins.

He went up to the crumbling wall and put his hand on the cold concrete, fraternally.

Bérangère went along the road with its royal blue macadam. She needed the exercise. Adrien the doctor had recommended it to her. The blond doctor who was looking after her daughter at Graye-sur-Mer. She sat down on a milestone. Presently, she crossed a field of clover. She had not gone far before she was attacked by a crowd of midges. Scratching only made the itching worse, but anyway she scratched. Caen! When? When she was a girl. When the world fell apart. Bérangère scratched her feet. The universe was really crumbling, the town collapsed and only midges were of any importance. Europe was aflame. Mad Meg went over. Bébé scratched herself. How was she to know that, a

279

few miles from her, there was a nineteen-year-old Canadian who was walking in her direction and would not come to her until sixteen years later! Destiny, the rose in the mud! How angry he had been, that night when she had been with the doctor! All the same, I shouldn't have done it to him! What is it that gets hold of me, sometimes? You wouldn't think I'm the same girl. Abel came too late. 'Abel, this is bad, worse than you know. When will you stop cutting me in two?'

I plead guilty, looking into the golden sky, in front of this tribunal of children who are playing in the evening light. I beat my breast. Not like the ape, in anger. I say: Guilty. Guilty at having, for sixteen years, embellished the bloody muddy story of Jacques until I had mutilated it. My God, I don't believe in You! I believe in Man! I know my wrongs. I've put Jacques through the hoop of gossip, as a result of fear, cowardice, shame, convenience, laziness and habit. I've talked about Jacques as one speaks of soldiers in the papers. I am guilty. Someone ought to set fire to the Museum of the Landings. History is an appalling lie! We must let nothing go. Everything lies. Everything helps forgetfulness. Perhaps they should have left something. A piece of land ten miles square, with the rusty barbed wire, the bunkers, the steel flowers from the burst shells, the fluttering letters, the dead men and horses, the gutted houses displaying the sad obscenities of water pipes and the bread of Pompeii on the table. The only monument which is worthy of the death is truth. Not the truth of the historian. But the truth true to themselves.

The things I know are: the rain, the nettles and the roses, dogs and the weather. In twenty years they will take on the allure of a fairground! So there's nothing to do. Nature, and life, is all forgetfulness. Every monument which is laid down never serves any purpose except to dam up forgetfulness for an instant! They put stones on the dead to be sure that they won't get up again, as they await forgetfulness. I myself am half gnawed by lichens, creepers, mosses, and the thorns of forgetfulness. And I don't want to forget! I am trying vainly to hold it back. Guilty! Guilty with the anti-Man, the Nazi, my brother Cain! Even those who fought for liberty are guilty. Guilty of having forgotten that we were beaten down for liberty. In Quebec I forgot. So, for the others, for the whole of life which forgets, which forgets all it can, I am a mad dog! There's an air of commiseration when you talk of the war. When you reproach them for forgetting! I've had the war! I must beat down the volunteer Abel Leclerc. Volunteer for what? I've had war, I've had war. Lord, Lord, I beat my breast and shout: 'Guilty, guilty, guilty!' Lord, if only I could believe in You! Understand me. Then You would force me to do all the work myself.

The twilight brought a return of warmth.

The sound of a motor was heard behind Bérangère. Perhaps the bus. She signalled to it. It was getting tiresome to walk. A Chrysler stopped. A heavily accented man, bronzed, dressed in a costly swimsuit of lemon yellow, asked her the way to Graye-sur-Mer. She answered with a smile. He invited her to climb in. She laughed:

'This is the opposite of hitch-hiking.'

He made her say it again. He laughed at last very loudly and two gold teeth shone. She got in. The stranger switched on the car radio.

The storm slipped in from the sea. The clouds made up an astounding picture in the forms of a goat, a unicorn, and a ship in which janissaries went past with drawn scimitars, skirted knights, black hussars and all the halbadiers of death behind Mad Meg, the mad woman with the broad sword. Round the pontoon, the children ran and chased, came together and grabbed at each other. Theirs is grace. Their running reproduced the ballet of the swifts around the *Escale*. A peaceful light spread over it all the soft soap of legend. The

281

shadow of the concrete lay on the grey sand where the sharp light emphasised the chalky whiteness of the shellfish. The seagulls had left traces which crossed each other between the footsteps, the heel prints, the foot prints of the little ones—oh, the little moon of the heels, the flower made by the hollow toes, as lightly imprinted as the marks of the birds.

Near the pontoon, a small boy called out.

'Hey, there, Canada, come and see!'

It was Olivier! What was new with him? In his mouth the hole had grown larger and now displayed a pink tongue.

'Well, Olivier, you've lost another tooth!'

'Buck up. We're setting sail!'

Olivier was holding a butterfly net in his left hand and he was rummaging in it with his right. A huge grey shrimp was splashing round in what was left of the water which was seeping slowly through the fabric. He must have fixed up his gadget himself, without concerning himself with getting the water to flow through quickly. 'That's what happened to me when I was fishing for tadpoles in the Royaume.' Ah, yes, but Olivier *is* in the Royaume. The other children were shouting and singing. Working his arms like pistons, a big boy came near. The steam engine had come up to look at the shrimp and he said: 'Your shrimp's not so big!' Then he went off to get some wagons at Caen.

'She's swimming round like mad!' said Olivier.

Of course, there will always be shrimps to make my life impossible. Abel considered the shrimp and the impatient child. Abel set his teeth, closed his eyes, comical without trying to be so, and plunged his hand into the bailer, felt the claws prick him, then the coolness of the living porcelain. Death entered into his entire being in cold waves. But he did it. The childish action took on a sense of the luminous. There was a great red sun inside him which was going to go down into the sea. Very small, in this immense landscape under the red sun and the small man who was holding a shrimp . . .

The kid put his little hands on the huge hairy hands. He

282

looked with admiration on his shrimp, an inch or so away, and danced for joy.

'I'm the one who caught it!'

'Of course, Olivier, I only helped . . .'

The idea shot into his mind: 'Like Bérangère did for me . . . Where are you, Bérangère? As soon as I get back to Canada, I'll write. I've an idea. Yes. I'll suggest that you come out. It will have to be arranged without too much scandal. But perhaps you won't want it? My darling! If I had closed my hand on you, I should have stifled you like a bird . . .

'Got a handkerchief, Olivier?'

He was in his swimsuit, how could he have a handkerchief?

'Well, then, hold it tight! You must ask your mother for a jar!'

'I won't ask my mother. I'll ask Simone.'

Valerie, leaning on a parapet, overlooked them without their seeing her. Abel took the child in his arms, lifted him up to the level of his eyes and the child pouted his lips for a kiss. He put two little damp red roses on Abel's cheek. Then Abel said, right into the child's ear:

'You'll be a free man! Free from fear!'

He threw him into the air, where but yesterday, or a thousand years ago, the birds of death were screaming. He repeated: 'Free from fear!' He caught him and threw him up again. Olivier shouted: 'Again! Again!'

'Free from fear,' said Abel.

'Free from fear,' repeated Olivier, his lisp turning it into: 'Feefomfeer.'

'Oh, Valerie, look. I've caught a kid who's caught a shrimp!'

'I've got to go and ring the bells,' said Olivier.

And he dashed off, so small, without letting go of his shrimp, preceded by a long shadow.

Abel went up the steps, washed by a supernatural light. A golden-green wave swept over the face of the old continent. He took out his pipe, the old chewed Dunhill. Jacques, my dear old Jacques, you're a poor old faker!

'Valerie,' he said with deliberation, 'You're a teacher. Tell me, would these children be playing there like that if we had been thrown back into the sea?'

'There are children playing everywhere.'

'Then it was all useless?'

'Of course not, Abel. Theirs fathers would be slaves.'

'But they are slaves. Jaouen, le Lucien and his father, the wedding party with the dead aunt, and the War Damage—and everything.'

He thought: 'And Bébé cut in two.'

'They are slaves by themselves, not belonging to other men. Perhaps not exactly; but don't ask too much of them.'

The light grew less under the clouds. In the booming caisson, the children were gathering while their mothers called to them. Their chattering re-echoed and their shouts were deafening, full of happiness and peace.

Well, was it then so simple? Was it just enough to watch children at play?

'Valerie, I don't know exactly when the answer came to me. Listen. If . . . What I've asked myself since I came here . . . if . . . if it were all to be done again . . . Eh? Do you understand? Everything . . . The war, Jacques, even . . . Valerie, I would start on it again.'

He choked and said it again, wildly:

'I'd start it again, again.'

The last shouts of the kids vied joyfully with the sharp calls of the swifts. Already, a breath of wind was announcing that the tide was on the turn. Olivier was going to sleep with his

284

shrimp, dreaming of the giant Canadian who had sent him right up to the sky. Feefomfeer, feefomfeer, Olivier!

At Vaugueux, Bibiche was touching up the curve of the wings of his Cupids, at the spot where they joined together. The problem of the stone on the angle is a difficult one. This must also be a functional piece. He had to find the perfect accord between art and utility. He gravely pondered the group. He went round the rectangular stone. That Canadian was right! By their two selves, with linked arms, the tender Cupids of Vaugueux were going to hold up an enormous weight, which would crush either of them separately. That's what one ought to meet 'in real life'.

At Verville, in front of the one-time Hotel de la Libération, the Courchinoux kid was humming:

> *Un oignon, ça s'ra-t-il bon?*
> *— — Un oignon, c'est trop rond!*
> *— — Un oignon, c'est trop rond?*
> *Ah, l'homme engagé*
> *Connaissait bien l'bobo d'la fille.*

He stopped, spat into the gutter, shrugged his shoulders and said, affectionately: 'That Canadian's a bit of a dope.'

The Chrysler stopped at the entrance of the road which led to the aerium. Bérangère and the stranger were chatting. Then Bérangère set out, alone, in the sunken road.

'Come on,' said Abel, 'You're lagging behind Valerie. We've got to put your bags in the car.'

She was astonished at the big man, now at peace, who had been watching the free children, with a smile. His hands always fell heavily at the ends of his arms, but they were always open.

Carrying her net carelessly, a slender little girl who was

staring wildly around her, sang out in as voice as clear as ice: *'L'école du Rouê la destinée, la rose au bouê.'* For one last time, the song brought back these words which were polished like the pebbles. Only Bébé could have told Abel that these strange words merely signified: *'La rose au bois m'est destinée.'* 'The rose in the wood is destined for me.' But Bérangère had gone. Henceforth, all vivacity, all lightness, the delights of life and irresponsibility, the sparkling joys of living will contain something of Bérangère, the princess cut in two. It is better that Abel should never know the flat explanation, it is better that he carry away his destiny, his rose in the wood, the rose of Arromanches, the rose of the bunkers and the geometrical graves in the maple leaf cemetery, the unforgettable rose of the dunes, wild and salty like tears, which flowers only in June, when the sea goes down.

Arromanches, July 1958
Chelles. Arromanches
St-Jean-Cap Ferrat
Chelles, May 1963